Published in the United Kingdom by Philly Books in 2013

ISLAND WOMAN
© Philomena Gallagher

First published in paperback in 2013 by Philly Books

Philly Books
18 Bridge Street, Portadown, Co. Armagh, N. Ireland, BT62 1JD
Email: sales@harrisonprint.com

Typeset, Designed and printed by
Harrisons
18 Bridge Street, Portadown, Co. Armagh, N. Ireland, BT62 1JD
Telephone: 0044 (0)28 38 330252
Email: sales@harrisonprint.com

Philomena Gallagher (nee Mulholland) was born in Portadown 1951 and educated at Corcain Primary School, Presentation Convent School and Portadown Technical College.

Returned to adult education 1989, graduated from the University of Ulster 1990, Queens University Belfast 1994 (BSSC Women's Studies & Sociology), Trinity College Dublin 1996 (M.PHIL. Women's Studies).

Divorced, two children, seven grandchildren. Retired Community Development Officer.

6

Island Woman

(Synopsis)

Although she held the aura of one born to command, one who was used to being obeyed and one who would not tolerate being disobeyed. Kachelle Harkin was dealt a poor hand in the game of life.

Set on Arranmore Island, Co. Donegal in 1930's through World War Two, 'Island Woman' is the story of Kachelle Harkin and Diarmuid Charlie McGinley, fellow islanders whose love was deep, pure and true, yet doomed.

Kachelle's lesson in love and the havoc it can wreak, leads her to being trapped in a loveless marriage, shackled to a life of hardship, all for the new love of her life, her son.

Determined to keep her son with her on the island and ensure he wants for nothing, Kachelle works hard at building a better life. Unfortunately fate delivers a cruel blow and Kachelle's life and her son's life are shattered.

'Island Woman' is a heart warming, heart breaking tale of love, loyalty, pain and loss.

PROLOGUE

Arranmore Island Co.Donegal 1920s.

Below the grey Atlantic sky lies a crescent band of rugged land, the island of Arranmore, Co.Donegal. Far to the West, great rollers of misty sea constantly demand attention and roar upon its beaches and staunch rocks. Crying gulls shriek and soar, attempting to ride the white horses on the restless tide.

One tiny pier with a scattering of boats offers scant shelter from the running sea. Low lying houses tucked tightly among hollows of earth seek protection from the bitter winds. Some thatched with heather, some with straw, restricted by hand made ropes, plead for release from their duty. The tiniest of windows peep like half shut eyes to keep in the heat.

Here the vast Atlantic Ocean holds domain. Cutting hail, wind and rain smite the island West to East. Rarely is the unruly ocean quiet, even on the calmest summer days, when bare-foot children venture forth and play on the beaches measled with small shaped stones and shells. The sea is the ruler here and man, woman and child obey.

In the late summer of 1923 nine year old Kachelle Harkin, spat on her small grubby hand, brought it down hard on to Tony Paul's large sea faring hand and said, 'It's a deal. Your bull services my cow and I'll see to Peggy Joe's needs while you are away fishing and you throw in a basket of fish to dry for the winter.'

'My but you are a hard one to deal with,' answered old Tony Paul teasingly. 'Leave out this fish and it's a deal. Here, slap my hand on it.'
And he spat on to his hand and offered it to Kachelle
'No. This is the best offer you're going to get. Take it or leave it.'

Kachelle bit down hard on her lower lip, the late summer breeze making it tremble. Her heart pounded in her chest so much so she was sure Tony Paul would hear it. The young girl prayed silently that a deal would be struck.

Brushing the unruly red curls from her small face, she smiled sweetly at Tony Paul.

'It's awful hard for Peggy Joe to cope when you're away and she gets so lonely now with all the family gone to America. She enjoys me reading their letters to her and she often talks of the fine handsome man she met and loved intently and the great family and life you have given her.'

Tony Paul's chest swelled with pride and his weather beaten face beamed red with embarrassment. 'My offer still stands. Is it a deal?'
Again she spat on her hand and brought it forcibly down on to his, while she crossed the fingers of her left hand behind her back.

'You know, it's a pity you're not a boy, you have the makings of a fine businessman! It's a deal.'

He spat on his hand and brought it down hard on Kachelle's upturned hand. The deal was sealed.

'I'll have my own business some day, right on my own doorstep,' answered an assertive Kachelle.

'Aye and pigs might fly. Women and business don't mix; you get yourself a good lad and rear a family, that's what women do,' and Tony Paul rubbed the top of her head.

'So that they can all leave me for America?' and she raised her right eyebrow at him. 'If I ever get married and have children I'll make sure I'll have a business, a means of keeping them all at home so we'll be together for ever,' and she gave him a firm nod of her head.

'Tell Peggy Joe I'll be over tomorrow,' and turning her back she began to climb over the rocks towards the small narrow road with the grass growing down the middle.

On returning home, Tony Paul announced to his ailing wife that he had struck a deal with Tom Harkin's young girl.

'My but she is a fine colleen. She's like a young colt with those long legs of hers. She'll be a real beauty when grown, that red hair is like a sunset on fire. Tom can be proud of her and there we all thought that with the mother coming from the mainland that nothing good would come of that union. I thought sure after Tom's death that the mother would return to the mainland but that young one is an islander through and through. You know,' and he took a fit of laughing, 'she claims she is going to be a business woman, own her own business right here on the Island.'

'No doubt she will,' answered Peggy Joe as she fingered the warm silver coin between her large breasts. A deal she had struck with young Kachelle for visiting her, carrying out a few small chores but most of all to

5

read her childrens' letters and to sing for her.

'That young one will achieve anything she puts her mind to. There's a strong independent streak in her. Sure, hasn't she been running that house since her father died two years ago, may God rest him.'

'Aye,' answered Tony Paul. 'She'll keep her word too. She's a good girl and by God she'll turn heads in a few years time, she'll be a real beauty. But then her da was a fine handsome man like all us men on the island.' and he winked at his wife.

Peggy Joe was not listening. Staring into the turf fire she thought to herself, 'I wonder has she struck a deal also with the children in America?' Laughing to herself she muttered, 'I wouldn't doubt.'

CHAPTER 1

Kachelle Harkin, tall and statuesque, stared blankly at the bow of the boat which dipped and bowed gracefully before the waves. Her neighbours, Padraic and Diarmuid Charlie McGinley hung carelessly over the side dragging their hands in the foam tipped sea. The boat started its long slow turn to the right. Arranmore Island was now in view. It hugged the line of the shore, facing the heavy rolling seas with mute defiance. The sea was incredibly blue as it washed onto the golden beach, the foam that edged the waves was white and frothy in the sunlight. There her home lay in the bright warm sunshine. The clouds that had earlier obscured the sun had completely rolled away and a blue bowl circled above their heads. Children shrieked with laughter, trying to jump the ebbing waves. Small groups of women diligently collected periwinkles among the rocks, to sell on fair day. Small stacks of turf were piled neatly against the walls. Full washing lines blew gently in the breeze. The soft mooing of a distant cow, the baying of a lonesome donkey and the cuckoo bird added to the orchestra of sound. Kachelle smiled nervously at Diarmuid Charlie. The time had come. Truth will out.

Diarmuid Charlie McGinley stood 6ft.2", with blue eyes, fair hair, fresh complexion. His brother Padraic Charlie was a stocky build of 5ft.9" with eyes and hair as black as coal. Twenty one years old Kachelle Harkin had loved Diarmuid Charlie McGinley from the moment he had danced her at the cross roads ceile two years past. Many's a time she had planned a trip to the beach to collect periwinkles or dulse, just to get a look at him. Many's a wake she had attended just to get a chance to be near him.

Kachelle was 5ft 11" with a fine figure and a mass of bright red curls falling half way down her back. A lilting Irish singing voice and a humorous personality meant that she had many admirers on the Island and the mainland but she knew her heart belonged to Diarmuid Charlie. She well remembered the day Diarmuid Charlie had scrambled over the rocks into the sea and offered to help her collect the dulse. She had been embarrassed as she pulled the back of her skirt through to the front and tied it up at her waist, exposing her long fine pale limbs to the afternoon sunshine. Quickly she let her skirt fall into the on-coming tide.

'Oh there was no need to do that.' laughed Diarmuid Charlie. 'I was enjoying the view!'

'You cheeky rascal,' answered Kachelle blushing bright red.

'Kachelle you're the finest and best looking woman on the island and beyond. How about you being my girl and coming to the crossroads ceile on Sunday night?'

Kachelle was speechless. Her heart thumped in her chest with excitement and pride.

'Ah come on, I know you fancy me,' he said as he skimmed small stones across the waves. 'How about a kiss to seal our date?'

And with that he gathered her in his arms, gently brushed back the cheeky uncontrollable curls at the side of her face and kissed her gently full on the mouth.

'See you Sunday night,' he called as he scrambled back over the rocks towards his father's fishing boat.

Kachelle felt as if she was floating with the waves.

'Oh, God, please tell me I'm not dreaming!' she prayed. 'Sunday night I'll meet you, my love,' she whispered after him and gently pressed her lips together to hold on to his kiss.

Two years had passed and Kachelle , Diarmuid Charlie and his younger brother Padraic Charlie were inseparable. The two boys fished together, mended fishing nets and all three cut, stacked the turf for drying and brought it home for their families and others for winter fires. Cows were milked, fields ploughed, while the whole island spoke in hushed tones and on clear evenings when the sea wind rested, soft crying could be heard from homes all over the island.

The Arranmore Disaster of 1935, had stunned and shocked the tiny community. Each summer some of the young islanders would travel far afield to Scotland to earn a living gathering potatoes. 'Tatie Hokers' they were called, and at the end of the summer they would return home with money to help ease the family burden throughout the winter.

Winters were so harsh it was impossible for the men to fish. Sometimes even the mail boat could not travel to the mainland. The island would be cut off completely from the rest of the world sometimes for days, others for weeks. It was important to have left in, in advance what was needed to keep the family surviving until spring would appear.

The island boat would meet the 'Tatie Hokers' at Burtonport pier and the following day there would be great celebrations to welcome the young travellers home, many stories to hear and dancing at the crossroads until the early hours of the morning It was on a cool and dull November day that the skipper of the island boat with two of his sons and a few fellow islanders pulled away from the tiny pier on Arranmore to collect the young travellers at Burtonport. The skipper was looking forward to seeing his youngest son, Michael Hugh. His eldest son, Patrick Hugh, prayed silently that the young one would not have spent all his earnings, like last year. The Island children waved good-bye and the skipper eyed the sea and sky, filled his clay pipe and puffed complacently.

The silent crew enjoyed the easy motion of the small boat; rising and falling on the spacious swell, the ceaseless march of broad backed rollers passed expertly around and below the small boat.

When all sight of land was lost and the Atlantic roll swept unhindered from the distant west, the skipper suddenly pointed out a massive grey breaker, 'My God, look over there,' and he pointed to the Western bay. Young John Joe, who had been crouching in the bow, jumped up and shouted,

'I bet if we were over there we'd get wet!'

'Wet,' answered Charlie Hugh, 'Why you would be getting drowned.'

Even as he spoke the mighty roller, higher than a house, poised at its height then toppled down in seething surf where no boat steered.

'I'd be afraid to meet the likes of that,' spoke young John Joe.

'That's the highest wave I've ever seen,' stated the skipper.

'Aye,' answered Charlie Hugh as he took a pinch of snuff.

'There's an uneasy feeling with the sea today, Da, the sooner we all get home the better. Mother will be worried.'

Gradually the sea calmed and the waves lessened. The old man steered the well accustomed way and with practised skill landed his small boat at Burtonport pier.

Hurriedly they all made their way to the station to meet the young travellers with hugs and shouts of joy and laughter. The young travellers were glad to be home with money in their pockets for fuel, food, clothing and many stories to tell.

The girls newly dressed rushed to Brigid's shop for a drop of tea. The boys took responsibility for the luggage. The skipper called for everyone to hurry as he was anxious to be away before the dark quenched the light.

The sun through the mist shone for the first time that day while the exhausted travellers settled on board. The glowing red ball hung low above the sea out where America's the next country.

In a soft misty November sunset glow they called good-bye to friends and fellow travellers at Burtonport pier. 'May God and St.Christopher guide you all softly home,' called old Brigid from the shop as she blessed herself. Many years back she had called the same greeting to many of their parents but to-night a strange feeling had come over her. Pulling her black shawl tightly around her she stood firm until the small boat was out of sight.

They were a happy boat load. They shouted questions about loved ones at home to the skipper. Others were teasing each other about the boys and girls they had met and fallen in love with. Some sang softly their mother's favorite song or remembered a new song from Scotland. Twenty happy travellers longing to be home.

The weather grew worse, the fog thicker, the sea and night grew darker. They cared naught, they trusted their skipper and singing and laughter helped them to forget the cold and the wet.

The boat continued on its journey and still the fog came thicker, making the Islands dim outline vanish. Ned Paul lit a match and looked at the time, proudly displaying his new watch. A flicker of light gleamed in the distance.

'Take the short cut,' someone shouted.

'The water is high enough to go through the Gap of Clutch.' answered another.

Everyone agreed, to risk the short cut would gain them more speed and get them home sooner.

Reluctantly the skipper changed his course and headed to where the reef outside the Gap of Clutch had last been sighted. A hushed silence fell upon the boat for several minutes. Then came signs of relief followed by nervous laughter as everyone knew they would soon be re-united with families, and the singing began again. Men lit their pipes and settled down for the last turn of the journey.

John Paul Rodgers, in the bow of the boat suddenly shouted,

'Hi, bring her round to windward! Quick! We're going on the rocks!'

Quick as lightning the sail was dropped, the tiller jammed to port. Alas, it was too late. A huge passing swell subsiding lifted the boat liked a small shell and left it perched on the reef. It tilted over and spilled the contents into the sea. The next wave filled the boat full, then carried with the surging water the upside down boat.

Screams and cries pierced the still November air. Mad hands clutched anything within grasp. Many tried to grasp the boat's slippery sides. Within minutes several had drowned. Others thrashed about helplessly, desperately trying to stay afloat. Mary Ann Gallagher, just sixteen years of age, though in deep shock, quietly and perfectly prayed an Act of Contrition before slipping beneath the dark waves.

Others struggled and moaned in the icy sea. Some drowned at once, others were lifted by the huge breakers and dashed against the rocks where they lay stunned until coming waves sucked them back again amidst the rolling, boiling, surf, dead, numb to pain.

A night of torture began for three men clinging, desperately to each other on the up turned boat. Hours seemed like years. Fears and prayers accompanied each other. Young Michael Hugh held his father by the hair as his body got heavier and heavier. All the time, the soft lights of the island houses dimmed as the families prepared for bed, accepting that the young travellers were safely tucked in with friends and families at Burtonport.

The huge waves continued to stampede the small boat, crushing the defenceless victims. All things in life they considered important fell away. Now, they just wanted to live. Ashore, the clock hands crept past eight, nine, ten. One by one the families went to bed, unaware that their loved ones where so near, though three still shouted for help and clutched frantically to the small boat.

The skipper's wife knelt at the side of her bed, rosary beads in her hands.

'It's a wild night, Lord, and the fog is so thick. Thank you for guiding my family safe to Burtonport, for making the right decision to stay the night. May you bring them home safe to me in the morning.'

Climbing into bed, she reached over to her husbands side and clutched his blankets close to her and slept.

Out on the sea, the upside down boat continued to be battered, buffeted, tossed and wave-swept as before. The mist lifted slightly and the two brothers could see the island shore, see their mothers light dim and then disappear completely. A monstrous wave, black as the night bore down on them releasing Michael Hugh's hold on his father.

'Da, Da,' he cried frantically.

'Stay close! Feel for my hand. Jesus, Mary and Joseph help us this night.'

The sons possessed no powers or means to help him. He was gone. His skill as a boat man was known through out town lands, now the sea that he loved had claimed him.

Patrick Hugh clutched his brother firmer, tighter. He tried singing to keep their hearts hopeful and to keep his brother cheerful. He talked about their plans of fishing next spring and summer, teased him about a young island love, how one day he would bounce his babies on his knee and when they were older would tell of this night. Michael Hugh's face grew whiter, Patrick Hugh prayed for God to spare them. Thinking Michael Hugh was praying also he said,

'It won't be long now until morning. Paddy Joe is up from the crack of dawn, he'll see us we'll soon be home.'

A long silence prevailed. Michael Hugh was dead. Patrick Hugh shook him fiercely.

'Wake up, come on now, wake up and keep me company.'

Then he noticed the blood on the right side of Michael Hugh's head. He must have hit his head on the rocks before reaching the boat. Now he was alone. Tears poured down his face and with a heavy ache in his heart he prayed for all the souls lost that night. The sun crept slowly over the horizon. Sea gulls shrieked and soared searching for an early morning meal. Over the fields, islanders heard the chapel bell ring for early morning mass.

Patrick Hugh numbed blue, gripped his cold dead brother. Half dead himself, he saw his island shore, saw the smoke rise from his father's house, where his mother kindled her fire and prepared the morning meal. Then slowly, two, three, four, soon all cottages on Arranmore sent up their little wisps of smoke to heaven.

Excited, Patrick prayed that they would see him. Not quite dead, he managed to release his arm from about his brother's chest and raise a numb cramped arm above the swell of the green sea.

'Jesus, I'm weak,' he mumbled. His arm dropped dead upon the up-turned boat. His mind took him back to childhood days, the warm sun on his back and head as he helped his father and Michael Hugh paint the boat with pitch black tar and proudly display the name, 'The Island.'

The sea bumping against the side of the boat awakened him from his trance. Nineteen dead, his damage, the cold and pain hurting a hundred times worse than before. The restless sea, the boat, his island shore.

'They'll come for me. They're bound to see me,' and staring at the shore he made a last attempt to wave his almost powerless arm. Paddy Joe's attention was caught.

'O Holy Mary, Mother Of God,' he exclaimed and ran as fast as his seventy years old legs could for help. The Islanders quickly put to sea and tried several times to throw a rope to Patrick Hugh. Somehow he grabbed it with unfeeling fingers. Three men hauled him close alongside and bent to the half dead body of Patrick Hugh. His clothes were in tatters cut and rent by the powerful sea. When he was safe, they turned and hurried to pick up Michael Hugh, a stiffened human form. Only one word was uttered,'Dead!' Thus in a tiny boat the living and the dead were carried home with sorrow and thanksgiving.

Patrick Hugh clutched the large metal cup of hot poteen, tea and sugar and told the tale to the shocked weeping Islanders. Sixteen hours he had stuck the cold, fought his fight with death, alone, one dead beside him and underneath, eighteen others- the loves of some, the darlings of their mothers.

'I'll never be on the sea again, never leave my beloved island again. I should have died with them, I am already dead.'

'Nonsense son,' stated the parish priest. 'You're only twenty three years old, time will heal. Tell me.......' but he was stopped in his tracks. Michael Hugh held up his hand. 'No more, I will talk of this no more.' And he never did.

CHAPTER 2

Patrick Charlie was a shy, quiet lad who constantly lived in his brother's shadow. He adored Kachelle and was jealous of his brother. Kachelle tried many times to get him interested in girl friends of hers but he would sulk and go off in a temper whenever Diarmuid Charlie and she tried to match-make.

'I don't know what he will do when I go to America,' said Diarmuid Charlie one day as he lay by Kachelle's side on the green grassy slope that ran down to the school house.

'America,' exclaimed Kachelle half rising to face him. 'Surely you're not going there, Diarmuid Charlie. What about us?'

'Look Kachelle, it's 1937. There's great opportunities in America. A man can really make his fortune. This island has nothing to offer me. From the disaster, this Island is dead!'

'I know how you feel love,' said Kachelle softly wrapping her arms about him. Diarmuid Charlie shrugged her off.

'No you don't, women don't go out to sea to fish. I hate the sea. It claimed nineteen lives, nineteen people that I knew and loved, all in one night.'

'The Arranmore disaster was God's will, Diarmuid Charlie,'

'God's will! I suppose that's your mother's talk. She's not an islander. She doesn't understand how we depend on the sea for a livelihood.

Kachelle stopped him saying any more by placing her hand over his mouth.

'My mother might not have been related to those who died, but I was, through my father's family. The disaster affected us all. We have to bond closer together and help one another to get over this bad time, otherwise this island is doomed!'

'I don't care about the Island, Kachelle. I was to go 'Tatie Hoking that year. I had my bags packed only Da found out and there was a hell of a row. I could have been among the dead. The very thought sends shivers down my spine. I can't face the sea every day knowing that. I have to get away as far as possible from it.'

Placing her arms around him Kachelle comforted him.

'We are all mourning, but time will come when life will get back to normal. Padraic Charlie loves the fishing and the sea. He wants to work at nothing else.

'I can't understand him, why he wants to stay here. This is not for me, Kachelle. I'm going to America, if not by the end of the summer definitely by spring of next year. You will have plenty of time to make arrangements for your mother. Sure she'll not be the only woman living alone. We can earn great money in America. You can see to her financially. You've been looking after her since you were eight. You have to decide what you want in life. Most girls your age are married with families. This place is dead. Since the disaster it is as if life has stopped. This island will never laugh again, Kachelle. I feel as if I'm suffocating. Please come with me.'

Cupping his face with her hand to reassure him, Kachelle softly said, 'We are all mourning, but time will come when life will be good again. Our people will sing and dance at the cross-roads and all this sad time will be behind us. I cannot leave my mother. She is not an Islander, has never really been accepted, she only has me. Please, Diarmuid Charlie stay, I love you! We can make a go of it, start a business..........'

'Don't make me laugh,' Diarmuid Charlie stated scornfully. 'The only business here is fishing and you have to go to sea for that. Have you not been listening to what I have just said? I'm afraid to go to sea. Me, a fisherman, afraid!' and he sobbed loudly.

Kachelle embraced him and kissed the top of his head, his forehead, eyes, nose and finally his mouth. He pulled her firmly into his arms and kissed her back passionately. They clung tightly together kissing and caressing, nervously at first, then with a passion that surprised them both. It was as if they both knew their love would be short and sweet.

'We are as one, Kachelle. You belong to me now and for always,' he whispered as he lowered his fair head into the nape of her neck.

'Oh God,' Kachelle groaned as she snuggled closer to him. 'What we have done is wrong.'

'Sh, shh....my love. Don't fret. We will be together always, I will always take care of you, be there for you, I love you.'

They lay in silence. His fair hair tangled among her bright red curls which glinted and shone in the hot afternoon's sun. After a while Diarmuid

Charlie spoke.

'We must keep my going to America between us, even Padraic Charlie does not know. If my Da got wind of my going to America there would be hell to pay. You will come with me?'

'This is all so sudden, I have to think. My mother, I would have to make arrangements, save some money. Look, love, one day at a time. I must go, love. See you tomorrow.' And Kachelle hurried away. She needed time alone to think, something she couldn't do while staring into his beautiful blue eyes.

Two months later and she, Diarmuid Charlie and Padraic Charlie had been to market in Dungloe. It had been a good day. A fair price had been made on the dried and fresh fish. Kachelle had sold her mother's eggs, dulse and periwinkles and in return was bringing home bacon, tea, sugar and other little luxuries that made the long summer days' hard work worthwhile. She had sung at the fair and had collected six shillings which she intended to give Diarmuid Charlie along with the other four shillings she had saved all year towards her fare to America.

'Yes,' she smiled nervously at Diarmuid Charlie as the boat pulled ashore. 'Meet me at our ususal place, as soon as you can, my love,' she whispered in his ear as he helped her ashore.

'I'll try,' he muttered among the calls from other men to join them in the local pub. There would be a night of celebrations for the men who had done well on market day.

At eleven o'clock the moon sank behind the dark clouds, throwing a heavy blanket of darkness around the island. Kachelle shivered and pulled her shawl up and over her head.

'Oh please, God, let him come soon!' she prayed. 'I must talk to him, tell him tonight. He'll know what to do!' Her heart thumped widely in chest with fear. 'He'll stand by me. I know he will. He loves me. We'll go away, nobody will know. Oh Sacred Heart of Jesus, please let him come soon.'

Kachelle's prayers went unanswered. By twelve thirty she was still alone. In the distance she could hear singing coming from the pub and soft candle light through the small windows made a welcoming gesture. She daren't go near the pub. That was a man's world from which women were barred. It was best to go home. She would have to wait until tomorrow.

Kachelle awoke to the whispering of a soft Irish rain against the bedroom window.

'Alana, Alana what ails you this morning?' asked her frail mother. 'You're usually up at the cock's crow and have half a day's work done. No doubt you're tired after the market day. You lie on a while and I'll mash some tea. Always remember if you get the name of being an early riser you can lie all day,' chuckled the old woman.

'God bless all here,' shouted auld Biddy Joe Boyle as she loosened her shawl and entered the tidy kitchen. 'God love you, Sheila, sure I smelt tae half way down the road and couldn't pass!'

'You know you're welcome any time, Biddy Joe,' said Sheila, 'You don't have to use a cup of tae as an excuse. I'll give you the tae and sure you can read my cup. Sure fair exchange is no robbery!'

'Here, have you heard the latest? There was murder in the McGinleys last night.' Kachelle, startled and alert, crept to the kitchen door and quietly entered.

'Murder there was. Blood and snatters everywhere!'

'What in God's name happened?' asked Sheila, and she quietly poured three mugs of strong tea.

'Sure that Charlie Hughie McGinley was never right in the head. He rules that house with an iron fist. Apparently he got drunk and was fighting with Pat Joe. Diarmuid Charlie and Padraic Charlie intervened and tried to get him to go home, but you know once the drink is in, the wit is out! He started on his two sons and when he got home poor Lizzie and the girls got it too. He wrecked the house, calling everybody all the whores of the day and knocked poor Lizzie into the corner. Diarmuid Charlie got laid him into to protect his mother and I hear he threw Diarmuid Charlie out! Poor Lizzie has a black eye and a busted lip. I heard her sobbing out at the turf stack where she had spent the night. Father Connolly has been sent for. I suppose Charlie Hughie'll come off the drink for another wee while. Sure what are we poor women to do at all, at all!'

Sheila blessed herself and thanked God that her late husband had never lifted a hand to her.

'Well, no man will ever hit me,' stated Kachelle.

'Sure love, no woman will ever beat a man. We just have to put up with it,' said Biddy Joe as she patted Kachelle's arm comfortingly.

'No we don't,' affirmed Kachelle. 'He has to sleep sometime. Be Jesus, I'd get him when he would be sleeping!'

'Language, language young lady,' remonstrated her mother. Biddy Joe lifted her apron, threw it over her head and laughed loudly.

'Oh girl, you don't have that red hair for nothing. Sure half the men on the island are frightened of you. Get him when he's sleeping! That's a good one, it is, it is!'

And with that all three fell about laughing. After a while a quietness descended on the small, dark kitchen. All three were thinking of poor Lizzie.

'He'll kill her one day,' stated Biddy Joe. 'if Diarmuid Charlie doesn't kill him first. I believe he gave him a good going over last night. He'll be lucky if the Gardai on the mainland are not looking for him.'

'More likely his uncles Micky, Diarmuid Charlie and Hughie will get to him,' confirmed Sheila. 'The madness in them McGinleys's can be traced back for generations.'

'That's what is wrong this place. It needs new blood. There is too much inter-marrying. Everyone is bloody related. It's as well you joined us from the mainland and yet look at the hard time you got from everyone when you settled here with your Tom. You'll always be considered an outsider, even though your Tom and the McGinleys's are full cousins. Why, what is wrong with you child?' asked Biddy Joe, 'You've gone as white as a sheet!'

'I didn't know Da and the McGinleys were full cousins, Ma. Why that would make me related to Diarmuid Charlie and Padraic Charlie,' cried Kachelle.

'I wouldn't worry about that,' said Biddy Joe. 'Sure if you traced us all back we'd all end up from the one couple. It's the island way of life. That's why we don't like outsiders- no offence Sheila.'

'None taken, Biddy Joe. If I hadn't had you for a good friend all these years I believe I would have ended up mental!'

'Where are you going, child, in that rain?' Sheila asked her daughter. Something about Kachelle frightened her. She glanced at Biddy Joe who was studying Kachelle carefully.

'Just out, Ma. I need some fresh air.'

Biddy Joe reached for Kachelle's cup.

'Ah God, Sheila, there's trouble ahead. But it can be sorted out. A fair haired fellow is involved but a black haired one will take the blame!'

'Oh God, tell me more, Biddy Joe' exclaimed Sheila.

'No it's Kachelle's cup. You'll know in good time.'

Kachelle hurried to the main road, grateful that she had not met anyone. She climbed the steep ridge to the lighthouse. On reaching the top she made out the outline of a man standing beside a huge rock.

'Diarmuid Charlie, oh Diarmuid Charlie, I'm glad you're....... Why, Padraic Charlie, what are you doing here?'

'I know this is where Diarmuid Charlie and you meet. I've often watched yous.'

Kachelle blushed.

'You had no call to spy on us. Where is Diarmuid Charlie?'

'Your precious Diarmuid Charlie is gone,'

'Gone? Gone where?' she demanded.

'To America!' he stated bluntly.

'He can't have! I was to........'

'I tell you he has gone. He rowed over to the mainland after the fight with me Da. Said he would get a lift to Derry, make his way to Belfast and his next stop would be America. You don't seem surprised. Tell me. Kachelle, did you know that he was planning to leave?'

'Yes I did, but he wasn't to go until the end of the Autumn. He is sending for me!'

'Forget it Kachelle. Diarmuid Charlie will never send for you,' and he made to clasp her hands.

'Don't touch me. You're lying! He will send for me, he will!' And she made a dash down the slippery slope.

On reaching home her bright red curls clung desperately to her head and face. She was soaked through, sobbing uncontrollably. Sheila and Biddy Joe were startled when she entered the safe, warm kitchen.

'Alana. what ails you? What has happened?' begged her frightened mother.

Biddy Joe took control. She guided Kachelle to the turf fire, undressed her taking off her damp clothes and placed a warm towel around her shoulders and started to dry her hair. She pressed her finger to her lips and urged Sheila to pour a drop of poteen into hot water for Kachelle to drink. She took the warm strong liquid and eventually her sobs subsided.

'Now, love, when you are ready, tell us what is wrong,' urged Biddy Joe . Sheila locked the front door, drew the curtains across the small kitchen window and lit the single candle.

'He's gone to America, mum,' she sighed.

'Who has, love?' asked Sheila.

'Diarmuid Charlie, the love of my life,' and the tears started to flow again.

'I'd no idea, love,' whispered her mother. 'I thought you, Padraic Charlie and Diarmuid Charlie were just good friends! Perhaps he'll write when he gets settled. There was always a longing in Diarmuid Charlie to travel. Perhaps he's just following his destiny!'

'What about my destiny Ma?' And Kachelle took another sip of her now cold drink. Biddy Joe with her sharp eyes and mind studied Kachelle.

Straightforwardly she asked, 'What's really wrong, Alana? You can tell your mother and me. We love you. Why, you've been like the daughter I never knew.' Kachelle looked puzzled at Biddy Joe.

'Biddy Joe, Ma, I'm pregnant!'

'Oh Jesus Mary and Joseph,' cried Sheila falling onto her knees and blessing herself.

'There's damn all them three can do about it Sheila. Get off your knees, woman. She's not the first and she won't be the last,' affirmed Biddy Joe. 'Did McGinley know?' she demanded of Kachelle.

'No, no-body knows only you two. I was planning to tell him today but he's gone and he doesn't know. Oh what am I to do?' and once again the tears started to flow.

'Oh Biddy Joe, Father Connolly will demand that I send her to one of those Magdalene laundries in Dublin,' and she raced over to Kachelle and put her arms around her protectively. 'My beautiful Kachelle can't go to England, that den of iniquity. She doesn't know anybody there and besides who'll look after me? Oh Kachelle, Kachelle girl, what have you done?'

'She didn't do it on her own, Sheila. We have got to think what is best for Kachelle and you. Put the kettle on and make some tea, while I have a think. You, me girl, go and take a lie down. Let me turn this through my head for a while.' and with that Biddy Joe drew out her clay pipe, lit it and settled down to her smoke, staring into the turf fire. Sheila went on her knees and started to recite quietly the Rosary. Kachelle lay on top of her bed rubbing her hand over her stomach.

'Oh little one, I know if your father knew he would stand by me. He loved me, he did. I know he did and I will always love him.'

After a while she fell into a soft sleep.

Kachelle woke with a start. She had a splitting headache. Her mouth was dry and her eyes were swollen and puffed from crying. She made her way to the kitchen following the soft murmers of her mother and old Biddy Joe.

'Come in love, come in,' urged her mother pulling the chair closer to the fire.

'Now Kachelle, Biddy Joe has something to say and I want you to listen carefully without interrupting.'

Kachelle gratefully accepted the large chipped mug of sweet tea and settled back to listen to Biddy Joe. Right now she couldn't care less if she died.

'How far gone are you?' urged Biddy Joe.

'Almost two months,' whispered Kachelle.

'Well girl, here's your options. One, you can go into one of those horrible laundries and probably spend the rest of your life there. You'll eventually lose your child after a month never to see it again. Two, you can travel to England, that den of iniquity, have your baby and try to earn a living and rear a child on your own. A pretty girl like you wouldn't stand a chance in England, love. Many a good Irish girl has had to take to the streets to prostitution just to survive. Three, you can marry Padraic Charlie McGinley.'

Kachelle was so startled that she dropped her mug of tea.

'Marry Padraic Charlie? Never, Biddy Joe, never!'

'Hold on my girl, think about it. He has adored you from afar for years now. With Diarmuid Charlie out of the way, he'll probably make his move soon,' said Biddy Joe.

Kachelle remembered Padraic Charlie reaching for her hands. She felt sick.

'I don't love Padraic Charlie,' she explained. 'I love Diarmuid Charlie.'

'Yes, but Diarmuid Charlie is not here and Padraic Charlie is. He'll eventually get his father's boat and house once his sisters are married off and he'll never leave the island,' stated Biddy Joe. 'You've no option, Kachelle, it's your only choice. Your mother needs you and do you honestly want to leave this island?'

'No, no, I don't but.......'

'No buts about it. Padraic Charlie McGinley's it is then,' stated Biddy Joe. 'We have to make plans.'

Sheila sat opposite the two, the Rosary beads clasped in her hands. Thank God, Biddy Joe was here, she could depend on her friend Biddy Joe to help them, she thought to herself.

'But when he hears about the baby....'

'No, no, on no grounds do you tell him' quickly answered Biddy Joe. 'Sure what man can be sure of any of his children? You'll pretend it's his. 'We'll bind you up so you don't show too much, then your mother and I will deliver your baby six to eight weeks early.'

'Oh Biddy Joe, I can't, I would be betraying Diarmuid Charlie!'

'To hell with Diarmuid Charlie. Did he send you a note or a message? He could have called at the house on his way to the boat. No, he had had enough and got off. You'll probably never hear from him again. You've to mind number one, girl, that's you, then your child.'

'And Padraic Charlie, what does he get?' asked Kachelle.

'Why he gets the finest looking woman on the Island. He'll be the envy of all the men here and on the mainland. He's getting a good worker, good breeder and in time you will give him children. So on the whole he doesn't lose out,' stated Biddy Joe.

'What if my secret gets out?' asked Kachelle nervously.

'Sheila, have you a Bible in the house?'

'I do, yes,'

'Well get it out' demanded Biddy Joe.

Rising she took the bible from Sheila and held it close to Kachelle's stomach. Placing Sheila's, Kachelle's and her own hand on top she intoned,

'We swear by the Holy Bible to keep this secret this night!'

All three women answered, 'I do.'

A roar of thunder and a flash of lightning vibrated through the small house. Kachelle shuddered and the hairs on the back of her neck rose.

'OK,' she said meekly. 'I'll meet Padraic Charlie..' She rose to leave the room. Halting, she stared at Biddy Joe. 'Biddy Joe what did you mean when you said I was like the daughter you never knew?'

'Like I said, love, you're not the first nor the last. I was young and pretty once. I loved my man but he deserted me like a rat leaving a sinking ship. I entered one of them laundries to pay for my so-called sins, while the local priest there couldn't keep his hands off me! I eventually escaped, but I had to leave my beautiful daughter, Kathleen, behind. For one month I had her. Then they took her away from me and I have never seen her since. One man has hurt and deserted you. Make sure no man ever does that again. So now you know my secret,' and slowly she lowered herself into the chair.

Kachelle crossed the room and hugged Biddy Joe and then her mother.

'I'm here for you both; I love you both. I'll marry Padraic Charlie McGinley, but my heart belongs to Diarmuid Charlie!' With a hardened heart she left the room.

Biddy Joe's plan worked. Seven months later, Kachelle, married to Padraic Charlie, had settled in his father's house and produced a beautiful red haired baby girl whom she christened Philomena. She thought the name Philomena rather appropriate. After all, Saint Philomena had been a martyr and a virgin. She had been a virgin for Diarmuid Charlie and a martyr to their sin.

Life was difficult in the McGinley household. Lizzie sat quietly in the corner with her black shawl wrapped tightly around her, mourning over the loss of her beloved son, Diarmuid Charlie. Diarmuid Charlie had been her first born and her favourite. Padraic Charlie was a good lad, but quiet and surly. Diarmuid Charlie was constantly smiling, had a song in his heart and regularlyly defended her from his father's blows and harsh words. She had accepted that she would never see him again and was heart broken. She only left the tiny house to walk across the strand to the chapel to pray and light a candle for his safety. She never questioned Padraic Charlie's sudden marriage or off-spring. If any of her neighbours wondered at his decision it would never be questioned, as this was Arranmore, their island, and they were all very clannish. Most of the people on the Island were related and their biggest fear was the numbers inhabiting the Island dropping so low that the Island would become deserted, so Padraic Charlie and Kachelle were welcomed, as would be their family. No questions would be asked.

Charlie Hughie McGinley senior was a different kettle of fish. He was glad Diarmuid Charlie was gone. His favourite was Padraic Charlie and now with Diarmuid Charlie out of the way the boat and land would come to his second son Padraic Charlie. He was suspicious of Kachelle. What on earth would a fine woman like that see in his surly son Padraic Charlie? Deep down he fancied Kachelle and was often caught gazing at her fine legs while she worked in the bog and he always made her uneasy while she breast fed the baby.

'Put those eyes back in your head old man,' Kachelle would snap at him, though she never told Padraic Charlie. The two girls of the household had left soon after Diarmuid Charlie. Mary Charlie was accepted as a priest's house-keeper in Glasgow and quickly left to take up her new post. Ann Charlie married Jack Seamus Connaghan from the island, but Jack Seamus detested fishing and they moved to Glasgow where he would gain employment in a large factory.

The year was 1938 and the McGinley household had settled down to a routine. The father and Padraic Charlie earned a living fishing and selling their goods at Burtonport. Kachelle fulfilled all household tasks as well as looking after her mother's household and livestock, and she was expecting again. Some evenings when Charlie Hughie and Padraic Charlie were away fishing and all her household chores were completed, livestock settled for the evening, she would settle Philomena at Lizzie's feet and go for a quiet stroll.

Her feet always seemed to bring her to the meeting place of herself and Diarmuid Charlie. Sitting quietly she would stare out to sea, a heaviness in her heart. She would think of Diarmuid Charlie. What was he doing? Did he think of her? Had he met someone new? This last thought always brought tears to her eyes. After a quiet weep she'd pull herself together and say,

'Come on girl, this self-pity won't do. You've made your bed- now lie in it! Life could be worse. You have a roof over your head.'

Padraic Charlie could be demanding at times but she could handle him. She had quickly learned that all she had to do was turn her back to him in bed for a while and he would soon come to heel, glad to be allowed to put his arms about her, to kiss her, fondle her and eventually make love to her. She knew she had this power over him, hadn't all women this power? No, she did not feel as if she was using him. She kept his home spotless, earned a living by looking after his livestock and selling their goods on market day and caring for her mother and his parents. Yet sometimes she was acutely aware that something was missing in her life. She was twenty four and yet felt eighty. She no longer felt like singing. The only joy in her life was Philomena. Now she was expecting again, Padraic Charlie's child and how would she feel about this child?

Life was hard on the island. There was talk of a second world war. Many young people's, parents, were leaving for England where work was plentiful, because young English men were joining the forces. Dark clouds had been gathering over Europe, yet the island people believed that this war would not affect them.

On Friday 1st September 1939 Kachelle gave birth, assisted by old Biddy Joe and her mother, to a healthy dark haired baby girl who was quickly named Sheila. She was the image of her father and he was delighted. While Kachelle cradled her in her arms amazed at her love for this child who sucked quickly at her breast, her mother whispered in her ear, 'Everything has turned out alright, love, God is good!'

Only old Biddy Joe was quick enough to see a dark veil come over Kachelle's eyes. Her heart went out to Kachelle. She really does love Diarmuid Charlie, she thought to herself. Lifting her head as Padraic Charlie came into the room, his face beaming with delight, Biddy Joe could only pray,

'May God help you both!'

September the third 1939 and McGinley's kitchen was packed with neighbours. This was the only house on the north side of the Island with a wireless and everyone waited with bated breath to hear the news.

Two days earlier, German forces had stormed the Polish frontier. Supported by screeching stuka dive bombers, a total 1.25million men swept into Poland and nothing could halt their advance. Now the British

Prime Minister Neville Chamberlain was to make an announcement. At 11.00a.m. the tired, strained voice of Chamberlain announced,'This country is at war with Germany.'

The old women quickly blessed themselves though many men cheered.......Everyone seemed to be talking at once. Many were arguing that Ireland had no love of the British and would stay neutral. The younger crowd, with excitement showing on their faces, was already planning to travel to England to seek work, which would be plentiful now with the English away fighting. Kachelle sat quietly with Sheila in her arms and Philomena at her feet. She didn't have any particular worries. Padraic Charlie would never leave the island.

Life on the island continued in its laid back easy-come, easy-go lifestyle, but every day would bring fresh news of the war. Kachelle's life continued as usual. Up early every morning to light the fire and prepare breakfast and see to her two daughters' needs. Feed the livestock and then race over to her mother. Biddy Joe would always be there before her, doing her best to help out. By lunch time a full day's work had been completed. Yet there were many more chores to do.

Some days Charlie Hughie would be very helpful and pleasant, others he would fume with temper over the slightest thing and rant and rave like a mad bull. Philomena would hide in a corner, her eyes bulging with fear. Sheila would give him one of her dark menacing looks and go back to what she was doing. One day ran into another, with Padraic Charlie constantly talking about the war. By the Spring and Summer of 1940, the situation worsened as first Denmark and then Norway, the low countries and and France all fell to a new wave of Nazi onslaughts. Mussolini's Italy entered the conflict on June 10th 1940, while the Germans surged towards Paris. Stalin's Russia had started the war as a partner of Germany but shortly before June22nd 1941, Hitler launched a surprise attack. The German army swept eastward along a thousand mile front, leaving towns devastated and airfields littered with burning planes. War was to come to the U.S.A. with similar suddenness. Pearl Harbour was hit by Japanese bombers at 7.55am on the morning of Sunday 7th 1941.

Still Kachelle struggled on. Life was harder now. Crowds were smaller at market day as many people from Donegal had left to work in England or join up, even though Ireland had stayed neutral. Padraic Charlie was worried. His father's mental health appeared to be failing. Some days he seemed confused and would get very irritated and annoyed with everyone. One minute he could be quite pleasant and the next he would be shouting and insulting everyone. He had become forgetful and he was drinking heavily.

The family boat was in need of repair. Their fishing nets were in need of replacement and Kachelle was being damn difficult. She was determined to have no more babies until the war was over. The last attempt had resulted in a miscarriage. He had threatened to talk to the priest about her refusing him his rights but she had laughed in his face. In the end he had agreed with her. Food and clothing were scarce. Little money was now made at the fishing. The younger men had gone to England and wrote home of the great fortunes to be made as work was plentiful. Padraic Charlie toyed with the idea of going to England.

On the first of March 1941, Ernest Bevin, Minister of Labour for Great Britain, called on British women to help in the war effort. One vital need was for women to work in the ammunition factories, filling shells with explosives. But there was a wealth of other options also. More and more women were going out to work. They found employment in tank and aircraft factories, Civil Defence, nursing, transport and other key occupations, and in so doing, they released men for the armed forces.

By 1942, the first United States service men began to arrive in Britain and set up military bases. 1.5million would pass through the United Kingdom before the war was over. The 'GI's,' as they became known, were well paid and in their spare time were determined to enjoy life.

CHAPTER 3

Back home on Arranmore, life was very difficult. The winter of 1942 had been particularly harsh. Violent storms racked the little Island and the boats were unable to travel to the mainland for supplies. Flour was scarce, as was tea, sugar, tobacco and alcohol. The McGinley's were lucky to own a cow, so at least there was milk for the children, a little butter and cheese. By now the family boat was in much greater need of repair but money was scarce. Padraic Charlie was silent and surly. His father, while sober, was cantankerous, contentious and contrary who constantly complained of having extra mouths to feed. Philomena and Sheila, although young, knew to keep out of his way.

'I'm going to England,' announced Padraic Charlie one evening. 'I'm sick of drinking watered down milk and making do. The fishing is finished unless I get the boat repaired. There's no option. Work is plentiful and the money good. Within a year I should have the boat back on the sea.'

Kachelle was astounded. He was addressing his father. He hadn't talked it over with her. A grown man seeking his father's approval! Angrily she grabbed her shawl and raced towards her mother.

'I am so tired of life,' she meekly admitted to Biddy Joe and her mother. 'I'm struggling and getting nowhere. Now Padraic Charlie is going to England there will be even more for me to do, and to be honest, I don't trust Charlie Hughie! Every minute of the day I catch him leering at me with those evil eyes. At least with Padraic Charlie there he wouldn't dare make a move!'

'Well then, there is only one solution,' said old Biddy Joe who had moved in with Kachelle's mother after the thatched roof had fallen in on her house.

'Go to England with him.'

'To England!' exclaimed Kachelle. 'How could I? I've two weans?'

'We'll look after them. Your mother and I could do with some young company, couldn't we, Sheila?' said Biddy Joe. 'Two earning will get you home sooner, and believe me, the change will do you good. Go with him, girl!'

'I'm going too,' announced Kachelle when she returned home. 'My mother and Biddy Joe will look after the weans. Two earning will get the boat on the sea sooner.'

'There's no call for you to go,' roared Charlie Hughie, 'your place is here.'

'This has nothing to do with you,' said Kachelle determinedly.

Padraic Charlie said nothing, yet his expression made it quite clear that he agreed with his father.

By the first of January 1943, it was almost impossible for a woman under forty to avoid doing her bit for the war effort in Britain. Kachelle safely deposited her daughters with her mother and Biddy Joe. She and Padraic Charlie headed for the boat to take them to Dungloe. Two days later, they docked at Liverpool and made their way to London.

Kachelle felt excitement stir within her. So many people, so much noise. She embraced it all. Padraic Charlie had grumbled from the moment they had left the island. Although a fishing man, he had been violently sea-sick on the journey. To comfort him, Kachelle had suggested that it was more nerves with going to a strange place, among strange people. He begged her to tell no one at home about his sea-sickness. Now they stood together at a London railway station, clutching two battered old suit cases, eyes scanning the crowd to see Padraic Charlie's cousin, Joe Martin Flynn who was to meet them.

'Hi Padraic Charlie. Kachelle. Over here,' shouted Joe Martin as he pushed his way forward through the crowd. 'Jesus, it's great to see you both,' he said as he threw his arms around them. 'God, but it is good to see someone from home. How is everyone? How's my ma and dad? How's the fishing Padraic Charlie? Did you have a good journey?'

'Whoa! Slow down,' laughed Kachelle. 'Plenty of time to catch up later. Where are we staying?'

'OK, OK, it's just so good to see yous. Come on, I've a place for yous to stay and I've arranged with you both to meet the foreman at one of the factories. You'll probably start the day after tomorrow.'

'As soon as that?' said Kachelle astounded.

'Ya, there's a demand for workers Kachelle, Jesus, I forgot you were so beautiful, Kachelle, you'll knock them dead- and wait till they hear you singing!' babbled Joe Martin.

'We're here to work, earn our money and get home as soon as possible,' stated Padraic Charlie flatly.

'Ah Padraic Charlie, that's you all over, all work and no play! Jesus, a German bomber could kill us any minute. Relax! Enjoy life! This war can't last forever. You'll be home soon enough! Come on, come on now till I get you settled.'

Joe Martin deposited them in a small two-up two-down in Amelia Street, not far from the train station. The landlady checked their identity cards, even though she knew and had a fondness for Joe Martin.

'Carry those with you at all times,' she stated while she showed them to a small, dark room. The room was stark. It contained a double bed and a small bedside table. A picture of the Blessed Virgin hung over the bed and a crucifix hung over the door. A large basin and jug were placed on an old rickety table as their washing facilities and a heavy dark wood wardrobe put the finishing touches to what was to be their home.

Then she led them downstairs to the small, dark kitchen which was filthy. There was a wooden table with four chairs, an old range that gave out some heat and would be used for cooking purposes also, and the outside toilet was next to a small coal shed. A clothes line that stretched from one end of the small enclosed back yard to the other completed the picture. Padraic Charlie was disgusted, but Kachelle didn't mind. She already had plans for their room and when the landlady asked for five shillings rent in advance she readily handed it over. Accommodation was scarce. They were lucky to get a place at all.

'Come on, it's your first night here. Let's go for a jar,' suggested Joe Martin.

'No we'll leave it and have an early night,' stated Padraic Charlie.

'Ah Padraic Charlie, let's go please,' begged Kachelle.

With reluctance he gave in and after freshening up they followed Joe Martin to the Crown Bar, just off Amelia Street. The place was warm and smelt of stale beer and sweat. Three whiskeys were ordered by Joe Martin. Kachelle had never been in a pub before and she hungrily drank in every sight and sound. The golden whiskey warmed her from her throat down and she soon forgot that there was a war on and her two daughters were back home across the Irish Sea. The crowd was friendly and eager to enjoy themselves. They were right, thought Kachelle, we could be killed any minute. We should enjoy life while we can.

'Come on, Kachelle, give us a song,' said Joe Martin. 'Shssh,' he urged the crowd.

'Silence please,' he called. 'Silence for the singer! One man one song'

The crowd laughed. They all knew Joe Martin and gradually the noise settled to a low hum.

'I have great pleasure to present to you, the beautiful Kachelle McGinley, all the way from the beautiful Arranmore Island, Co.Donegal in Mother Ireland.'

Kachelle hesitated. Singing on market day was much different to singing to an audience in a pub.

'Don't you dare sing,' whispered Padraic Charlie threateningly in her ear. 'These women in here are nothing but whores. Don't you dare show yourself up.'

Kachelle stared at the young women. Many were her own age; several with a yellow tinge to their faces. Joe Martin had told her this was because they worked in the ammunition factories handling the explosives for the shells.

'Go on, love,' one urged her. 'We're for the night shift. It would be nice to hear you before we leave.'

'I'm warning you,' stated Padraic Charlie.

The whiskey seemed to have changed his personality. He had become like his father.

'Don't you warn me,' she stated as she looked him directly in the eye.

Standing up, she looked around the room, smiled at Joe Martin and opened her mouth. A hushed silence descended on the little bar room. 'A Mother's Love is a Blessing,' rang out sweet and clear and brought forth a thunderous applause when finished. 'More, more,' the crowd urged. Kachelle immediately broke into 'Danny Boy,' and there wasn't a dry eye in the house when she had finished!

'God Bless you. Thank you,' people said as they filed out at closing time. Joe Martin was delighted with her.

'Kachelle girl, you're a star. It's the stage you should be on and not a factory floor.'

At this Padraic Charlie stormed out shouting back at her, 'Come on.'

'What the hell did you ever see in him?' asked Joe Martin as he pushed his flat cap back on his head. 'He's the image of his da, you know I always thought that you and...,' Kachelle cut him short.

'Please, Joe Martin, I've got to go. It's been a long day.'

'OK, love,' and he offered his arm. Her first night in London and Joe Martin walked her home. Padraic Charlie tore on in front, muttering to himself.

By 6.00am. The city of London was alive. People were going to work. People were heading home after their night shift. Already queues were forming for fresh bread, milk and meat. Kachelle and Padraic Charlie were up and ready. Padraic Charlie complained of a headache but wouldn't admit to the whiskey disagreeing with him. He was in a foul mood, verbally abusing Joe Martin and her for singing in the pub.

'Look here, Padraic Charlie, I may be married to you but you don't own me. My life belongs to me. We agreed to leave home, earn some money and eventually return home. Now we have living expenses here so we'll equally contribute to these, we'll both save the same amount and any over belongs to each of us to do with what we want. We both need some new clothes and shoes, plus other little personal items, so just let's get on with it and don't dare ever, ever tell me what to do. Loving does not entitle anyone to possession. I'll sing where I want, go where I want and dress as I wish. If you can't handle this situation go back to Donegal. I'm staying!'

A silence fell over the small room. Padraic Charlie was motionless for a while. Eventually he lifted his cap and gruffly said, 'Come on. We'd better go and see the foreman.'

The foreman diligently took all their information, checking again and again their identity cards.

'Why is a young man like you not in the forces?' he asked.

'I'm Irish,' stated Padraic Charlie firmly. 'Ireland is neutral. This war has nothing to with Ireland!'

The foreman took an instant dislike to Padraic Charlie but he needed the workers. Now the girl beside him was a different kettle of fish. He could hardly keep his eyes off her, He would make sure she was on his shift.

'You can have the day shift 7.00am until 7.00pm. You,' and he pointed at

Padraic Charlie, 'can have the night shift- 7.15pm until 6.45am.'

'Why can't we both be on the same shift?' demanded Padraic Charlie.

'Why can't this war be over?' answered the foreman. 'Take it or leave it,' he said flippantly.

'We'll take it,' said Kachelle

'Right. You start now,' said the foreman, taking in Kachelle's fine figure and long legs as he opened the office door for her. She had only time to call a quick good bye to Padraic Charlie.

The foreman led Kachelle towards a long line of pasty faced women all wearing wrap-over pinnies with their hair tied up in head scarves, turban style.

'Here, Betty, show this one what to do,' he shouted over the noise of the machines.

'Hi, how are you? I'm Betty. I remember you, you sang in the Crown Bar last night. Welcome to our team.'

Kachelle had difficulty hearing Betty. The noise from the machines was deafening.

'You'll get used to it,' shouted Betty, and putting her hand in her pinny pocket she pulled out an old worn head-scarf.

'Here, tie this around your head. It will help keep your hair clean.'

Kachelle struggled to tie up her curls which seemed to have a life of their own. Betty took control and showed her how to tie it turban style. A shrill whistle pierced Kachelle's ears and the machines came to a grinding halt.

'Time for our tea-break,' explained Betty. 'You have less than ten minutes to use the lavatory and have a quick cuppa.'

Over two sweet cups of tea Betty filled Kachelle in on the rules and regulations of factory life and the two sowed the seeds of a firm friendship.

'I hate this bloody war,' stated Betty. 'But God, how I love having my own pay packet. For the first time in my life I'm in control. I'm free. My old man is in the forces. Glad to see the back of him, to tell you the truth. Never knew what it was to own a penny. Never had anything decent to wear. He never went short, though. Too fond of hitting out. Even if he does come back, I'm not taking up with him again. I'll live on my own first.'

'Oh, we're here to make enough money to repair Padraic Charlie's fishing boat and then we're back to Donegal,' explained Kachelle.

'Wait till I tell you love. A bloody great big German bomber could drop on us any minute, God forbid,' said Betty. 'Enjoy life while you can. You don't get a second chance. There's that bloody whistle; back to work.'

Kachelle's first day at work finally drew to a close. She drew in a sharp breath of fresh air on leaving the factory. Already a long line of workers was queuing up for the night shift. She spotted Padraic Charlie. It would have been hard to miss his dark surly face. She smiled and waved over. He slowly came across.

'I've had to make my own dinner,' he said sulkily.

'Jesus, you can't expect her to make it while she's in the factory,' laughed Betty. Padraic Charlie scowled at her.

'Look, we'll work something out,' said Kachelle. 'See you in the morning,' Betty linked her arm.

'Come on, tea is on me,' she offered.

'No, no I couldn't,' said Kachelle.

'And why not?' asked Betty. 'Surely you don't prefer to go home and sit alone, when you could be seeing London in the raw!' laughed Betty. 'Who else do you know in London? Look girl, you have to make the effort to make friends. Your old man is away until morning and to be honest I don't think you're too annoyed to see him go.'

'I'm not,' stuttered Kachelle, 'It's just.....ah you're on. What's for tea?'

And the two young women linked arms and walked briskly down the street.

'The finest fish and chips you have ever tasted,' said Betty and she led her to a small café.

Kachelle had not realised how hungry she was. The fish and chips were delicious.

'Don't look now, but you have clicked,' laughed Betty.

'I've what?' asked Kachelle.

'You've clicked. Your man over there can't take his eyes off you. Bet he asks us to go for a drink.'

'Oh Betty, I couldn't, I'm married,'

'So what? We would only be having a drink. Where's the harm in that? If your old man was on the day shift I bet he would be in the pub every night. Come on, live a little.'

With that the young fair haired soldier approached their table.

'Hi you girls. Just finished work, have you? Would you make this my lucky day and let me take you two girls for a drink?'

Betty rolled her 'I told you so eyes' at Kachelle.

'Look I'm off sailing tomorrow I just don't fancy being alone.'

'No, neither do we,' said Betty. 'Sure we'd love to go for a drink. Come on,' and she linked Kachelle on one arm and the young soldier and his mate on the other.

The Royal Oak Bar was already busy. The drinks were ordered and the two young men chatted happily about their home and families. Kachelle felt herself relaxing and a few hours later when Betty called on her for a song there was no hesitation. At 11.00 o'clock the fair haired soldier kissed a slightly tipsy Kachelle on her lips and said good night. Kachelle opened the door to her new home and headed for the stairs. Collapsing on the bed she laughed to herself. God, if her mother and Biddy Joe could see her now! She had enjoyed herself. This den of iniquity appealed to her. Thank God she didn't have to see Padraic Charlie, 'The ideal marriage,' she whispered to herself and fell about laughing.

At 6.30am the noise of the city woke Kachelle. She had fallen asleep in her clothes. Christ! Work! And she rushed to get ready. At ten minutes to seven she was outside the factory gate. Betty was already there.

'Morning, girl,' called Betty. 'God but I enjoyed myself last night. My head is splitting. We had a good drink you know and it didn't cost us a penny, thanks to your looks and singing voice.'

Kachelle made to answer her but she had spotted Padraic Charlie away in the crowd. She waved and called his name but he seemed to be in a world of his own. He had either failed to notice her or ignored her.

Kachelle's jigsaw of life was coming together. Padraic Charlie and she passed like ships in the night. When they did get a few hours together it was to share out their living expenses and savings. He would snap at her new clothes saying that she was selfish and neglecting him. Kachelle paid no heed. Like Betty, she had her own money, a life at last. She pitied the poor men and women who were away fighting the enemy, yet this war had re-structured her boring life. She had even begun to wonder if she could ever live on the Island again.

The days rolled easily from one to the next. She and Padraic Charlie were now nine months in London. Her mother's letters assured her that herself, Biddy Joe and the girls were fine. They appreciated the money she sent them and she begged Kachelle to attend Mass and confessions regularly as that England was a terrible place. Kachelle placed the letter in her handbag. She and Betty were going to the pictures again to see 'Gone with the Wind'. This was their third time seeing it. The two girls would sit in awe and drink in every word.

'Frankly my dear I don't give a damn,' said Kachelle when the foreman would shout at her to work faster. Betty and the other girls would fall about laughing. The noise of the machines didn't bother Kachelle anymore. She could have a perfect conversation above the din and when the girls would call for a song Kachelle would delight them with the 'White Cliffs of Dover,' or imitate Lilli Marlene singing 'Underneath the Lamp Post.'

The bar at night would be packed with young soldiers, many of them American soldiers who had lots of money to spend. They taught the young British and Irish women to jive- a fast moving dance where the man would push and pull the girl into him and on occasions swing her over his shoulders or between his legs. Kachelle was a natural at the jive. She often wondered where she got her energy from after working all day. She and Betty didn't go home now after work. A quick sandwich or fish and chips would do them, and then off to the pub. If there was an air raid, Kachelle would soon get a sing-song going, often she did not close her eyes until 3.00am and when the all-clear sounded it was usually time to go to work.

The devastation of the bombings would bring home to her how safe her two girls were back home in Ireland. Faithfully every week she would send her mother two pounds, a little tea and sugar and plenty of chocolate. The American GI's gave Kachelle the chocolate and bubble gum. Her mother had requested no more bubble gum after Philomena got her hair and Sheilas covered in the stuff. They had to take the scissors to both of the girls' long hair. So now Kachelle gave the bubble gum to her work-mates.

CHAPTER 4

It was on a Saturday afternoon when she and Padraic Charlie were dutifully setting aside their weekly expenses and savings that he announced that they had almost enough to repair the boat. He'd had a letter from home, stating that his father wasn't too well and his mother was having difficulty coping.

'We'll go home next month,' he stated flatly.

Kachelle's heart lurched in her chest. Home? Oh God no, she thought. Not yet please- just a little time more.

'I can't,' she stammered.

'What the hell do you mean you can't?' demanded Padraic Charlie.

'Look, Padraic Charlie, this war has changed everything. Even the island. I was thinking, if we could save more I could perhaps open a small shop at home. You know, selling tea, butter, sugar, tobacco- perhaps a few household items.'

'No, you'll do as I say! You're my wife. We are going home at the end of the month . You'll look after my parents, the children, the livestock- and another thing! Your place is in my bed. You'll do my bidding. I want more children. I want a son!'

'Fuck you! Just who do you think you are? I may be your wife but you don't own me. I'll go back when I'm ready to go back- if ever! Yes Padraic Charlie, if ever! This is my life. I answer to no one. Why, I only have to click my fingers and I could have a dozen men. I don't need you. I don't love you!'

There! It was out at last. His shocked face was pitiful. She was tempted to race over and put her arms about him and apologise, but her legs wouldn't move. She was fighting for her life. She had made a big mistake marrying Padraic Charlie. It was best to finish it here and now.

'This den of iniquity has turned you into a whore! What about the island? What will our neighbours say when you don't return with me? What will my Da say? What about our daughters?'

'Philomena....' she was about to say 'is not yours', but his pained expression weakened her. 'Philomena and Sheila will see me again,' she answered softly, 'I love them dearly, and there's my mother and Biddy Joe. All I'm looking is a little while longer. You go on home now and start to repair the boat. Once I have enough saved for my shop I'll join you. We'll sort everything out. I can't go home now. Not now, Padraic Charlie.'

Padraic Charlie knew not to push her any more or he would lose her for good. Picking up the savings he quietly said,

'I'll be home for next weekend. No point in waiting a month. You do what you have to do. You're a big girl. You know where your home is,' and he quietly left the room.

Kachelle pulled her coat on and walked nowhere in particular. An hour later and she found herself outside St.Patrick's Chapel. Confession, perhaps she should go. She hadn't been in ages and she had promised her mother.

'Bless me Father I have sinned......'

And her story poured out to the elderly English priest. She told of her love for Diarmuid Charlie. She spoke about Philomena, why she had married Padraic Charlie etc,etc. 'I'm no whore either,' she stated defiantly. A kiss and a cuddle yes, but I'm no whore.'

'You have done very wrong, my child. You are walking the broad road to temptation. You must pray for forgiveness for your sins. God has granted you a roof over your head, two healthy children and a good Catholic husband who only wants to love and protect you. I'll give you absolution now, but you must promise me that you'll go home with your husband and do his bidding. To love, honour and obey were the vows you took before God. Don't throw theses vows back in our Lord's face, my child!'

'I will go home, Father, but not yet. Padraic Charlie is getting out of life what he wants. Why can't I?'

'You are a woman, my child, and a wife! Your place is with your husband. If you don't go with him I can't give you absolution!'

Kachelle saw red. Another man controlling her life. How dare he?

'You can keep your absolution, Father. My life belongs to me. Good night!'

And she slammed the confession box shut. On leaving the church she was confronted with a large statue of the Blessed Virgin Mary. The statue's peaceful, sad face bored through her. Tears welled up in her eyes. She slowly lowered her head and kissed the statue's feet.

'Oh Holy Mary, Mother of God, be with me always. Surely as a woman and my mother you understand me. I can't go home just yet. It's as if something is keeping me here. Please pray for me.' She dipped her hand in the Holy Water, blessed herself and left the church.

'He's away then?' asked Betty.

'Yes, he left yesterday,' answered Kachelle.

'How are you?' quizzed Betty.

'Fine! I'm fine. Now where are we for tonight?'

'Oh I believe there is a new crowd of GI's landed. We'll go to the cinema and then the pub. But first you need cheering up. Come on, treat yourself to something new to wear. I've a friend who has a stall at the market. She has some first class stuff. Got it off some big wig. Come on, we'll pay her a visit.'

'It's absolutely gorgeous. You must have it,' exclaimed Betty.

Kachelle stared at herself in the long mirror. The green crushed velvet dress followed the outline of her magnificent figure. The sweetheart neckline showed off her freckled cleavage and the shorter hemline showed her fabulous legs. Her red hair tumbled down her shoulders and back. Her fiery green emerald eyes completed the picture.

'I can't. It's too expensive.'

'Nonsense,' said Betty. 'You've been saving for ages. Oh Kachelle you must buy it, please.'

'I'll tell you what,' said the stall holder. I'll throw in these couple of dresses. Perhaps you know a couple of little girls they would fit.'

Kachelle stared at the beautiful dresses. They would fit Philomena and Sheila perfectly. Her eyes caught a beautiful shawl and a pale blue cardigan.

'I'll tell you what! Throw in these also and it's a bargain.'
She waited with bated breath.

'OK, it's a deal,' and the two women shook hands. Kachelle handed over her five pounds and felt less guilty. She would have to write a note to her mother and Biddy Joe explaining why she wasn't home with Padraic Charlie and asking them to look after her girls a little while longer. These gifts would help ease her guilt.

When Betty called for Kachelle at 7.30pm all she could say was
'Whoa! Oh Kachelle you look like a film star. You're beautiful!'
'You're looking well yourself. Turn around and let's have a look at you!'
Betty was tall and very slim with short blond hair and blue eyes.

'Let's forget about the pictures tonight, Betty. Let's go up town, somewhere classy. Come on, we'll be snobs for the night.'

'You're on,' laughed Betty. 'That's what I love about you, Kachelle, you make life so exciting.'

The two girls took a bus to Piccadilly Square, linked arms and boldly walked towards the Queen Victoria Public House. The bar was already crowded. As the two girls made their way to a table, heads turned in admiration. A dance band was playing a George Formby tune. In no time Kachelle's feet were tapping. A couple of GI's asked the girls for a dance and they eagerly accepted. Afterwards they took them to the bar for a drink. Tom and Jack were from Boston, USA. They begged the girls to stay with them.

'We're meeting our sergeant later. He's from Ireland. I bet he would be delighted to meet you, Kachelle. Please stay with us a while,' begged Tom.

'Ok! Ok!' laughed Kachelle, 'but right now we're going to the Ladies.'

'I told you, you were looking stunning,' laughed Betty. 'That Tom is a dish and Jack is not bad either. They want to take us for a meal at one of those big hotels. Please say we can go, Kachelle, please. I've never had a big posh dinner.'

'Oh I don't think I could eat anything, Betty. Can we leave it for a while?' Let's join the boys for another drink.'

The girls linked arms and pushed their way forward toward the bar. Jack and Tom waved them over and produced two stools.

'Kachelle, Kachelle, our sergeant is here. Come and meet him. He's......
where did he go Jack?' asked Tom.

'There he is, over there. He has his back to you,' shouted Jack above the din. 'Come on Kachelle and meet him,' and Tom pulled a reluctant Kachelle by the arm.

'Sergeant, I would like you to meet this beautiful girl from Ireland,' started Tom.

The fair haired, broad shouldered man turned to face them. Kachelle felt her knees go weak; she felt sick and faint. Oh God, no! her brain screamed and she fell into a faint. The cool night air helped to bring Kachelle round. Betty was fussing over her trying to get her to take a glass of cold water.

'Are you alright love?' Asked Betty.

'Oh Betty, I thought......'

'Hello Kachelle,' said a broad Irish/American accent.

'Do you two know each other?' asked Betty curiously.

Kachelle pulled herself to her feet and smoothed down her dress. A quick toss of her head assured her curls were all in place.

'Yes, Betty. This is Diarmuid Charlie McGinley. Padraic Charlie's brother,' and she stared at Diarmuid Charlie in the face.

'Kachelle, oh Kachelle,' said Diarmuid Charlie as he caught Kachelle in his arms.

'What a small world,' exclaimed an excited Tom. 'Our Sergeant knows Kachelle.'

'Tom, will you and Jack take Betty for a drink? I need to catch up on old times with my friend and neighbour from Ireland.'

'Yes sir, no problem. Perhaps you two will join us later?'

'We might. For now have a few drinks on me.'

Diarmuid Charlie handed some paper notes to Tom. Betty had caught the shocked look on Kachelle's face and understood immediately that there was something between these two.

'Sure, Tom, come on. Let's dance. We'll see you two later.'

She caught Tom and Jack's arm and marched them back into the Queen Victoria.

Diarmuid Charlie McGinley, tall and bronzed, looked fantastic in his uniform He placed Kachelle's coat over her shoulders and taking her elbow he guided her across the road and away from the hustle and bustle of Piccadilly Square. They walked in silence for a while. Although not cold, Kachelle shivered.

'Here, love, you have had a nasty but delightful shock. We both have. Let's slip into this quiet wee pub and have a brandy.'

The brandy warmed Kachelle and helped her relax.

'Kachelle, I can't believe it is really you. You look marvelous. Why did you leave the Island? What are you doing here? How long have you been in

England?

'Why did you leave me, Diarmuid Charlie?' asked Kachelle quietly.

'Ah Kachelle, I hadn't time. My da was exploding. I thought I had killed him. I was afraid I would go to prison. I meant to get in touch. I couldn't get work right away, I made my way to Canada. I was many months living hand to mouth, I finally got work on a building site. This didn't last long so in desperation I joined the army. I feel as if I'm following my true path in life at last. I was promoted to Sergeant and they say I have potential.'

'Why did you not write to me? Why did you not send for me?' begged Kachelle.

'Kachelle love, it was difficult. There was so much to do. I couldn't write home or send for you until I heard how my da was. I missed you Kachelle, I love you.'

'Stop it, stop it, you coward. You promised to send for me. I waited that night for ages. I needed to talk to you but you never came, and then it was too late!'

Kachelle beat on Diarmuid Charlie's chest with her fists.

'Oh God, why didn't you send for me like you promised? I love you Diarmuid Charlie but I have messed up my life. Please hold me Diarmuid Charlie.'

Diarmuid Charlie wrapped his arms around her and drew her head onto his shoulder. His fair head was resting on her bright red curls.

'I'm sorry, Kachelle, so sorry. Why are you here in England? How have you messed up your life?'

Kachelle took a large gulp of her brandy and slowly related her story. Diarmuid Charlie interrupted her every now and then with:

'You married Padraic Charlie! I have a daughter!

'I knew I was to stay here for a reason, Diarmuid Charlie. Padraic Charlie is just away home. I refused to go. It's fate. If I had gone home I would have missed you. How long are you here for?'

'I've only three days Kachelle and then my company is moving on. We don't know where we are going and anyway I wouldn't be allowed to say!'

'Three days! Oh Diarmuid Charlie, please, please let's spend those three days together. I'll take the time off work. Please don't leave me.'

'I won't, my love, I won't.

He gently pressed his lips to hers and kissed her passionately. Diarmuid Charlie helped her on with her coat. He slipped his arm around her waist and pulled her close to him. Kachelle placed her head on his shoulder and slipped her arm around his waist and slowly they walked home, pausing now and then to kiss gently.

Kachelle placed the key in the lock and pushed open the door. Quietly she led Diarmuid Charlie to the small room she had shared with Padraic Charlie. They just seemed to naturally fall into each others arms and slowly begin to undress each other. Her breasts ached for his touch and she couldn't believe how natural and comfortable they were with each other when naked. It was if the right key was finally in the lock. Her soul mate had returned to her. One minute she was gently whimpering like a little puppy then she was clutching and tearing at Diarmuid Charlie like a lioness. She couldn't believe this person was her.

Diarmuid Charlie just kept repeating: 'Ah, Kachelle girl, I love you, I love you, thank God I found you.' Exhausted they fell asleep in each others arms.

The sunlight poured through the small, filthy window. Diarmuid Charlie eased himself out of bed dressed quietly and left the room. Within a half hour he had returned with fresh bread, milk, ham, tomatoes, cheese, tea and coffee. He brushed Kachelle's curls aside and kissed her softly on the lips. Kachelle awakened stretched her arm above her head exposing her young firm breasts and pulled Diarmuid Charlie to her.

'Come on, girly, up you get. You're bound to be starving. See what the man of the house has brought you!'

'Oh Diarmuid Charlie, where did you get such luxuries?' squealed Kachelle.

'Ah it's marvellous what a few nylon stockings and chocolate will do,' laughed Diarmuid Charlie. 'Thank God for the black market.'

'You have nylon stockings?' asked Kachelle,

'Well, I might have a few left. Now where did I put them?' said Diarmuid Charlie pretending to search his pockets. A few seconds later he threw three pairs of stockings on Kachelle's lap.

'I love, I love you,' laughed Kachelle, as he pulled her up out of the bed and held her close.

'Ah Kachelle, I love you with all my heart and soul. What about you and me heading up to Brighton for a few days? Let's get the sea air around us and lie in the sand dunes like we did before.'

'I'd love to. Brighton it is. We'll eat first and be away for twelve.'

By twelve thirty Kachelle and Diarmuid Charlie were settled in the train. The train was packed with soldiers, young nurses, women with shopping bags. What was noticeable was an absence of children. Kachelle explained that the majority of children had been sent out of London to the countryside.

'Thank God mine are safe in Ireland,' she said.

Diarmuid Charlie's jaw tightened at the mention of the children. As of yet he hadn't asked about Philomena. They booked into a small guest house and immediately went for a walk along the sea shore. Arms entwined they walked slowly along the beach, the ebbing tide just missing their feet. They breathed in deep gulps of sea air and watched the seagulls soar above their heads. They both fell silent for a while.

'A penny for your thoughts,' said Kachelle.

'Oh I wasn't thinking of anything in particular. All this just reminded me so much of home, and I haven't thought of home in so long,' said Diarmuid Charlie.

'Dear God, Diarmuid Charlie, what are we going to do?' pressed Kachelle.

'Look love, for now we're going to be together and enjoy every moment. We'll talk later. Come on, time for a pint.'

Grabbing her hand he pulled her up the beach. The pub was warm and cosy. Everyone chatted friendlily together. Diarmuid Charlie suggested Kachelle for a song and she gladly volunteered a lilting Irish ballad which brought a hushed silence to the room. She soon raised their spirits with 'Pack up your Troubles,' and 'It's a Long Way to Tipperary.'

Diarmuid Charlie's heart swelled with pride and he applauded loudly with the rest of the crowd. Yet there was a deep pain in his chest,

'Oh God, Kachelle, just what are we going to do?' he asked himself.

Kachelle, a little worse now for drink, threw her arms around him.

'I love you Diarmuid Charlie McGinley!' and she kissed him firmly on the lips- which brought another roar of applause.

'Time you were in bed,' laughed Diarmuid Charlie as he swung her up in his arms and out the door.

Once they were safely in the privacy of their own room they explored each other's body with a passion and finally fell asleep, exhausted.

After breakfast next morning they asked the landlady for a packed lunch and agreed that they would spend the day at the beach. The sun was shining brightly out of a clear blue sky. Brighton was bustling and for once war was forgotten. Diarmuid Charlie stopped for some ice-cream and noticed a sign encouraging people to have their photos taken.

'Come on, Kachelle, I want a photo of you.'

'We'll get one taken together,' suggested Kachelle.

'No I want one only of you. You can have one of me and then we'll get one together!'

They entered the small dark shop and was greeted by a bald man who made them very welcome. Diarmuid Charlie looked handsome and proud in his American uniform. Kachelle was tall and beautiful with her red hair falling about her shoulders. Together, a close loving couple. Kachelle lowered her head on to his shoulder. He put his arms about her and looked lovingly down into her eyes.

'Beautiful, beautiful,' exclaimed the small bald man. 'Now where do I send them?'

'One of each to my company,' said Diarmuid Charlie and he gave the addresses and a more than generous tip for the extra postage. 'And one of each- where to Kachelle?' he asked. Kachelle gave her address and was assured that she would receive them within two weeks.

After lunch they walked along the promenade hand in hand. Kachelle spied a sign for a fortune teller.

'Oh Diarmuid Charlie, I must have my fortune told.'

'You women and your fortune tellers! I suppose old Biddy Joe is still reading tay leaves back home. On you go, though mind if she tells you anything about me, I want to know,' he laughed.

'No, you can get your own fortune told,' teased Kachelle and she entered the small shop.

'Come in, come in,' welcomed the old woman. 'Sit yourself down. Now what can I do for a pretty girl like you?'

'I want my fortune told,' said Kachelle and wondered why she felt fearful.

'Tea leaves, playing cards, tarot cards or crystal ball?' asked the fortune teller.

Kachelle studied the items on the small table.

'I've only ever had the tea leaves done. What's special about the tarot cards?' asked Kachelle. Her eyes seemed drawn to them.

'The others love, can see your life like a long road. They can only tell so much. The tarot cards sees that road but can take you to the cross-roads of life. They can advise you whether to turn left, right or to make a move on or back. They give a much better reading. Of course they are more expensive. It's five pounds to have a tarot card reading.'

'Five pounds!' exclaimed Kachelle, but she felt herself pulled stronger to the tarot cards. 'OK, she laughed, I'll spoil myself, read my tarot cards.'

The old woman handed her the pack of long cards with the faces turned down.

'Clear your mind, love. If you want a reading on yourself and a loved one just think of that while you're shuffling the cards.'

Kachelle shuffled the cards thinking all the time of Diarmuid Charlie and herself. She handed the cards back. The old woman placed them carefully in her hands spreading them out.

'Choose seven and don't go back on yourself, always go forward.'

Kachelle chose seven cards and placed them face down on the table. The cards were turned over and strange shapes appeared before her. A Goddess, a hangman, stars. Before she could take in any more the old woman spoke.

'You wear a wedding band even though you don't love him. You have deceived him twice. He does love you. Watch yourself, there's a vicious streak in him and indeed in all his family. There's something wrong here. I see your family tree and his entwined. It's as if you are too closely related, parents too closely related. You know, there's a fine line between intelligence and insanity with close breeding. Your children will carry this gene also, but not some of your grandchildren.'

'Does Diarmuid Charlie love me?' asked Kachelle.

'You've asked a question of the cards; I'm duty bound to tell you. He does love you, but he has other responsibilities. He will stand by you in other ways. You will travel across water soon and you will rock the cradle again. There is a bad time ahead for you. There will be times you will despair; only your children will keep you going. Your son will take the pride of place in your heart. You'll fight tooth and nail for him. The black haired one will eventually settle down. Check out your family tree and his. The true facts can be used as a weapon over him. Your place is across the sea. You're a strong, independent minded woman who will battle for her son's birthright. You're a born leader who looks at life and religion through independent practical eyes. You've broad shoulders; you'll carry your cross. By the time the primrose blossoms you'll have resigned yourself to your fate. For now, go and enjoy what is left of your three days with the love of your life,' and she quietly folded the cards.

Kachelle stumbled out in amazement. 'Oh Diarmuid Charlie, she knew you were here waiting for me,' she explained.

'Possibly saw me though the window waiting for you,' he laughed.

'But she knew we only had three days, Diarmuid Charlie, she knew I didn't love Padraic Charlie.'

'Oh Kachelle, you and your fortune tellers. They see you coming, they do. Come on let's go back to the guest house where I can show you how much I love you,' and he pulled her close and nibbled her left ear. Kachelle put her fortune teller's words out of her head and followed Diarmuid Charlie's advice.

On their last day together they awoke early and lay in each other's arms. Diarmuid Charlie lit a cigarette and slowly inhaled before handing the cigarette to Kachelle.

'Will I ever see you again?' asked Kachelle nervously.

'I don't know, love. I'd love to take you now in my arms and fly away with you. I don't know where I'll be posted to or if I'll survive this war but if I do, I'll contact you.'

'Oh God, I'll pray hard that no harm will come to you and when you send for me I'll take the girls and join you in Canada. The fortune teller told me I'd cross water, you know.'

'Hold it, Kachelle, you don't understand, love. I can't send for you until....' he nervously pulled on the cigarette.

'What's wrong love? You've turned quite pale. What is it?' she pleaded.

A silence fell on the small room.

'There is someone else, isn't there?' she asked.

His silence told her the truth.

'Do you love her too?' she asked, puzzled.

'She's….. she's my wife!' he whispered with bowed head. 'Oh Kachelle, how come we messed up both our lives? I love you as I have never loved anyone.'

Kachelle's chest was heavy. The pain started in the pit of her stomach and spread to her chest. She felt as if someone had tightened a great belt under her bust and kept tightening it. She found it hard to breath. The tears welled up in her eyes. Diarmuid Charlie reached to put his arms around her but she pulled away.

'We've got to talk, Kachelle. Would it be fair to Padraic Charlie to take his two daughters, yes two daughters, 'cos I'm sure he loves Philomena, away from him?'

'What about you? Do you have children?' Again there was silence.

'Yes, two boys, twins. They're almost two years old. Their mother is a lovely girl and a good girl, she was good to me when I had nothing and no-one. She's twelve years older than me. I don't want to hurt her. I can't leave her and my boys, Kachelle. If I came home to Ireland, my boys would have to stay in Canada. We have to think of the children. Oh please, Kachelle, be strong for me.'

'I'm sick of being the strong one! Kachelle's strong, she'll cope with anything. She can take everything in her stride. Right now, I want someone to hold me, for them to be strong and to tell me that everything is going to be alright.'

Sobbing uncontrollably she allowed Diarmuid Charlie to take her in his arms and heard him whisper, 'Hush now Alana, hush, hush.

They stayed like this for ages. Finally her sobbing subsided. She walked to the small table, poured some water into a basin and washed her tear-stained face. Pulling on her coat, she stopped Diarmuid Charlie from following her.

'Please love, I need to be alone. I promise to be back soon,' and she headed out the door. The sharp sea air caught her breath as she made her way to the highest point along the sand dunes, where once again alone she broke down in ears, arms wrapped around her knees. She didn't even bother to wipe her tears away. They rolled down her cheeks, into the crevice of her young, firm bosom.

'Oh God,' she prayed, 'help me! What am I to do? Jesus, Mary and Joseph, I place all my trust in you. Oh remember oh most gracious Virgin Mary, please help me. How am I going to let him go?'

Again the tears rained down. Sometime later, exhausted, she dried her tears. Anything could happen she thought. He might not return home from the war. God Forbid. Right now he was back at the guest house waiting for her. Time enough to make plans when the war was over. On her way back she found Diarmuid Charlie out looking for her. He looked drained.

'Oh darling, I was worried about you. I feared you might......'

'Shh love, shh. Let's go back.'

Arms entwined they made their way back to their small room. There was no drinking or singing now. They both knew they only had a few hours left together and they wanted to savour every moment. Their love-making was slow and gentle. Gently caressing each other with butterfly kisses and declaring their love for one another, they clung together, fearful of letting go.

They didn't sleep that night. There would be plenty of time later for sleeping. They loved and comforted each other.

'I'll always love you, Kachelle, please remember that.'

'I love you too, Diarmuid Charlie, I always have and always will. Please promise you'll take care and come back to me, even through a letter. Please keep in touch. One letter a year is all I ask, just to let me know how are you. I'll write one to you, once a year.'

'Won't that cause rows between you and Padraic Charlie?'

'Don't send them directly to me. Send them to my mother. I'll make arrangements with her. One letter a year, please Diarmuid Charlie, promise me.'

'OK. Love, one letter a year. And when you get the chance you will forward me a photo of Philomena and I'll send one of her brothers?'

'I promise,' she yielded.

Their journey back to London was silent. They sat close together, hands clasped. There was nothing to say. Time was running out. He had to report back to his barracks at 2.30pm. There was just an hour and a half left. She found herself constantly staring at him, drinking in every detail-his fresh complexion, his beautiful silky fair hair and those twinkling baby blue eyes which could make her heart skip a beat every time he smiled. All too soon they arrived in London. Kachelle's heart was pounding in her chest. She held him close, fearful of letting go. The crowds pushed and shoved about them. She could feel his heart pound. He held her tight.

'Ah, my love,' he whispered hoarsely. She felt and tasted his silent tears.

'Don't, darling, don't,' she begged wiping his cheeks with the palms of her hands. A gentle wind lifted her bright curls and pressed them full in his face. He buried his lips in the nape of her neck.

'Be strong, love,' she begged. 'We must be strong. Let's leave it all in God's hands. May He watch over you and protect you. Perhaps after the war there will be some way we can be together. I'll pray to St. Jude of Hopeless Cases,' she teased, trying to put a smile back on his face.

Their last kiss was bitter-sweet. He cupped her face in his hands, kissing her forehead, nose, cheeks, eyes and finally again her lips.

'Goodbye, my love, take great care, I love you only and always.'

Stepping back, he saluted her and, lifting his hold all, he walked away. Kachelle's legs buckled. She grasped a near by hand rail. 'Damn this war,' her brain screamed. 'Damn you, Diarmuid Charlie McGinley for not sending for me. Damn you, for allowing this to happen. I love you, my darling, I love you only and forever,' she whispered after him.

He was gone. She had lost sight of his broad shoulders. There was nothing to do but go home.

CHAPTER 5

Kachelle couldn't remember reaching home. She must have slept nearly twelve hours. She had lain down fully clothed on top of the bed. Her head ached. She felt faint and exhausted. Someone was hammering on her door.

'Come on, Kachelle, open up.' It was Betty. 'Please Kachelle, come on, open up.'

Reluctantly Kachelle opened the door.

'Oh God, what has happened to you? You look awful!' exclaimed Betty.

'He's gone, Betty. I'll probably never see him again,' and she collapsed in Betty's arms.

'Come on, girl, a hot bath will do you good. Sit down till I get you a cup of tea and a bath and then you can tell me all about it.'

Two hours later, Kachelle had related all her tale to Betty. She explained about Philomena, Biddy's advice, marrying Padraic Charlie, meeting Diarmuid Charlie and their three days together. Betty wrapped her arms about her.

'To see you singing your heart out and keeping everyone's spirits up you would think you hadn't a care in the world and the whole time your heart was breaking you were crying in your heart. Come on now, girl. I'll get you something to eat and then it's back into that bed. I'll call for you tomorrow morning for work. The quicker you get back to work the better. By the way, you and I have been made supervisors!'

'What?' asked Kachelle.

'Yeah, I couldn't believe it either but we have. A few of the men are raging they weren't made foremen. We'll show them anything a man can do we can do better,' laughed Betty.

'You're a good friend, Betty. Thanks for coming round. I'll do you a good turn some day too!'

'Enough of your nonsense! Into bed with you and get a good night's sleep. I'll see you in the morning.'

Turning to put the light out, Betty noticed Kachelle's eyelids were already closing. 'The whiskey in the tea did the trick,' she thought to herself as she let herself out.

Kachelle was up and ready for Betty callingthe next morning. She looked pale, which only enhanced her beauty. She and Betty had been promoted to supervisors and she threw herself into her work, working all the hours she could. She wasn't in the mood to go to the pictures or the pub or singing. Work and sleep seemed to be her motto. Kachelle was so much caught up in herself that she failed to notice a change in her friend.

Betty was not her usual self. She had stopped asking Kachelle to go out. She wasn't eating and seemed depressed. Kachelle turned quickly to talk to her one day at work and for the first time in weeks she noticed the change in her friend. When their shift was finished, she put her arm through Betty's and said:

'Right, we're going for a drink and a chat. Something is wrong with you. Who are you in love with now?' She teased, guiding Betty towards their local.

Two brandies were ordered.

'Come on girl, spill the beans. Who is it this time?' enquired Kachelle.

'Oh Kachelle, I have messed up my life!'

Kachelle was confused.

'How? What have you done? asked Kachelle, puzzled. Betty took a sip of brandy.

'It's my husband; he's been injured. He's lost both his legs.'

'Oh I'm sorry Betty, but I thought you and he were finished?'

'I thought so too, and he wrote me a letter releasing me from our marriage vows saying he loves me too much to be left with half a man! Life's strange Kachelle. I love my job, I'm now supervisor. I've my own place, good money but you and I know that when the men come home from the war we'll all be made redundant. It will be jobs for the boys. Women were needed. We answered the call, we did a good job but it will be back to the kitchen sink for us and I'm pregnant!'

'You're what?'

'I'm pregnant and I don't know who the father is. How will I survive trying to work and raise a child? My husband is a good man but I would get this thrown in my face till the day I die. I couldn't bear that. What am I going to do?'

'I was so wrapped up in myself I wasn't there for you, Betty, but I'm here now.'

'I'm planning an abortion!'

'You're what?' exclaimed Kachelle. 'No, good God, no, Betty, please don't think about it. You can't kill your child.'

'Well, we all haven't got someone waiting in the wings to step in and think it's his,' answered Betty sarcastically. The look on Kachelle's face pained her. 'I'm sorry, please forgive me I didn't mean to hurt you. Please help me!'

'It's okay pet. Hush now, alana, come on home. We'll talk there,' and Kachelle helped her gently out of the chair.

Over several strong cups of tea the two girls studied what was best to do. Betty was three months gone but had been assured that an abortion could still be performed. Kachelle begged with her not to consider this an option. Long into the night the two friends tossed back and forward what they could do and finally decided that Betty would put the child up for adoption. Secretly Kachelle hoped she would change her mind once she would hold the child in her arms. Betty finally fell asleep on top of Kachelle's bed. Kachelle pulled a blanket up and over her and for the first time in months her arms ached to hold Philomena and Sheila.

The days passed slowly and many nights were spent in air raid shelters. London was taking a fierce bombing. Sights familiar to the girls were destroyed. Their local pub and the cinema where they had both enjoyed 'Gone with the Wind,' had disappeared. But the people were resourceful. They picked themselves up and started over again. Kachelle had letters from her mother and Biddy Joe and Padraic Charlie. Her mother wrote of saving a nice little nest egg for her from the money she sent every month and stating that Padraic Charlie wanted to take the girls to his parents, but who would look after them? Padraic Charlie wrote about the work he was accomplishing with the boat and that her place was now at home looking after him, the girls and his parents. Kachelle placed the letters at the side of her bed. Maybe it was time to go home, but she missed Diarmuid Charlie so much. Padraic Charlie would notice something was wrong. Besides she wasn't feeling well lately. She feared that working in the ammunition factory had damaged her health and she checked frequently for the tell-tale yellow tinge to her skin. Betty had advised her to see a doctor if she was so worried and an appointment had been made for the next afternoon. She smoothed down the letters, staring blankly at them. She did miss her mother and Biddy Joe and especially her daughters. Deep down she feared they might not know her on her return. Perhaps it would be best to go home, settle down and wait patiently for Diarmuid Charlie's letter.

The following day at four thirty, Kachelle was facing the politely spoken doctor. After an array of tests, she asked nervously, 'Has working in the ammunition factory damaged my health, doctor?'

'No dear, your problem is no different to hundreds of other women, you're pregnant!'

'Pregnant, pregnant!' she kept repeating, 'You'll rock the cradle soon,'- the fortune tellers words pierced her brain.

'Yes, my dear. When one has sexual intercourse without protection one runs the risk of having a baby,' said the doctor sarcastically. 'When was your last period?'

Kachelle couldn't think. Stupid girls, he thought to himself.

'Mrs McGinley, your last period?'

Kachelle stumbled over the date.

'I think it was the, the mmm, the fourth of August.'

'Then I reckon you are due on the.......' but when he looked up from his calendar she was gone.

Kachelle rested against the wall and gulped in air.

'Pregnant! Jesus, Mary and Joseph, I'm pregnant. No! No! Dear God, no please I beg you no. It's a mistake.'

Deep down though she knew what the doctor said was true. Not again! How will I tell my mother and Biddy Joe? Jesus, Padraic Charlie, what am I going to tell him? Her eyes filled up with tears. Her heart pounded in her chest and she turned quite pale. A passer by asked if she was alright. 'Fine, fine, thank you,' she replied softly. 'You stupid bitch,' her brain screamed. Pregnant again, and Diarmuid Charlie gone. Oh God, how could I be so stupid? Betty, Betty- she must talk to Betty.

'You're what?' asked Betty, shocked, as she poured two cups of tea. 'Oh

Kachelle, what are you going to do? You were thinking of going home too. An abortion is the only answer Kachelle. We'll go together. No one will know. I can get on with my life with my husband when he returns; you can go home to your little girls.'

'No, no, I can't,' shouted Kachelle.

'For goodness sake, Kachelle, will you be sensible? If you keep it, you'll have to stay here until it is born. What if Padraic Charlie decides to come here to see you? What if your girls fall ill and you have to go home? How will you explain things, Kachelle? Please listen to me. This can be ended once and for all before the end of the month. Your only about six weeks gone. It will be easier for you than me. I can arrange it for the both of us. We're earning good money so we can afford it. Please think about it!'

Kachelle's mind was in a turmoil. What was she to do? Padraic Charlie might well return to England to encourage her to return home. What if anything happened at home? Counting roughly she reckoned the baby would be due in April.

'Oh God, how could I be so stupid?' she asked Betty.

'Now hold on there, Kachelle, it takes two to tango. Diarmuid Charlie has a part to play too. Sure them GI's are given pocketful of Johnnies. He should have made sure he used one. It was different in my case- the damn thing slipped off.'

'Ah Betty, we didn't stop to think. We just loved each other so much using a Johnny didn't come into it.'

'Well I bet now you wish you had,' answered Betty tartly.

'I just wish Diarmuid Charlie was here. I just can't believe this has happened twice.'

'Listen, I have to go. Please, Kachelle, think about an abortion. Why wreck Padraic Charlie's life, your girls, your own? Have the abortion with me and then you can go home as if nothing has happened. I'd say good night and sleep tight but I know you'll not close your eyes. Remember, I'm here for you.'

Betty kissed her on the cheek before gently closing the door. Kachelle threw herself on top of the bed. Her knees were drawn tight up to her chest, her head almost resting on her them. She felt the tears swell up in her eyes. She chided herself. 'No point in crying girl. Tears won't help. Nobody can help you now. Diarmuid Charlie is gone. You might never see him again. You have to think for yourself, think what is the best thing to do. Abortion is a mortal sin, but it isn't really a baby yet. Nobody back home would have to know. I could go home in a few weeks. To go home with her belly full or a child in tow would cause some talk on the Island. And Padraic Charlie, how would he react? He had always been jealous of Diarmuid Charlie. Should she pretend it was someone else's?'

She could just see his father's face. Her mother, her poor mother and Biddy Joe who went to so much trouble to help her before, she had let them down.

'I couldn't have better luck,' she thought to herself. 'I broke my promise, after putting my hand on the Bible to tell no-one. I told Betty and Diarmuid Charlie. Oh God, what am I going to do?'

Though mentally and physically tired, Kachelle could not sleep. When the siren went off she refused to move to the air raid shelter. Right now, she didn't care if she died. She sat alone with her thoughts for company. Finally she fell into a disturbed seep, awakening after a few hours from a frightening dream. She dreamt she had been drowning, trying to catch the side of Padraic Charlie's boat but the boat was on dry land. She blessed herself. To dream of a boat on dry land was a bad sign to Islanders.

Making herself a cup of tea, she lit a long American cigarette. Betty was right. Abortion was the only solution. She would ask Betty to arrange everything whenever she called this morning. Kachelle washed, combed her hair and dressed. A noise at the door alerted her. The post had arrived. Perhaps there would be a letter from Diarmuid Charlie. She rushed downstairs to find a neat package in a brown envelope addressed to her. She did not recognise the writing and could not make out the postmark. Hurrying back upstairs she poured another cup of tea and set about opening her package. A small note of apology fell out.

'I apologise for the delay but I was ill with 'flu!'

She opened the parcel wider. A smiling attractive Diarmuid Charlie stared her full in the face. The photos! She had forgotten all about them. She held them carefully in her hand. One of Diarmuid Charlie, in his uniform, his eyes twinkling and one of her and Diarmuid Charlie. She had her head on his shoulder and he was smiling lovingly down on her. 'He does love me,' she said to herself and this time the tears did come. Memories of their time in Brighton came back to her.

'You'll fight tooth and nail for your son!'

'Oh my God,' she exclaimed. 'The cards turned up a son for me! My son, Diarmuid Charlie's son, our son!'

She clutched at her stomach. Going to the large bowl from which she had just washed, Kachelle vomited. Rinsing her mouth she sat down, feeling weak. She lifted the photographs and stared at them. What if anything happened to Diarmuid Charlie? She might never see him again, even if he did survive. God willing, at least she would have his son.

'I'm sorry little one,' she said as she patted her stomach.

'Fuck them all. You're mine and I'm keeping you. I don't care any longer what Padraic Charlie, my mother or the Islanders say. I'm not the first and I won't be the last. You're mine and we'll go home.'

'Morning, Kachelle, are you ready for work?' came Betty's voice from the doorway.

'Why, Kachelle, are you OK? You look settled, have you come to a decision?

'Yes, Betty, I have. I got up this morning convinced the only solution was an abortion.'

'Oh Kachelle, you've done the right thing.'

'No, Betty, you don't understand. I was going to have an abortion and then I received these,' she threw Betty the photos.

'They're lovely- but I don't understand.'

'Diarmuid Charlie McGinley and I love one another. It's not lust or drunken passion, We really and truly love one another. It's unfortunate the way things have worked out. But you know we Islanders have an old saying.'What's lotted can't be blotted.' It has been left out that this would happen to me. I now understand the fortune teller's words; 'You'll cross over water, you'll rock the cradle soon, I'll fight tooth and nail for my son, there are hard times ahead.' I know this baby is my son, our son and I won't kill him. I intend to have my baby.'

'What about Padraic Charlie, your mother, what will you tell them?'

'I don't intend to tell anyone any more lies, Betty. I can't tell Padraic Charlie about Philomena. I promised my mother and Biddy Joe that I wouldn't, but I will tell them who the father of my son is. In fact, I intend to call my son Diarmuid Charlie McGinley after his father and I hope and pray to God he is the spitting image of him!'

'Kachelle, you can't,' said Betty nervously. 'Think of the trouble it will cause!'

'Fuck them all, Betty. This is my life. I'm taking control. I answer to no-one. My son will have the best.'

A silence fell over the room. Betty was astounded at her friend's strength in her thinking,

'What about you, Betty, what are you planning to do?'

'I know I said I wouldn't have an abortion, Kachelle, but I know I haven't your strength and courage. Not only would I suffer, I know my child would be made to suffer and I don't think that is fair, so I'm going ahead with the abortion.'

Kachelle rose from her chair and put her arms around Betty.

'I'm sorry, love, for judging you and coming across all high and mighty about abortion. No one can really understand until they are in that position themselves. You know you are the strong one. It takes courage to face what you are facing. I guess we both have a tough time ahead of us.'

'Aye, it's a man's world alright. I wish to God I'd been born a man,' weakly laughed Betty. 'If I can arrange everything this week will you come with me Kachelle?'

'Of course I will love. Come on, we'd better get to work.'

CHAPTER 6

Betty's abortion was arranged for 8.30pm Friday night. At 7.30 the two young women sat quietly in their local. Kachelle had ordered Betty a brandy.

'Maybe I shouldn't?' she asked Kachelle.

'Go on love, it can't do you any harm.'

'God, I'm nervous, Kachelle.'

'Look, love, are you really, really sure this is what you what you want to do?'

'Yes, my mind is made up, the sooner it is over the better. We'd better go.'

As she rose, Betty knocked over the brandy glass. Glass splintered everywhere and golden brandy trickled down on to the floor. All heads turned to stare at Betty.

'I'm sorry, I'm sorry,' she kept repeating.

'It was an accident, love. Come on, don't annoy yourself,' comforted Kachelle, as she linked Betty's arm and guided her out of the pub.

They walked in silence to the bus stop. The female conductor took their fares and went off chatting to two young soldiers at the back of the bus. Fifteen minutes later the bus pulled into Victoria Square and the two girls jumped off.

'It's No.92,' said Betty in a timorous voice.

A small square of derelict houses faced them. They followed the numbers until No92, tucked neatly in the corner, challenged them. A dark green front door with its paint peeling stared defiantly back at them. Kachelle blessed herself.

'What's wrong Kachelle?' asked Betty feebly.

'Nothing love, nothing. It's just that the door is green. I'm freaky about anything green. We have an old saying that green is for grief.'

'Oh, Kachelle, you're making me more nervous. But your pound notes are green and I've never seen you refuse them,' giggled Betty nervously.

'You're right, I'm being foolish. Come on, you knock.' Betty knocked the door half heartedly.

'She'll never hear that,' said Kachelle, 'Knock again.'

Before Betty could raise her hand a large bulk of a woman whispered angrily, 'Come on in. You needn't let the whole street know you're here. 'Come on, come on.'

The two women were shown into a dark, damp hall. The smells of urine and cabbage met in their tonsils. The large woman wore a grubby, dirty wrap-over pinny. Her large hands were black from coal and she rubbed them down the front of her fat belly before showing the girls into a dimly lit back room.

A small wooden table covered with dirty looking lino stood in the middle of the room. The room was dimly lit and something wrapped in greasy looking brown paper sat alongside the table.

'Which one of you is it?' asked the woman. 'Right then, off with your underwear and up on the table,' ordered the woman.

Betty squeezed Kachelle's hand.

'Are you really sure this is what you want? asked Kachelle as she faced Betty, holding both her hands gently.

Betty stared at the table, the woman then Kachelle. She swallowed hard. 'I have to.'

'Right you, out into the hall and none of your interfering. She knows what she's doing. I'll have the twenty five pounds now,' said the abortionist.

Kachelle kissed Betty on the cheek saying, 'I'll wait and pray for you.' She reluctantly left the room. Falling to her knees in the sordid hallway, Kachelle blessed herself and started to pray,

'Remember O most gracious Virgin Mary that never was it known......'

Her prayer was interrupted by Betty's scream.

'Jesus, Mary and Joseph, pity us poor sinners....' And again Kachelle's prayer was drowned out by Betty's screams for someone to stop the pain.

A short while later a pale and shocked looking Betty opened the door. Kachelle slipped her arm around her waist, so fearful was she of Betty fainting.

'Come on, love, I'll take you home.'

Betty lowered her head onto Kachelle's shoulder, her silent tears already rolling down her cheeks.

Within an hour Betty was tucked up in bed. She hadn't spoken one word. Kachelle smoothed Betty's hair from her face and urged her to sleep, assuring her all the time that she was staying with her. Betty eventually fell into a sleep and Kachelle moved to a large armchair. The heavy curtains had been drawn and the only light was a soft glimmer from the dying embers of the fire. Kachelle struggled with her decision to add more coal to the fire. She was afraid of wakening Betty and eased her mind that the room felt warm and Betty seemed warm enough. She pulled her coat off the table and eased it over her legs. Slowly her head rested on the arm of the chair and Kachelle drifted off to sleep. How long she slept she didn't know, but Betty's mutterings awoke her with a start.

The small bedroom was dark and cold. On reaching Betty she found her delirious and very hot. Kachelle immediately went into action. She brightened the room, eased the covers from the top half of Betty and got a cold damp cloth to place on Betty's forehead. Betty was struggling to sit up and seemed to be in terrible pain.

'Shh, shh, love, I'm here. You're going to be alright,' she consoled Betty.

It was of no use. Betty didn't know where she was. Her eyes were wide with fear. She clutched the bedclothes tightly and drew her knees up to her chest.

'Help me please, the pain the pain,' she cried.

'OK, OK, I'll eh....I'll get your neighbour, Mrs Clarke, to get the doctor. I'll be back in a few minutes,' and Kachelle rushed off. She knocked wildly on Mrs Clarke's door of the adjoining room.

'Mrs Clarke, please! Betty is ill. Can you get a doctor to come right away?'

'Yes, yes, but what's wrong, can I help?' asked the startled frail woman.

'I don't know, but she is in great pain. Please, please get a doctor as soon as you can,' and Kachelle hurried back to Betty's room.

On entering the room Kachelle found Betty's spasming body almost out of the bed. She raced forward and struggled to help her back pleading with her to calm herself and assuring her that the doctor was on his way.

After a few minutes a somnolent Betty settled in Kachelle's arms.

'There now, love, you rest easy,' and Kachelle eased her down on to the bed. A calmness had come over Betty. Her breathing was shallow and her limbs were limp. She's far too hot, Kachelle thought to herself and began easing the bedclothes further down the bed.

'Oh my God! No! No!' cried Kachelle to herself.

The bed was saturated with Betty's bright red blood. Suddenly her body convulsed and a gurgling sound came from her throat.

'The death rattle,' exclaimed Kachelle and she blessed herself.

'Please Betty, hold on, I beg you. The doctor is almost here. Betty please hold on, everything is going to be alright. Mrs Clarke! Mrs Clarke!'

But she knew it was too late. Her dear and only friend was gone. Bringing her mouth to Betty's ear she recited an act of contrition.

'Bless me, Father, for I have sinned,' she prayed while her tears rolled down her cheeks. 'Have mercy on me, a sinner. Dear Jesus, I cannot receive you sacramentally, but come at least spiritually into my heart.'

The prayers went on and on until the local doctor interrupted her solitude.

Three days later Betty was laid to rest. Kachelle sat in isolation in her own small room. She constantly clutched her belly and assured her child that no harm would come to him. She had spoken with Father Murphy and told him everything. He had ranted and raved when he had heard about the abortion but Kachelle had got equally angry with him and demanded an answer to her question.

'Could my act of contrition have helped Betty?'

Secretly the priest admired Kachelle for her strength and forth-rightness and assured her that if Betty was sorry for the abortion then the Good Lord had forgiven her.

'You see, Father, I didn't know until afterwards that Betty had been reared in an orphanage and that was why she couldn't bring herself to give her baby away.'

'Better away than dead,' was the priest's retort.

'What's lotted can't be blotted,' answered Kachelle leaving his presence.

Now she sat alone. Diarmuid Charlie was gone and so was Betty. Hopelessness engulfed her. There was nothing to keep her in London. She would give in her notice at work, tie up a few loose ends and prepare to travel home. Lifting a pen to paper she wrote:

'Dear Padraic Charlie,

Betty fell ill and was buried on Monday. I have a few things to do here and then I am coming home. We need to talk. Kiss the girls for me.

Yours, Kachelle.'

Three weeks later Kachelle knelt at Betty's grave side. Absent mindedly she arranged some fresh flowers and talked to her friend.

'I'm away now, love. May you rest in peace. Thank you for your friendship and support. I'm really sorry I couldn't have done more. If only, only I hadn't fallen asleep in the chair. I promised to look after you and I failed you. Please forgive me.' A gentle breeze disarranged Kachelle's work. 'I'll never forget you, Betty. I'll pray for you and you please pray for me and this little one.'

Easing herself up, she stared at Betty's grave.

'You're right, you know. It is a man's world. I'm going back to Ireland. I promise to return some day. Please rest in peace. Please watch over me.'

Kachelle shivered in the cool night air. Pulling the collar of her coat up, she lifted her small case and joined the queue at the Liverpool dock for the Belfast boat. She had no wish to sit with the drunken crowd and found herself a small seat at the bow of the boat. She knew she wouldn't sleep.

'You'll cross water.' The fortune teller's words raced round her head. She laughed to herself,

'There was me thinking I would go to America but it's back to Arranmore!'

'There is a difficult time ahead of you.' Again she remembered the words.

'Well life hasn't been that great up to now. If it gets any tougher I'll handle it,' she whispered to herself. 'No matter what Padraic Charlie and the Islanders may say or do, my daughters and my son are my life. Oh Diarmuid Charlie, how I wish you were here now. Please God, watch over him and keep him safe.'

She tightened her coat around her and drew her legs tightly under the bench, resigning herself to fate.

'Welcome home. Kachelle, it's good to see you,' shouted Paddy Joe, the boatman.

'How's things in England? Are you home to stay? He persisted.

'Later Paddy Joe, later, I'll fill you all in later. Right now I need to see my girls.'

Lifting her case, she made her way along the quay. 'Home at last!' she thought to herself and she lifter her face to the weak afternoon sunshine. Padraic Charlie was not there to meet her. There were few islanders about. Many of the men were still in England and those at home were probably out fishing. A soft Irish rain fell gently about her head and shoulders as she made her way to her mother's home.

On reaching the brow of the hill, children's laughter reached her ears. She could see her two little girls chasing one of her mother's best laying hens.

'Philomena! Sheila!' she called to them.

They stopped and hesitated, unsure of the tall stranger.

'My darlings,' she called as she fell to her knees and stretched out her arms to them. Philomena stood her ground, unsure, but Sheila ran on her small fat legs towards the house shouting,

'Nana, Nana.'

Kachelle's mother appeared, wiping her hands on a worn towel. She stopped short. Her Kachelle had returned! Something was wrong, she could tell.

'Please God,' she prayed, 'Don't let her be ill.'

Kachelle stared in disbelief at her mother. The frail woman she had known was gone. Her once pale face was brown from the sun. Her hair was tied up in a neat bun and her hands were covered in flour from baking. Obviously, looking after two weans agreed with her.

'Alana, alana,' called her mother as she took Kachelle in her arms. 'You have come home child. At last, you have come home to me,' and she kissed Kachelle on both cheeks before hugging her again.

'I'm dying for a cup of tea, Ma,' laughed Kachelle nervously.

Her heart was heavy with grief at the news she would be telling her soon. She loved her mother deeply and had no wish to hurt her.

The small kitchen was turned into a commotion of activity. Her mother rushed about making tea and talking nineteen to the dozen about island life, who had died, married, given birth. The two girls squealed with delight at the presents their mother had brought them and in the midst of everything, Biddy Joe arrived.

'God bless you, God bless you,' whispered Biddy Joe as she hugged Kachelle. 'Thank God you have returned safely to us.'

Taking control, she gave her attention to the children.

'Right now, you two. Out to the field and enjoy your chocolate and leave the hens alone,' warned Biddy Joe.

The two girls practically stood to attention at Biddy's words.

'Come on, give your mother a kiss and out you go.'

The two girls shyly gave Kachelle chocolate kisses and then escaped eagerly to the wide open field that was their back yard.

'Well they look healthy enough,' laughed Kachelle. 'They have got so big I hardly knew them and, mother, you're looking so well.'

'Well now,' said Biddy Joe as she eased herself into the old worn chair that had been Kachelle's father's.

'There's nothing like looking after young ones and a few extra pounds coming in to give you a new lease of life.'

'Oh Biddy Joe thinks I spoil them, Kachelle, but I love them dearly. You know, I used to wonder how a woman would feel about her grandchildren but I love them as if they are my own. Biddy Joe can keep them in tow though, and it's not a bad thing.' laughed her mother.

'And what about you Kachelle?' asked Biddy Joe quizzically as she lit her pipe. 'Does Padraic Charlie know you were coming?'

'Yes, I wrote him last week, again,' answered Kachelle.

'And he didn't come to meet you?'

'No, no he didn't,' said Kachelle and quickly changed the subject by stating that she would go and check the girls.

'There's something wrong,' said Biddy Joe.

'No, she's just tired, Biddy Joe, and don't forget she has just buried her friend, Betty. Life in that factory and Betty's death are bound to take their toll. Thank God that factory didn't claim our Kachelle,' answered Kachelle's mother who quickly blessed herself.

Later when the two girls had been bathed at the big open turf fire and safely put to bed, Biddy Joe made another cup of tea. She had noticed that Kachelle had eaten almost nothing at tea time and that she seemed worried.

'Are you staying here tonight, love, or are you going to Charlie Hughie's house?' her mother asked.

A sombre silence filled the small kitchen. Biddy Joe glanced at her friend. Something was definitely wrong. Kachelle lit a long American cigarette and slowly inhaled.

'Kachelle, you're smoking!' said her surprised mother.

'And so am I,' stated Biddy Joe. 'Now, girl, what's on your mind? If you want to talk we're here for you and if you want to go to bed just you go on ahead. You're bound to be tired.' Kachelle inhaled the cigarette again.

'Look it's my problem. I can handle it.' she answered quickly.

'Whoa, whoa,' chided Biddy Joe. 'We're only trying to help.'

'I'm sorry, I'm sorry! I didn't mean to go on the defensive. There is no problem really. Well, there was one, but I have made a decision and the problem is gone, simple as that,' stated Kachelle.

'Why don't you start at the beginning?' suggested Biddy Joe as she pushed Kachelle's mug of tea forward.

The three women settled down and slowly Kachelle related her story. When she spoke of meeting Diarmuid Charlie again her mother paled and clutched her heart. Biddy Joe just nodded her head. Kachelle held nothing back. She told of her three days in Brighton, of his marriage, twin boys and the possibility of forthcoming letters and of Betty's death. After a few minutes silence she said,

'I'm pregnant to Diarmuid Charlie McGinley. I believe I'm carrying our son. He should be born in April. I am not going to hide the fact that it is his child. In fact I'm calling him after him. So if you wish to disown me now, mother, I accept that,' and she sank against the back of the chair.

There! It was over. They knew, and she longed to tell them how sorry she was to have hurt them again but she was afraid her apology would be taken as a sign of weakness and she must stay strong.

The silence in the kitchen was broken only by the ticking of the clock and the whispering of the dying turf fire.

'You've become a hard woman, Kachelle,' stated her mother quietly.

'Well, life made me that way,' replied Kachelle.

'What about Padraic Charlie and the girls? What will happen to them? quizzed her mother.

'I intend to tell Padraic Charlie all,' began Kachelle.

'About Philomena?' asked her mother, startled.

'No, no, he'll never know that. I mean what happened in England. Look, I don't care if he doesn't forgive me. He means nothing to me. But he does need me. To look after him, his parents, home and children. I'm willing to do all that provided he accepts my son!'

'You're looking for a miracle, girl,' shouted her mother. 'Look, how far gone are you? Why don't you go home to Padraic Charlie to-night. He'll be delighted to see you. Perhaps you could pretend it's his.

'No,' shouted Kachelle, 'No Ma. It wouldn't matter if I was only a week gone. I'm not denying the father of my son. I would die for Diarmuid Charlie. I could never love Padraic Charlie in that way. I will always live in hope of Diarmuid Charlie sending for me, and if he does I'll gladly go to the far end of the world to be with him, even if it means leaving my daughters.'

Kachelle's mother blessed herself and stared at her beautiful daughter who had become a stranger to her.

'On your head be it,' she said flatly.

'What have you to say Biddy Joe?' asked Kachelle.

Biddy Joe tapped her pipe into the fire. It was some time before she spoke.

'Well, girl, you certainly have made up your mind. There'll be talk you know. But then sure you know that. You have got courage, I give you that and you're young and strong. This will certainly test how much Padraic Charlie loves you. He was always jealous of Diarmuid Charlie. You'll need eyes in the back of your head to protect this wee one. All I can say is I'm here for you, Alana. You have a heavy cross to carry but then they say God only sends crosses to those who are able to carry them. It will be tough, but your shoulders are broad. Walk tall and proud, never show a sign of weakness and you'll get through. I just thank God you didn't have an abortion like your friend, Betty,' and she stared at Kachelle's mother.

At the thought of her beautiful Kachelle dead, her mother rushed forward and put her arms around her.

'You can always stay here if you want. Biddy Joe and me will do all we can to help you, love. 'What's lotted can't be blotted,' and she patted Kachelle's shoulders.

'Thank's Ma, Biddy Joe.' And Kachelle gathered them both in her arms and hugged them. 'It's best I be off. Padraic Charlie is probably working at the boat after the days fishing.'

'May God be with you,' whispered her mother sprinkling some holy water on her daughter's head. Biddy Joe watched in silence as Kachelle, walking tall, straight and proud climbed the brow of the hill to talk to Padraic Charlie.

CHAPTER 7

Every step of the way to Chaplestrand was like a knife piercing Kachelle's heart. She recalled how she used to skip with delight at the prospect of seeing Diarmuid Charlie. On approaching the McGinley household she thought it best to call and say hello. Perhaps Padraic Charlie might be home. She entered the back kitchen and was surprised to find it reasonably neat. His mother was absent from her fireside position and was making some tea.

'God bless all here,' said Kachelle and startled her mother in law.

'Alana, alana, you're home,' and she rushed forward and hugged Kachelle. 'At last the girls can come home. This house has been far too quiet. I've missed them and you,' and once again she hugged Kachelle.

'Is Padraic Charlie here?' asked Kachelle.

'No, alana, he's down at the boat. He'll probably be there for a while yet.

'His father?' enquired Kachelle.

'He's bedridden now, thank God. His drinking and kicking days are over. He's not fit to lift his hand to me now. God works in mysterious ways you know. He's down in the wee room. Mind you his tongue is as sharp as ever!'

Kachelle was shocked by her mother in law's attitude to her husband's illness. The whole island knew this woman hadn't the life of a dog, so could she really blame her now for the way she was thinking? No! She stared at her mother in law. She had been an attractive woman in her day. Her pale blonde hair was now tinged with silvery grey. Her twinkling blue eyes, oh why hadn't she noticed before that Diarmuid Charlie looked so much like her? Unfortunately her nose was splattered across her face, no doubt by Mr.McGinley in a drunken rage. She has been given a new lease of life, thought Kachelle to herself. He wasn't fit to beat her up any more and this woman could now enjoy what was left of her life.

'Who the hell is there?' came a roar from the bedroom.

'Best go down and see him, but if he's sharp with the tongue just leave the room and close the door tight. He can shout at the walls then.'

Kachelle walked to the small bedroom at the back of the house.

'Hello. May God bless you,' she said as she entered the bedroom.

'So you're back then. Why? What brought you back? An attractive girl like you wouldn't come back just for my son Padraic Charlie,' he quizzed.

'You're forgetting, I've two daughters,' said Kachelle quietly.

'Two daughters to Padraic Charlie. Well you didn't need them when you were in London, did you?' he said provokingly.

'I'm an Islander too, you know. My mother is still here!'

'Your nothing but a fucking blow in! Your mother is a......' But Kachelle had left the bedroom, closing the door gently behind her.

On entering the kitchen again she gave her mother in law an understanding look.

'You'll have a mug of tea with me?' invited the older woman.

Kachelle was about to refuse and then quickly realised that it was the company of another woman she sought.

'What was London like? Is it really crowded with people? What was the factory like?'

'Slow down,' laughed Kachelle. 'Tell me, have you ever been off this island?'

'Na, Only a couple of times on fair days with my Da. That's where I met him you know,' and she gestured towards the bedroom door. 'I was born in this house, you know. I was an only child. My mother was frail and died when I was only two years old. My Da reared me. There's a right bit of land comes with this house. I have often thought of why himself married me. I believe now it was because of my inheritance. Them mad McGinley's came originally from Scuttle Island. When the numbers became low there they transferred here and settled on the other side of the Island. He's almost five years younger than me you know. My Da was getting on in years and there wasn't too many young men about and I suppose my Da thought he would look after me and care for me. Da died within six months of himself moving in. All that I own is going to Diarmuid Charlie. From three years of age he used to try and defend me from his blows. Many's a night he would leave his warm bed and join me out by the turf stack where I would be hiding from himself. Many's a time I was ready for throwing myself of a cliff edge, not caring that I would be committing a mortal sin. As far as I was concerned, I was already in hell.

Then Diarmuid Charlie's wee hand would slip into mine and he'd ask me not to cry and he would tell me he loved me. He favours my Da you know, quiet and gentle. Now Padraic Charlie is a different kettle of fish. I remember him as a baby. Once when he was about fifteen months old, I was lifting him to put him to bed when he sank his teeth into my shoulder so hard that I had to throw him off me with force. He had drawn blood. I was in agony but when I looked at my son he seemed delighted with my pain. You know I thought one time that my Diarmuid Charlie and you would marry. He used to talk to me about you. I imagined your children running about this house.'

Kachelle's stomach churned at how close part of the woman's dream was coming true.

'I never expected you and Padraic Charlie to get married. But you are, and we have two lovely wee girls and you're home now. God's good. Perhaps soon I'll hear from Diarmuid Charlie and then my heart will be content.'

'I have to go. I have to find Padraic Charlie. We need to talk.'

'Yes I understand, love.' Rising, she placed her arms about Kachelle and hugged her close. 'Don't ever let him hit you or the children, love. Once is enough. Now God bless and take care.'

Kachelle bid farewell and started out again on her journey to find Padraic Charlie. She thought over the old woman's words. 'Hit the children.' God, the day and hour Padraic Charlie would hit one of her children she would leave him for dead. She could defend herself but if anyone hurt her children she would leave them for dead, particularly the wee one she was carrying, her son!

Without thinking, her feet had carried her down to the strand. Padraic Charlie worked alone at the boat. The strand was deserted except for the cry of an odd seagull. Their piercing screams were like a warning to her. She felt herself chill. What is it Biddy Joe used to say, she thought. Ah- go in fighting and the battle is won, she whispered to herself. Kachelle, straightened her back, tossed back her head of red curls and composed herself.

Padraic Charlie caught sight of her.

'Oh God,' he thought to himself, 'She's beautiful' and he drew in his breath.

Kachelle had the aura of one born to command, one who was used to being obeyed and one who would not tolerate not being obeyed! As she drew level with the boat he spoke,

'You're home then,' he said sourly.

'Yes, I'm here. But whether I'm home or not is yet to be decided,' she answered very controlled and self assured.

'My mother will be needing you now that my father is ill.'

'What about you, Padraic Charlie, do you need me? I've spoken with your mother. She looks well. In fact strength has replaced naivety.' He stared at her, puzzled.

'Where's the girls?' he demanded.

'They're with my mother. She's putting them to bed.'

'Why are they not with my mother? Are you going back to London?'

'That depends on you Padraic Charlie. If I go to London again, the girls with me.' He stared at her, confused.

'What nonsense are you talking?' he demanded.

Kachelle swallowed convulsively, then took a deep breath and quietly said.

'I'm pregnant. My baby is due in April. If you and I cannot come to some arrangement I'll either live with my mother or my children and I will return to England.' A look of contempt came over his face.

'I knew this would happen. It's that whore's fault, that Betty. I knew from the start she was no good but you wouldn't listen, oh no, you had to run with her. Show me your company and I'll tell you what you are. You're a whore. You dirty slut! Ah what's in the marrow comes out in the bone. As my father always said blood will out. You filthy dirty blow in, you're a whore just like your mother and auld Biddy Joe. I rue the day I ever married you. You've brought shame and degradation on my good family name. I could kill you for this,' and in his rage he lifted a large piece of wood and, catching Kachelle off guard, brought it down on her left shoulder.

Kachelle sucked in her breath, the rolling nausea receded. Glancing up she saw him lift the wood again but his time she acted quickly. She flung herself at him pushing him against the boat and bringing up her right knee she violently lodged it into his groin. He collapsed to his knees groaning in agony.

'Don't you ever, ever lift your hand to me again!' she said forcefully but quietly. 'For your information Betty did not get me pregnant. I'm no whore. The man that I love, yes truly love, made me pregnant. The man I should have married is the father of my child and I intend to let the whole Island know the father of my child because I will call my child after him. Diarmuid Charlie McGinley is the father. Yes, your beloved brother Diarmuid Charlie, and if he could send for me I'd take my children and go to Canada. So don't ever attempt to strike me again because I'll get you back. You have to sleep some time, only I promise you I'll not just strike you, I'll kill you!' Lifting her hand she brought it violently across the left side of his face. She turned her back on him and slowly walked away, her stance defiantly aggressive. The soft autumn wind carried his insults in a different direction.

'You worthless trollop. You slut. You whore!'

Kachelle couldn't face going home to her mother just yet. She needed time alone. Her shoulder was aching and an ocean of tears needed to be released. She made her way to the lighthouse, back to where Diarmuid Charlie and she had met often. Oh God, she thought to herself. I stood here before with Diarmuid Charlie's child, waiting eagerly to tell him. She needed time to think. Easing herself down on a large stone she dropped her head into her hands and released the bitter pain of tears. They came with a force. Never in all her life did she feel so alone. 'I never meant to harm anyone,' she whispered. I couldn't help falling in love with Diarmuid Charlie. Oh if only things had worked out different. Again she allowed her tears to flow. What was she to do? Should she go to England? To stay would see her trapped in a loveless marriage.

How long she sat for she had no idea. Thoughts ran rampant through her brain. She thought of Padraic Charlie's harsh words about Betty and silently said a prayer for her.

'Judge not and you will not be judged, Padraic Charlie McGinley,' she shouted to the wind. Finally, her temper subsided and her tears became gentle and slow, and she admitted to herself that her priority was her unborn child. He had to be protected, while in her womb and when born, perhaps Diarmuid Charlie would send for her, perhaps.......

She was startled by footsteps. Turning swiftly around she was relieved that it was only Biddy Joe.

'Ah, Biddy Joe, you put the heart across ways in me. I thought you were Padraic Charlie,' and she eased her shoulder against the rock.

'I was worried about you, alana, as was your mother. It's late. Here, wrap this shawl around you. You're in pain. Did he hurt you?'

'Yes, he caught me off guard and swung at me with some driftwood. I caught it on my shoulder. But I taught him a lesson. He'll not hit me again.'

'Alana, alana, you've made a large cross for yourself. You'll have to keep strong to survive.'

'He called me my mother and you whores Biddy Joe. He........'

'Sh, sh, love, I know. And you'll hear worse. Sure he's been hearing those words from he was a baby. It's his way of hitting back. You'll hear worse than that. There will be times you'll wish for a dig in the mouth because the pain of that will eventually go away but harsh cruel words stay forever. Have you decided what you're going to do?'

'Aye, Biddy Joe. I'm staying home. I'll stay with my mother and you until I talk to Padraic Charlie again. I'll tell him that I'll cook, clean, nurse his father, foot the turf, see to the livestock and contribute to the finance of the house, but I won't lie with him. I could never bring myself to do that again. I have the girls and this little one. I will never sleep with Padraic Charlie again. Not after Diarmuid Charlie!'

'You've a hard road to travel, love. He'll make your life hell. There's a deepness in Padraic Charlie that has always frightened me. It's like there's something mentally wrong but then that is to be expected after all....'

'After all what?' interrupted Kachelle, pulling the shawl around her as there was now a sharpness to the evening air.

'Enough for now. Come on, girl, let's get you home and a strong mug of tay in you before you catch a chill. I'll have a look at that shoulder too. Come on, link my arm and mind your step, this hill is steep and I'm not as young as I used to be.'

The two women travelled home in silence. Kachelle and Biddy Joe gladly accepted two mugs of sweet tea. Not a sound was spoken until her mother kissed her good night and left the room.

'You're exhausted, alana. Let me have a look at your shoulder and then get yourself off to bed. I'll tidy and lock up.'

'My shoulder is OK, Biddy Joe. It's only badly bruised. I'd rather my mother didn't know. Here, read them for me please,' and she passed Biddy Joe her cup.

'Ah sometimes ignorance is bliss, love.'

'And fore warned is fore armed,' retorted Kachelle quickly. 'Please, Biddy Joe, hold nothing back. I want to hear it all.'

Biddy Joe accepted the large mug and turned it upside down on the saucer and turned it clockwise three times. When she had lifted the mug again a few tea leaves had fallen on to the saucer leaving a few scattered on the side.

'You haven't much to work on,' joked Kachelle half heartedly.

'Believe it or not, you get a better reading with fewer tea leaves,' explained Biddy Joe.

The small kitchen was quiet except for the tick of the clock and the whispering of the dying embers of the turf fire.

'I see a baby, a boy. His name will begin with a D.'

Kachelle's heart leapt with joy. The fortune teller in England had been right.

'Will I see his father again?' quizzed Kachelle. Another silence.

'I'm afraid not love. You will be in contact with him. But I don't ever see you meeting him face to face again. You've a long hard road to travel. Life will not be a bed of roses. You'll shed many tears. You'll pay hard for your son!'

'Will the baby be OK?' nervously asked Kachelle, whispering softly in case her mother heard.

'The baby will be fine and healthy yet there's something here I don't understand, there's not an illness, yet there is something. Padraic Charlie will never accept him.'

'I don't care about that, Biddy Joe. I'll have so much love for him he'll not need his.'

'I see you grieving over a death, a sudden death of a woman.'

'Oh that's been poor Betty,' and Kachelle blessed herself. 'Oh Biddy Joe, I can't believe that I will never see Diarmuid Charlie again. Surely he will come home for a visit or perhaps send for me?'

'I'll tell you what. We'll see what your marriage bed turns up for you,' and rising from her chair Biddy Joe went to a kitchen drawer and withdrew an old worn packet of playing cards. She offered them to Kachelle to shuffle. Kachelle obliged. Then, having searched out the Queen of Hearts, she placed the other cards fan shape in her worn hand, and she offered them to Kachelle saying:

'Choose one and place it face down over that one. Now choose another and place it at your head, one at your feet, one at either side and one at each corner. Now if your marriage is strong when I join all these cards up and turn them over, the cards should stay together and a dark haired man, possibly the King of Spades, should lie across your back.'

Taking an odd card from the pack Biddy Joe used this to help turn over the joined-up cards. When she turned over the cards they did not hold together but fell apart. Biddy Joe set about arranging the cards in a circle around the Queen of Hearts.

'You have no man at your back. There's one dark haired man on the outskirts. He loves you but it's a jealous possessive love. A love-hate relationship. Always be on your guard. Never show any weakness mentally or physically towards him. There's your baby- a boy. In fact he's the only man in your life. There's the fair haired one,' and she pointed to the King of Hearts. 'He loves you truly and dearly but.... he's tied. He has made a new life across water. I see a wedding ring and children. He will always be in contact with you. I see a lot of money coming your way from this man. He will provide for his son, but he will never get to meet with him. You'll survive all that is being thrown at you. There's a difficult time ahead regarding the dark haired one but you'll cope, you're a survivor,' and she quickly and neatly folded the cards away.

Kachelle sat with her head down. Biddy Joe's readings had proved right so many times before that she believed now what Biddy Joe told her.

'Forewarned is forearmed after all,' she said to Biddy Joe. 'It's God's way of helping me. I accept his holy will.'

'Now go to bed love and try to get a good nights sleep. Tomorrow is another day,' and Biddy Joe patted her softly on the shoulder.

A week had passed and Kachelle had not seen Padraic Charlie. She spent her days helping her mother and Biddy Joe and getting acquainted with her daughters. The difference in their personalities amazed her. Philomena was gentle, quiet- a day dreamer. Sheila was demanding and given to sulks. She seemed suspicious of Kachelle's hugs and kisses and cuddles and preferred to play alone. Alone in her bed at night Kachelle would gaze at Diarmuid Charlie's photograph. On the back she had penned: 'A picture taken having a merry week end at Brighton 1943. Diarmuid Charlie McGinley. Blue eyes. Fair hair, fresh complexion. The love of my life. Father of my Son.'

The following Sunday Kachelle had just finished the dishes when Padraic Charlie called. The two girls rushed up to him and threw their arms about his neck. He swung them round and kissed them both, calming their excited laughter by offering them each a handful of dulse to fill their mouths.

'We need to talk,' and he looked at Kachelle. 'We'll go for a walk he suggested. Kachelle caught Biddy Joe shaking her head telling her no.

'No,' answered Kachelle quickly. 'My mother and Biddy Joe will take the girls for a walk. We'll stay here. After all every cock crows loudest in its own backyard.'

The two elderly women quickly called the children and headed for the door. Padraic Charlie stood aside to allow them to pass but Biddy Joe halted in her tracks. She placed her small hand on Padraic Charlie's chest, gently yet forcefully pushing him back.

'Hit her again and it's me you will be dealing with. I'll leave you that you'll never walk again and yet I'll not lay a hand on you,' she hissed quietly.

Padraic Charlie visibly paled. Many of the islanders were fearful of old Biddy Joe. The children called her a witch and the elders suspected her of having powers because she could so accurately read their fortunes. Many blessed themselves when passing her. Biddy Joe often laughed at them arguing that if she had powers that her own life would have been different. Never the less the suspicion remained.

'Well what have you come to say?' demanded Kachelle.

'People are asking why you are not living with me.'

'So? That's no concern of mine.'

'You listen to me,' he said aggressively moving forward. Kachelle faced him.

'No, you listen to me. I don't love you, but I have known you all my life and once we were good friends. I love you as a brother but I'm not in love with you. I could care for you. I hate to see you suffering and please believe me I'm really sorry that I have hurt you. I know you need to be with the girls and them with you. I know your mother needs me and that we have to live on this island so to stop any scandal which you are afraid of, I'll tell you what I will do. I'll clean your home, cook, wash, care for your parents, the children, the livestock but I will not sleep with you.'

'And the bastard you're carrying?' he stated.

'Don't you dare, don't ever call my child a bastard or I'll leave you completely, taking my girls with me,' she furiously shouted at him. 'Now get out of my sight and don't come near me again until you have decided what you are going to do,' and walking slowly she opened the door and held it wide for him to pass through.

Sitting down on the worn kitchen table chair, she lit a cigarette and inhaled deeply. When her mother and Biddy Joe returned they quickly set about preparing tea. No one asked Kachelle what had taken place between her and her husband.

It was well into the evening with the two girls asleep and the three women preparing for bed when a knock came at the door. The three quickly looked at each other, puzzled. Kachelle, who was nearest the door, opened it wide.

Father Connolly said, 'God bless all here,' and he invited himself in. He stared at the three women noticing that only Kachelle's mother seemed nervous. He gave eye contact only to her.

'As a good Irish mother it is your duty to order your daughter back to her husband. Her place is with him, honouring and obeying him.' He only looked at Kachelle when speaking the last four words.

In a disciplined voice Kachelle answered.

'What happens between my husband and myself is my business Father.'

'Please, Kachelle, now be respectful. We don't want any trouble,' whispered her mother, nervously wringing her hands.

'There would be no trouble,' answered the priest looking directly at Kachelle's stomach, 'If you had forbidden her to travel to that den of iniquity, that most pagan of countries. If she had stayed at home and looked after her in-laws and her family, poor Padraic Charlie would not be in such a state today. You,' and he looked directly at Kachelle, 'should go down on your knees and thank God that a good man like Padraic Charlie would be willing to take you back, after you committing adultery, with a complete stranger in London.

'Oh is that what he has told you?' asked Kachelle. 'Well Father, I did commit adultery, but with the man I love and will always love- his brother Diarmuid Charlie.'

'Holy Mother of God,' prayed the priest. 'This is even worse. Poor Padraic Charlie. I want you two to leave the room and I demand that you go on your knees, Kachelle, and make a good confession now, or you will not enter my chapel again!'

'There's nobody going anywhere, Father,' said a calm and cool Kachelle. 'If I have sinned that is between me and my God. I will answer to him alone. He had his reasons for this little one to be born,' and she patted her stomach. Don't you ever tell me what to do. The house of God is open to everyone. I will enter when I wish. I will receive when I wish. Judge not and you will not be judged.' Placing her hand on the door latch she made to open it wide.

'This is what you have reared,' he roared at her poor mother. 'You will answer to God for this.' Kachelle's mother paled and fell sideways into her chair.

Biddy Joe, who had been silent, now spoke quietly and firmly to the priest, 'Father, I think it would be best if you took your leave.
Your housekeeper gets rather annoyed if you're missing for long, doesn't she?' and she cocked an eyebrow and looked him directly in the eye.

'You look here, Biddy Joe Boyle,' bellowed the priest. 'My housekeeper is....'

'No ,Father, I think it's best if we don't discuss your housekeeper. That's your business..and God's,' answered a perceptive Biddy Joe

He swallowed hard, his face mad with rage but he turned quietly and walked quickly into the dark. A stillness fell upon the small kitchen. The three women were speechless. The first to speak was Kachelle's mother.

'I'm glad your father is dead. I love you, child, but why oh why did this have to happen?'

No one spoke. Defeated, she took her leave. Kachelle made to follow her to the small bedroom but Biddy Joe gestured not to.

'He's been to the priest then,' said Biddy Joe to no one in particular. 'God, when I think of the women on this island who have had the priest sent to them. God help them. The Catholic Church is a male dominated Church for men. They forget Jesus Christ died for us all.'

'Oh Biddy Joe you'll be saying there should be women priests next,' replied Kachelle quietly.

'And why not?' demanded Biddy Joe. 'It was the women who were there from the beginning. Didn't the apostles desert him on Good Friday? Didn't one betray him? Didn't the women kneel at the foot of the cross until he died? Wasn't he laid in his mothers arms? Women buried him. Weren't they the first on the scene on Easter Sunday morning?'

'Whoa, whoa.' exclaimed Kachelle. 'OK, OK, you have a point, but I wouldn't mention it to himself,' and she gestured with her hand towards the door. 'His housekeeper what......?' She was halted in her tracks.

'I don't give scandal, girl. There are lots of things about this place. You keep your eyes open and you'll see for yourself, but also keep your mouth shut. It pays to keep your cards close to your chest, Kachelle. Now I'm going to see your mother. I expect we'll be seeing Mr Padraic Charlie McGinley within the next twenty four hours. Good night, Kachelle, and you did right to stand up for yourself.'

Biddy Joe was right. Padraic Charlie did appear next day, but only to take the two girls to his mothers. Kachelle's mother had taken ill during the night and a doctor from the mainland had been sent for. Padraic Charlie spoke not a word to Kachelle, collected a few belongings of the girls and quickly left. Kachelle and Biddy Joe sat alone quietly. It seemed ages before the doctor entered the small kitchen.

'Kachelle I'm sorry. Your mother is very ill. It's her heart, and she has taken a stroke.'

'Will she pull through?' pleaded Kachelle.

'It's hard to say. She is in God's hands. Look, it's too late for me to get the boat back. I'm staying at McCauley's. You can get me there. Don't hesitate to send for me,' and he quietly walked out the door.

'Biddy Joe, ah Biddy Joe, this is all my fault. I should have stayed in London. If my mother dies, I'll have killed her.'

'Nonsense,' answered Biddy Joe, quickly putting her arms around Kachelle. 'What's lotted can't be blotted. Whatever happens to your mother is your mother's fate. From the minute she was conceived her whole life was laid out for her. She made the decisions. She chose her paths. Just like you and I do. Now go to her and be with her. The next twenty four hours are crucial.'

Kachelle quickly pulled her chair to the side of her mother's bed. Sheila was pale and her breathing was shallow. Gently Kachelle stroked her mother's long thin fingers. Flashbacks came rapidly. Her young mother teaching her to foot the turf on a hot summers day. Mending the fishing nets. Baking the finest bread she ever tasted. Brushing her hair and complaining, yet loving her unruly curls. Comforting her when she was sick from eating to many blackberries. Scolding her for her childhood pranks. Most of all, her peaceful hands joined in prayer, morning, noon and evening.

'Oh God, please don't let her die,' she prayed silently to herself. Aloud she said, 'I love you Ma, and I am deeply sorry for all the hurt I have brought you. Please get well. I need you.' Her plea went unheard. After an hour Biddy Joe entered the room with a mug of sweet tea for Kachelle.

'I'll sit for a while now, love. You get some rest. It will be a long night.'

The long night came to an end at 3.00am. At 2.15 am the mother opened her eyes and seemed agitated.

'She's trying to tell us something,' said Biddy Joe.

The more Kachelle tried to understand her mother, the more agitated she became. The priest had been sent for but still her mother was determined to get her message across. Lifting her once paralysed arm she pointed to the trap door in the ceiling and then stroked Kachelle's face. Amazingly she played a little game she had always played with Kachelle as a child. 'A long index finger touched her right eye, 'I,' whispered Kachelle. Then Sheila laid her arm across her chest. 'Love,' said Kachelle, the tears now rolling down her cheeks. At last her arm pointed to Kachelle, 'You,' offered Kachelle.

Imitating the actions, Kachelle sent back the message, 'I Love You,' with an ache in her heart.

Then with laboured breath her mother offered a strong hand of friendship to Biddy Joe who clasped it tightly and said,

'Dearest friend, go in peace. I'm here for Kachelle and the weans.'

Kachelle's mother smiled and lowered her now-useless arm to her side. Staring at the Sacred Heart picture she uttered nonsense words which Kachelle took to be the 'Act of Contrition' and slowly, peacefully she passed away.

In the small island graveyard, surrounded by sorrowing neighbours, Kachelle stared at the brown, dry, sandy wound in the green earth that would be her mother's final resting place. Padraic Charlie stepped forward to help bury her mother. His harsh words rang out in her head, 'Your mother's a whore1'. She moved as if to stop him but Biddy Joe gently eased her back. When the last spadeful was patted into place the islanders departed. Kachelle and Biddy Joe placed a small bunch of flowers and sat down on the edge of a neighbouring headstone. It was customary to leave the family alone at this point. Padraic Charlie's mother had taken the girls home and the men had gathered in the local pub for their dutiful drink. Kachelle lit a long cigarette and stared ahead. The scene was breathtaking. Her mother lay next to the small graveyard wall which looked down on the wide open stretch of a golden beach. The deep blue sea gently ran away leaving ripple patterns of wet sand. Her children had laughed and played here while her mother watched over them.

'She's at peace now love. Lying next there to your Da. God, I remember the day he brought her home. Tom Harkin had married a mainlander! It was the talk of the island. They were suspicious of her and shut her out as only they can do. Life wasn't easy for her and she started to fail like snow off a ditch. I befriended her and when your da went fishing I would stay with her. Her health improved. Did you know I was with her when you when born? God, there was a fierce storm that night and she was worried about himself at sea. She said the storm fitted the hour of your birth, you with your head of mad red hair born in the eye of the storm. She always admired your courage and strength. She told me, she did you know. When I joined her that last evening after 'he' had left, she admitted to me that she knew if you hadn't stood up to the priest that he and Padraic Charlie and the other islanders would make your life hell. They're now scared of your courage so they'll leave you alone.

'And I am alone now, except for you, Biddy Joe. I'll always be here for you. You've always been like a mother to me.'

Kachelle placed her arms around Biddy Joe and held her close. After a few minutes Biddy Joe took her leave and Kachelle sat alone, absently rearranging the flowers on her mother's grave. The sun now shone out of a clear blue autumn sky and the island children who had been absent from the beach as a mark of respect now gathered, quietly at first but then their games and laughter rang out.

'Life has to go on, they say,' whispered Kachelle to herself. 'I have to go now, Ma. Thank you for everything and please pray for me!'

CHAPTER 9

When Kachelle returned home Biddy Joe had a roaring fire blazing up the chimney and even though the sun was hot, Kachelle felt chilled to the bone.

'You haven't slept in three nights, love, that's why you're cold and probably the shock of it all is just hitting you now. Sit yourself close to the fire and I'll pour you a mug of tea,' advised Biddy Joe.

Unknown to Kachelle she was prepared to add a good measure of whiskey to help her sleep. The two women sat staring quietly into the fire.

'Is it really possible, Biddy Joe, to read the flames?' asked Kachelle.

'Ach aye love, many's a one has the gift of reading fortunes that way. My great granny used to be able to do it, and she could have told you if there was to be a storm or not just by the colour of the flames.'

'Look at those beautiful blue and orange flames, Biddy Joe. I tell you there's no fire like a turf fire. I missed my turf fire in London,' quietly murmured Kachelle.

Biddy Joe smiled to herself. The tea was helping her to relax; a good nights sleep was ahead.

'I wonder why my Ma kept pointing at the ceiling? Was she trying to tell us she was going to heaven?' asked Kachelle childishly.

'She did get herself in an awful state, didn't she? No, she wanted us to know something. Her eyes were on the trap door. Could it be.........'
Before Biddy Joe had finished Kachelle was on her feet.

'There must be something in the loft she wanted us to know about. Come on, Biddy Joe, hold a chair for me until I have a look.'

'Can't this wait till morning, love. You need a good night's sleep.'

'No, Biddy Joe, I must look now,' said an urgent and curious Kachelle.

The small wooden chair didn't reach Kachelle high enough so the two women struggled with the kitchen table into the bedroom. Kachelle could now reach with ease. Her head and shoulders were lost within the dark hole.

'Pass me a lighted candle, Biddy Joe, please?' she asked, and her request was granted. Kachelle pulled forward a small wooden crate which resembled an old box that would have had been used to store fish in. She passed the candle to Biddy Joe and then lifted down the mysterious box. When the trap door was replaced and the kitchen table returned, she and Biddy Joe sat down and stared at the box.

'Go on, love,' gently urged Biddy Joe. 'Your mother wanted you to have it.'

Kachelle started to lift out the old newspapers that formed a protective covering. To her amazement there were tiny bundles of English paper money.

'Oh Biddy Joe, it's the money I sent her from England for looking after the girls. She has hardly spent a penny,' exclaimed Kachelle.

'Well your mother was always careful with money. She certainly knew how to stretch a penny.'

'There's almost six hundred pounds here, when you count her own savings from selling Da's boat,' offered Kachelle and then she started to sort out various papers. 'What on earth is this?' And she opened an official looking envelope. 'Deeds of a house, Biddy Joe. This house, Ma had the deeds of this house. How?'

'Look here,' said Biddy Joe. 'It's your father's will. Apparently he bought his sisters and brother out and owned this house. He has left it and a fair size of land to your mother and you. That's what she was trying to tell you, love. You have security.'

'And so do you, Biddy Joe. It's your home too.'

The rest of the evening was spent quietly looking at some old photographs of people, many of whom Kachelle and Biddy Joe didn't know, but assumed were relatives from the mainland. There was a lock of Kachelle's hair, with a small blue ribbon attached. Biddy Joe laughed,

'I remember the day you cut that off. You were about four and said you were fed up with your curls, you wanted straight hair like your friend.'

'Look at my first tooth in this small pill box- and there's another smaller lock of hair, Biddy Joe, blonde in colour.'

Biddy Joe was silent for a moment.

'That's from your wee brother.'

'My brother?' exclaimed Kachelle.

'Yes love. It was a very difficult birth, but there was something wrong with the wee mite. Mind you, he was a very big child. We reckoned about eight pounds, and beautiful. There must have been something wrong with his wee heart. His breathing was laboured and he was a blueish colour. The doctor reckoned he would only live a few hours. Your mother was demented! Your father was at sea and her baby son was dying. She walked the floors with him. It was as if she wanted every minute with him. She hardly slept. God gave him to her for ten days. He just finished feeding and fell asleep at her breast. When your Da came home it was all over. She never spoke about him again.'

'Poor Ma, she had her heartaches too,' wept Kachelle gently. 'You're tired love. Go to bed. I'll open your Mother's bedroom window and set her spirit free. Tomorrow is another day,' advised Biddy Joe as she helped Kachelle up out of the armchair.

Three months passed and Kachelle had not heard from Padraic Charlie. His mother visited her and the girls often but she didn't mention Padraic Charlie's name or Kachelle's condition. The talk of the island was that Padraic Charlie McGinley had hit the drink, The fishing season had come to an end and his mother had had to rely on friends and neighbours to bring home the turf for her. Night after night Padraic Charlie was to be found in the pub knocking back pints and whiskeys. The whole island waited with bated breath and if the situation was discussed it was in private and in hushed tones.

The war raged on and Kachelle, like her neighbours, had a quiet peaceful Christmas. It was on a January Sunday morning with a bitter frost on the ground so that Kachelle and her daughters carefully chose their steps to morning Mass, when Padraic Charlie called with Biddy Joe. He had obviously been drinking all night and was in a foul mood. He stood in the doorway, unsure whether to enter or not.

'Well are you coming in, lad, or am I going to lose all this heat to the fields?' asked Biddy Joe. He staggered towards the armchair and fell down with a force.

'You'll take a cup of tay?' asked Biddy Joe, already filling the pot. He never spoke.

'You are frozen through. Kachelle and the girls are away to Mass.'

'Yeh, I know. I watched them go. It's you I want to see.'

'Me?' asked a curious Biddy Joe, offering him the tea.

He accepted it gratefully and just stared into the fire. The silence was broken by his large sobs.

'Oh God, thought Biddy Joe, anything but tears. Why is it when a man cries it's so painful to watch?'

'Look son, finish your tea and then get it off your chest what you've come to say,' offered Biddy Joe.

He drained the tea and then surprised Biddy Joe by passing over his cup.

'You've read the whole island's, now do mine. What does the future hold for me?' he sneered. The tears were now replaced by contempt.

'Are you sure this is what you really want? You might not like what I tell you,' she explained.

'Just read it,' he snorted.

'First tell me how do you feel about Kachelle?'

'She's mine, mine, not that git Diarmuid Charlie's. I love her, she belongs to me,' he bellowed.

'No, son, you may love her but you can't make Kachelle love you. Love is not about owning someone. You can't demand that she loves you. Love and respect have to be earned.'

'He always had everything. He's my mother's favourite. He could have had any girl. Why did he have to take Kachelle?' he asked, his head I his hands. 'I hate him, and I hate her.....no, no I love her too it's just...' but he never finished his sentence.

'What's in a man when he's sober comes out when he's drunk,' offered Biddy Joe. 'Here, give me your cup son. I know you're hurting. I can't put it to right but let's see what lies ahead.' Biddy Joe turned the cup around.

'I see a bond with your brother broken,'

'Will he take her away?' Padraic Charlie asked eagerly.

'No, no I don't see that happening. Kachelle has feelings for you, son. She hates to see you suffering. There's a lot of love but it's not the love there should be between a man and a woman. She loves you like a mother. Your wedding ring is badly cracked but not broken.'

'What does that mean?' he interrupted again.

'It means there is a possibility that you and her will get back together. You're going to have to stop bending your elbow, son, or else you'll have a serious problem with the drink. You make your own life hard and difficult.

No-one else. You find it hard to forgive and you never forget. You are your own worse enemy. Try to sway a little in this relationship, you're too rigid. You have two little girls to think of and way down your cup..........'

'What does that mean?' he interrupted again.

'It means a long way off, possibly years away..... I see you with a son.'

'To Kachelle?' he asked eagerly.

'Well it's to a red haired woman, unless you know two red haired women. But there's a long hard road ahead and no one is making it difficult but you. You are your own worst enemy. Always remember you catch more flies with honey than vinegar,' and she set the cup down, but Padraic Charlie had fallen asleep in front of the fire, his drunken snore soon vibrating throughout the small house.

Kachelle met up with her mother in law coming out of Mass and was grateful for her arm as she felt all eyes in the church upon her.

'Hold your head high and smile as you talk to me,' instructed the old woman.

When well out of ear shot of the other islanders her mother in law spoke again.

'Will you come in for a cup of tea? We need to talk, Kachelle.'

Kachelle nodded her reply. She knew the time had come to tell the truth. The two girls were sent to the back bedroom to keep the Granda occupied and the two women faced each other across the table.

'They say this war will be over soon,' offered her mother in law. 'I hope Diarmuid Charlie is safe. My heart aches to hear from him. I did get a letter you know, before himself took to his bed but he burnt it before I could get reading all of it. It came all the way from America. Diarmuid Charlie probably thinks I'm angry with him for leaving but I'm not. He drove him away. I'll never forgive him for that.

Kachelle sat in silence for a while before going to her bag and bringing out the photos of Diarmuid Charlie and herself. She handed her mother in law the one of Diarmuid Charlie in his Canadian uniform.

'I met him in London,' she said quietly. He loves you deeply and I love him. Next to my breath he's all that I need. My heart aches to see him too. Please read the back.' Slowly the photo was turned over and her mother in law sucked in her breath. 'Oh Kachelle, Jesus Mary and Joseph,' and she blessed herself. 'Does Padraic Charlie know?'

'Yes,' answered kachelle. 'that's why I'm not back with him.'

'You must be very careful, Kachelle, there's a jealous streak in Padraic Charli. He could be dangerous. If he were to really lose his temper he's capable of murdering you. He's my son and I love him but at times he's like a stranger to me.'

'You're not angry with me?' queried Kachelle quietly.

'No, love, just scared for you. You're carrying my grandson, Diarmuid Charlie's child, how could I be angry with you? Please tell me all. How did you meet? Is he well? When did he join up? I know my Diarmuid Charlie loved you and if things had been different I know you two would be together.'

Kachelle toyed with the idea of explaining why she married Padraic Charlie but decided to keep her secret. Instead she slowly began relating how Diarmuid Charlie and she met and she showed the other photo of Diarmuid Charlie and herself together. She explained about him being married with a family and that it was very unlikely that they would ever be together. Sitting in the quiet kitchen with only the tilley lamp for light and a hushed turf fire the tears quietly rolled down both women's faces.

'We can't help who we fall in love, pet, but you have big decisions to make.'

'I know. I explained to Padraic Charlie that I would do anything to give him a good home life but I can't bring, myself to lie with him, I'm sorry I just can't.'

The old woman listened to all carefully and then in a hushed voice she spoke.

'Kachelle, now listen to me. I'm older than you and wiser. You must do all you can to get back with Padraic Charlie.'

'No! Why? I've security for myself and my children, I don't need him,' explained an agitated Kachelle.

'Shh, shh. Don't upset yourself. You're right, you do not need him but you need his good family name. You tell me you're carrying your son. Do you want him to be known all his life as the 'Bastard McGinley? Because that's what this island will name him and his children. Your daughters' future husbands will be warned off they will say, she might end up like her mother. I know this sounds harsh and cruel but this island will make sure your sin will be handed down from generation to generation. Another important point. All that I own is for my Diarmuid Charlie and his son. You say it's hardly likely that Diarmuid Charlie will ever come home here so this house and land is for your son, but an illegitimate child cannot inherit. At the moment the Islanders don't know what to make of the situation, that's why I linked your arm coming out of Mass. If you take my advice, move back in here. For your son put up with whatever Padraic Charlie throws at you. You can handle him, but do it for your son. People will think you stayed with your mother because she was ill and afterwards you didn't like leaving Biddy Joe on her own. I know exactly the woman to tell that tale too- Mary McCauley. She'll have it round the island in no time. But come home!'

'What if Padraic Charlie doesn't accept my decision....about not lying with him?' asked Kachelle nervously.

'There's been many a Mary and Joseph marriage. Who knows what goes on behind closed doors in any marriage. I'm sure there has been manys a row in every household over a woman unwilling or unable to have sex,' stated her mother in law firmly. 'Padraic Charlie will keep quiet. He wouldn't want the other men to know, especially his da, that you're carrying another man's child. He'll go along with the pretence.'

On her way home Kachelle thought carefully about her mother in law's advice. She knew she was right. She didn't want any stigma attached to her children. She had to leave her mother's home and return to the McGinley household. On her return she was surprised to find Padraic Charlie in her father's armchair. Biddy Joe kept her silence on the reason for his visit.

'Talk to him,' she urged. 'This problem has to be solved one way or another,' And she took the two girls off to feed the chickens.

Padraic Charlie stared, unsure of where he was at first. Kachelle lit two cigarettes and offered him one. She stood with her back to the fire her swollen belly staring him in the face.

'Have you decided what you want to do Padraic Charlie?' she asked.

'I don't want my girls talked about at school and shunned in later years. What man in his right mind would marry them, when they have a wh..... when their mother and father are split up?' he hissed. 'I will not be made to look a fool on this island, so on account of my girls you can come home and see to my parents and children like you suggested.'

'I won't sleep with you,' she stated firmly.

'I wouldn't touch you with a forty foot pole,' he sneered. 'As far as this island and my father are concerned, we live as man and wife. That's all I ask,' and he stood up.

'Well, we did marry for better or worse. I guess this is the worse.'

'You can bet your life on it,' he said with contempt. 'I'll expect you at my mother's shortly,' and abruptly he left.

Later when the girls were settled for the night Kachelle confided in Biddy Joe what had taken place between her mother in law and her and Padraic Charlie.

'Well, she does have a point, alana. Sure this island never forgave your father for marrying a mainlander. Even to this day, you wouldn't really be seen as a real islander and you born and reared here. Your children would have it thrown at them at school and believe me children can be very cruel. Your son would suffer the most. When they would come to courting age, oh their 'pedigree' would be discussed throughout the length and breadth of Arranmore. This island is too clannish, sure we're all too closely related. They can't see that strange blood is good for this place.'

'Oh God, Biddy Joe, what am I to do? I have my own house and capable of rearing my kids myself, yet to save my children any embarrassment I have to be trapped in a loveless marriage. Life is too unfair!'

'I know, love, and no matter how well you cover up your son's father, truth will out. Maybe not now, but some day the truth will be known. Only you can make this decision. I'll say good night and leave you,' and she kissed Kachelle on the top of her head and ruffled her hair.

Kachelle didn't go to bed. The baby kicked violently as if forcing her to make the right decision and no matter what she took, the heartburn raged within her. She prayed hard to the Sacred Heart picture and then would go giddy telling herself it was St. Jude of hopeless cases she needed. Before long, morning broke. A dull, damp day lay ahead. She quickly reset the fire and put the kettle on to boil. Philomena and Sheila came quietly into the kitchen and rushed towards the struggling fire. She patted her knee and the two girls fought to gain access.

'My darlings,' she said, and stroked their heads on her chest and they snuggled in close to gain warmth. When Biddy Joe entered the room she smiled at the small gathering and her heart went out to Kachelle.

'What do you think you will do?' she asked Kachelle gently.

'Look at them, Biddy Joe. Aren't they beautiful and innocent? I can't let them suffer because of my sin. I will have to go back to Padraic Charlie and work for some resemblance of a happy family for these two and this little one,' she said, patting her stomach. 'My son will have the best. Nothing will be too good for him. I'll sacrifice my life if necessary.'

'Well, you've made your bed, so now you'll have to lie on it,' offered Biddy Joe. You sit there with the girls, I'll make a bite to eat,' and Biddy Joe set about preparing the last breakfast for all of them.

By seven o'clock Kachelle and the girls were re-instated in her mother in law's home.

'Bless you, child, you have made the right decision. You're welcome, very welcome,' and she kissed Kachelle on both cheeks. Himself in the back bedroom had to be confronted yet.

'Will you take him supper?' meekly asked her mother in law. Padraic Charlie spoke not a word until he got his mother out of hearing.

'Don't tell him it's Diarmuid's he pleaded.'

Kachelle looked at her husband; he was like a frightened school boy, afraid to confront his father.

'OK if that's what you want,' and she lifted the small tray of baked soda bread and cheese and a glass of milk.

'So it's yourself then,' came the voice from the dark. Kachelle lit the candle. 'You took your time coming home...Jesus Christ! Now I see why. Who's is it? An English man's bastard no doubt! So he's given in and taken you back, the trollop that you are. You are a dirty whore, get out of my house! Why he's no man. If he was he would have kicked it out of you! Padraic Charlie, come here! How many times have I told you a woman is like a field, she needs a good digging to keep her under control. Padraic Charlie! Padraic Charlie! This whore needs a good hiding!'

'Like you would have done?' stated Kachelle. 'Well it's as well your kicking days are over or I would be leaving you for dead too! You dirty old man, I caught you leering at me, what does that make you?' And she turned to leave the room.

'You whore. You come from a long line of whores. Ah.... my innocent lad has been caught by a dirty whore! Your mother was a whore from the mainland who snared poor Tom Harkin,' he squealed savagely after her.

Kachelle stopped in her tracks and then slowly returned to the bed. Calmly she lifted the glass of milk and flung it violently into his face.

'Perhaps that will wash your mouth out,' and then she took her leave. His mouth was open in shock. He spluttered and coughed. Never, never had a man dared to do such a thing- never mind a woman! He was speechless at last.

On entering the small kitchen Kachelle found the girls and their grandmother on their knees anxiously praying the rosary.

'Oh Kachelle, I was so scared. Even though he can't leave the bed the old fears come back on me. He's so quiet now, he's up to something. Padraic Charlie raced out when he started to call for him. What's he doing?'

'Nothing,' replied a composed Kachelle, 'I threw the milk at him, full in the face.'

'Oh Kachelle, you didn't,' gasped her mother in law and the two women suppressed their laughter by placing the palms of their hands over their mouths.

The two girls thought the whole situation ridiculous and joined in on the adult laughter. Within a few minutes the whole house was filled with female laughter.

'Witch! Bitch! Whore!' rang out in the background.

When Padraic Charlie returned home he found his mother asleep on the old black settee which had become her bed since his father fell ill. The two girls were settled in the small box room off the kitchen, a room that had always frightened him as a child. He recalled how Diarmuid Charlie had always comforted him and told him not to be afraid of the dark.

'The bastard,' he muttered to himself. On entering the only room left, he quickly saw that Kachelle had made a makeshift bed on the floor for herself.

'Good enough for you, you whore,' he hissed at her quietly for fear of awakening his father. 'Yous are all whores, every damn one of yous. Dirty filthy whores!' And he fell on top of the bed.

Kachelle pretended to be asleep, hoping he would leave her alone. Alas, a pattern was set that would continue for many years.

On 17th April 1944, after a long hard labour, Kachelle finally gave birth to a baby boy. Her heart swelled with pride and joy when Biddy Joe placed him in her arms. The two girls had been sent out to play in the wide open space of golden beach. Padraic Charlie had not returned from a heavy night's drinking and her mother in law had laced her husband's tea with a good measure of whiskey so that his verbal abuse would not reach the ears of her new baby grandson. The three women gazed lovingly at the newborn infant. The grandmother vividly remembered the birth of her Diarmuid Charlie, Biddy Joe of her daughter, and Kachelle gazed at her first son. All three hearts ached as only a womans can.

'He's beautiful,' whispered Biddy Joe.
'He's the image of his father, God Bless him,' offered his grandmother.
'He's mine, all mine, Thank you, God,' gently murmured Kachelle.
'He's going to have your red hair,' suggested Biddy Joe.

'He has his father's and grandmother's eyes,' said Kachelle gently squeezing her mother in law's hand.

'What are you calling him?' she asked eagerly.

'Why Diarmuid Charlie of course, Diarmuid Charlie McGinley after his father,' said Kachelle calmly.

'He'll go berserk!' panicked her mother in law, nodding her head towards the back bedroom, 'and so will Padraic Charlie.'

'Well they can go berserk together then, exclaimed a determined Kachelle.

'Come on,' offered Biddy Joe taking the other woman's arm. 'We'll let her get some sleep,' and they quietly left the room. Kachelle stared sleepily out of the small, grimy bedroom window. The April sun shone delicately on the fresh primroses. Spring, she thought. A new beginning.

'Yes, my darling boy, you're now the love of my life. I will protect you. You will want for nothing,' and she cuddled the child closer to her breast as she fell asleep.

How long she slept she had no idea, but she was awakened by the kicking of her bedroom door. A drunken Padraic Charlie stood in the doorway.

'So you've had your bastard then. What are you going to call him?' he demanded..

'Why, Diarmuid Charlie of course, after his uncle Diarmuid Charlie in Canada. Isn't that right Padraic Charlie?' she declared.

Padraic Charlie stumbled towards the bed as if to hit out at the child.

'No! You touch him and you're dead!' she threatened.

'Get him out, get him out now, or I'll not be responsible for my actions!' he ordered.

Kachelle quickly placed her coat over her nightie and resting the child in her arms she backed protectively out of the room. Taking flight, she ran bare foot over the strand, her heart pounding like the Atlantic ocean a few feet away, over the pebbles and shells, until she reached the safety of Biddy Joes.

Unknown to her the same journey would be made time and time again until the child would be old enough to make the journey by himself, an action that would not only affect him but his wife and children thirty years on.

A startled Biddy Joe quietly ushered Kachelle and her son in and drew the large armchair to the dying fire. The infant, fragile and tiny, his skin translucent, slept in his mother's arms. A pale reddish fuzz covered his perfect little head.

'Sh, sh, Alana,' whispered Biddy Joe. 'Calm yourself while I make you a strong cup of tay. You look as if you need it.'

Kachelle drew in large gulps of air and fought back the hot, stinging tears.

'Let them come, love,' urged Biddy Joe. 'Your tears are your release. They'll help keep you sane in the years to come.'

At this time the infant began to cry, a thin thready wail. Kachelle unbuttoned her nightdress and held her erect nipple to the baby's lips until they closed around it. She stroked the petal soft cheek and the infant began to suck greedily, easing some of the misery in her heart.

'Damn you, Diarmuid Charlie,' she hissed at no one in particular. 'Why didn't you send for me? Why didn't you tell me you were married?' and she lowered her head against her sons.

Her thoughts flew again to Diarmuid Charlie, a deliriously virile man and herself a woman profoundly lonely in the flesh. How could they have avoided each other? With the child pulling strongly on her breast, her body ached for the release only Diarmuid Charlie could give her. He was a wonderful lover, with more finesse that Padraic. She knew she was a passionate woman, but not a wanton one. Yet all Diarmuid Charlie had to do was smile with his twinkling blue eyes and she was wet and willing.

Now something stirred in her where only longing for Diarmuid Charlie had been. It was a resolve she had not known she possessed. Fate had changed her life, She would protect this child, see to its every need. He was now, and would always be, the man in her life.

'Oh God, help me please to push all memories of Diarmuid Charlie out of my head and heart. You know that I love him and I thank you for sending me my son. Help me to protect him and see him reared. Please don't let any harm come to him and I promise to teach my children to know and to love you.'

Kachelle stared   the image of the Sacred Heart hanging above the fireplace full in the eyes and then meekly blessed herself. Then wetting her thumb with her own saliva she made the sign of the cross on the child's forehead.

'Have you thought of what you are going to do?' asked Biddy Joe.

Kachelle was silent for a while, then calmly said,

'It'll be alright during the day. Padraic Charlie will be sleeping it off. At night time I'll come to you. If something happens so I can't stay, I'll leave him with you.'

'He could be on the drink for years. How will you manage for money?' asked Biddy Joe.

'I'll go ahead with my plans for a shop. I'll buy an old van and get shelves put in. I'll sell everything the island needs. I can take the children with me until they start school. It will help keep me and them out of his way. Before he gets home from the pub, I'll come to you. It will work, won't it Biddy?' she asked nervously.

'It will take all your mental and physical energy to keep going, love, but I guess you need something now to divert your memories and feelings, and to give you a new interest and some money coming in.'

'I just know I can do it, Biddy Joe. I've got to do it, to give this little one a chance in life. He'll want for nothing I'll make sure if that!'

'Aye, but will it be good for him, love? Anyway you do what you have to do. Now ease yourself down and try and get some rest otherwise you'll have no milk for that little mite,' and Biddy Joe pulled an old coat over the two figures.

Next morning Kachelle crept quietly home. Her mother in law had lit the fire and was preparing breakfast. The two men were fast asleep, their snores complementing each other.

'He was furious last night, Kachelle, and when he gets like that he can be dangerous. We must protect this little one. I'll see to him while you do your chores and then we'll talk about what we'll do,' urged her mother in law.

Kachelle was exhausted and was losing quite heavily after the birth. Nevertheless she gathered herself up and set about her daily routine. Her arms were aching to hold her son. How was she going to bear to be parted from him? She would have to come up with a plan that would enable her son to be with her continually.

By mid day the fresh water was collected from the well, the turf was gathered in for the day's cooking and heating, the cow milked and moved to fresh grazing, the hens fed, the fresh bread baked, the salted fish cut down for the meals during the week, the household rubbish gathered up and burned and a full line of washing blew triumphantly towards the Atlantic ocean.

Kachelle's breasts ached for release. To her disappointment her son was fast asleep.

'He should be starving with the hunger,' worried Kachelle to her mother in law.

'He was, love, but you were away with the cow. I had to give him something. I was afraid the cow's milk would upset him so I dipped a clean rag in my tay and he supped the lot.'

'God I hope it doesn't do him any harm,' said Kachelle and she rushed forward to lift him.

'I didn't mean any harm. I had to stop him crying in case he would waken himself.'

'I know, I know. Look, it's O.K., I'll keep him with me. Have you an old sheet?'

'Aye, but what are you going to do?' asked her mother in law.

'I'll make a sling so he can be against my breast while I work. It'll do for now. I'll have to come up with something else when he gets bigger.'

Kachelle laid the child down and taking the sheet she tore it in the shape of a triangle. Tying the broadest end around her waist, she laid the child against her breast and pulled the pointed end up and over the child, securing the end piece with a safety pin at the waist. The child was held snugly against her, leaving her two arms free.

'See, that will support him and leave me free to do my chores,' and she patted the child's bottom. 'Now I'll have a bite to eat and then I'm off to the mainland. I've a bit of business to do.'

Her mother in law did not question her 'business.' She made a light lunch and then bade them farewell.

'God be with you both,' she prayed as she blessed herself with water from the holy water font and blessed Kachelle and the child with her damp thumb, before they left the house.

Kachelle returned to Biddy Joe and to the box of money which was her legacy from her mother. Extracting one hundred pounds she placed this between her breasts and bade Biddy Joe hide the box again.

It had grown dark outside with rain threatening. Biddy Joe offered her a large black shawl to wrap around her and to keep the child warm. Kachelle hurried to catch the mid day boat.

By four o clock Kachelle was on her home bound journey. She had called at Jackson's in Dungloe and purchased an ageing bus for sixty pounds. A further ten pounds would see the seats removed and shelves installed. With her last thirty pounds she had struck a bargain with the local grocer for tea, sugar, flour, bacon, soap etc. This was the first order for her shop. All her goods were to be delivered the following week to Burtonport Pier to catch the postal boat. Kachelle then struck a deal with Phil Bann to load these goods on the boat for her. She would be responsible for them at Chaplestrand Pier.

By evening, Kachelle was safely home. Her two daughters were settled for the night and her mother in law was preparing supper for the two men. A drunken roar from the back room signalled the men's entry into the day. Padraic Charlie appeared with a scowl on his face demanding something to eat. Kachelle calmly lifted her shawl, wrapped it over her head and around the child and left for Biddy Joe's. Her young daughters said nothing, calmly accepting the situation. And so the small household fell into a routine.

CHAPTER 11

The following week, Kachelle painstakingly collected her goods from the pier and stored them safely in the barn. Her son never left her side and she was contented. The two girls fussed over their new brother and asked no questions why he left every night. As the boatmen struggled to release the bus from its constraints the children laughed and squealed with delight at their efforts. At one time it looked as if the bus would topple over and fall into the ebbing tide. Kachelle stood tall and proud. Finally her hard work was showing some results.

'This is all for you, my love,' she whispered to her son as she snuggled him close.

At last with the help of the children and half the island population the bus was carefully placed on the wide dirt track of a road with the grass growing down the middle. Kachelle sat herself behind the large black steering wheel. Her son lay at her feet in the large blanketed fish box. John Joe McCafferty was on hand to guide her through the driving process.

'Now, Kachelle, check the gear is in neutral, left foot off clutch and turn the key. Right foot on the accelerator- gently. When you feel her biting, release the hand brake.' The bus moved slowly with the children running in front.

'Sound your horn, girl, and scatter the holy terrors,' he commanded.

Kachelle did as she was 'bid' and the children scattered, squealing with delight.

'Now, increase the pressure on the accelerator and change into second gear. Remember it's only a machine. It can only do what you tell it!

The journey home was guided by John Joe.

'There you are, girl. You'll soon get the hang of it. I'll tell you what. I'll nip home for a while and then we'll go down to the strand. The tide will be out and I'll talk you through reversing and stopping on hills. Sure you'll be driving in no time.'

'Thanks, John Joe, I appreciate you helping me. I'll see you later. God bless,' and Kachelle jumped down. Lifting her son she tied him to her bosom again and made her way inside.

Her mother in law was astonished.

'Good God, child you'll never manage a bus like that.'

'Where there's a will there's a way. I will so. I have to! There's no money coming in and I want the best for my children, for my son. It's not so hard. I saw women driving buses in London. Don't you fret yourself.'

'Child, you could be killed. Them women in London had proper roads. Why some of the roads you'll be driving on are nothing more but paths and they're steep. Dear God, I'll not do a bit of good thinking and worrying about you.'

She rose and reached for her bottle of Holy Water and she filled a small container.

'Now wait till I get one of my medals,' and she rummaged through an old tin box

'Come on girls,' she called to her granddaughters and made her way to the front. She chanted a prayer in Irish while sprinkling the Holy water on the bus. She climbed in and placed the holy medal on the dashboard along with the small container of the blessed water and continued praying and sprinkling.

'Now then, the Sacred Heart will protect her and keep her safe from harm.'

Kachelle watched from the half door. The gentleness of her mother in law's actions struck a chord within her heart.

'Thank you, mother,' she said softly as she clasped the frail hands. 'Now, I've my chores to finish and another lesson with John Joe. Then I have to collect more merchandise from the port. I hope to start the day after tomorrow. It's time for a drop of tay. You sit yourself down and I'll see to things.'

Kachelle prepared a meal of boiled potatoes mixed with raw eggs and a few spring onions, finished off a with glasses of fresh milk. Her father in law put the finishing touches to the meal with his ususal verbal abuse about herself and the bus.

By eight o clock the children were safely tucked up in bed. The merchandise was securely stored in the barn and Kachelle climbed aboard the bus with John Joe. Her son slept contentedly at her feet. She was worried about John Joe. His so-called errand had been to the pub, but she needed him. Carefully she guided her bus to Chaplestrand and awaited his instructions.

'Right now, girl, your gear stick goes like this for reverse. Pull about the length of your bus in front of where you want to turn into. Now slowly, the slower the better, reverse, keeping an eye in your mirrors at all times.'

Kachelle followed his instructions carefully, but swung the front of the bus wide.

'Try again, slower,' he urged. 'Jesus, Kachelle, a fine looking woman like you shouldn't have to be doing this. Why if you were my woman you'd neither work nor want,' and he placed his large warm hand on her left thigh squeezing it violently.

'No, John Joe,' she shouted. 'None of your nonsense. There's a bottle of whiskey in this for you, if you behave, that's all. Now try anything like that again and I'll take the head off your body!'

'OK, OK, no need to get your knickers in a twist! I'm sure I'm not the first and won't be the last to try you out. Padraic Charlie needs his bloody head examined allowing a beautiful woman like you to run about. Tell me, is that his?' and he kicked the bottom of the fish box that cradled the child.

'Out, get out you bastard! I'll teach myself to drive. Any more talk like that and I'll tell Mary Ann about you.'

'I didn't mean any harm,' he stuttered.

'Out, I said! Out!' and she made to rise from her seat.

'I'm away. Fuck you and your bloody bus! You stay away from my Mary Ann. I wouldn't allow her to talk to the likes of you!' and he slammed the door shut.

It took quite a while for Kachelle to calm down. She looked at her sleeping son.

'I've got to protect you,' she whispered. 'There must be no talk about you. I'll do all in my power to be there for you. Even if that means sleeping with Padraic Charlie, I'll do it. Anything, not to have your name tarnished. Sleep soft, my pet. I would willingly die for you. But now I have to practise this damn reversing, so I can get this show on the road.'

The roar of Kachelle's engine could be heard all over the small island. Some men in the pub were betting she wouldn't be able to do it. Others admired her courage and bet heavily that no matter what Kachelle put her mind her too she would accomplish. All the same they wouldn't have their women driving; All bets came to an end when Padraic Charlie entered the pub.

By ten o'clock Kachelle called it a day. She felt exhausted. Her shoulders and arms ached and she was hot and sticky from nervous perspiration and the mild weather. The child would soon be waking for his feed. Kachelle parked the bus, lifted her son and made her way across the darkening strand. Carefully choosing her steps she made her way to the lower beach to a spot where she and the other children used to play after school

The cool sea had left part of itself behind, caught among some rocks. It glimmered and shone in the approaching moonlight. Kachelle disrobed entirely, secured the child in a safe spot and entered the cool water. It rolled over her hot body, massaging her tired aching limbs. She felt herself relaxing. Lying back, her red, long hair spread out about her, her fine sculptured pale limbs gently caressing the water was the only sound to be heard.

Unknown to her, John Joe was watching from behind a large rock. The sight of her made him catch his breath.

'Bitch,' he whispered hoarsely. 'Fucking bitch,' and he rubbed his groin to satisfy himself. 'I'll get you some day and when I do I'll, I'll,' he leaned against the rock panting and perspiring heavily until he relieved himself.

The child whimpered. Kachelle swam forward. Standing waist deep she lifted him from the fish box. He felt hot.

'It's too warm for you, love,' she said and quickly stripped him of his garments which she placed on the rock. Singing gently she eased the child into the cool water. He kicked and fussed at first, his small face startled. Soon he settled down, enjoying the coolness as his mother did. Kachelle turned him on his tummy and lifting handfuls of water she allowed it to trickle down his back.

'You have broad shoulders my love. You'll make a fine man. Just like your daddy.' Thoughts of Diarmuid Charlie made her think of John Joe's hand on her thigh. Oh, if only it had been Diarmuid Charlie, she thought to herself and found herself trembling at the thought.

'Please God, no. Lead me not into temptation,' and she quickly fought to hold back all thoughts of Diarmuid Charlie. She turned the child round; he quickly sought her breast and sucked greedily.

'Wait, my little one,' urged Kachelle. But the child fought and struggled back. He had found his satisfaction. Kachelle was not to find hers. Her half naked figure, feeding her son, silhouetted in the moonlight would have inspired any artist or poet. Only John Joe witnessed the beautiful sight.

Kachelle was so engrossed in feeding her son that she did not hear or see the figure behind her until it was too late. Startled she spun round to face John Joe, his eyes drinking in her nakedness. He pulled her roughly to him.

'No, John Joe! Please! Mind the child,' she begged.

'Fuck him, he's only a wee bastard. It's you I want. The ice queen of Arranmore! Well a man like me will soon melt you,' he sneered.

He gripped her free arm like a vice, her other was supporting her son. He made to loosen the buttons on the front of his trousers. Kachelle panicked when he produced his responsive penis and started prodding her instantly. She feared more for her son than for herself. Walking backwards with John Joe almost between her legs, her back soon came in contact with the rock. Reaching quickly she placed the child on his back on the cold stone. He squealed and kicked furiously.

'No you don't, you bastard!' and with her free hand she hit out wildly at John Joe. They both lost their balance and went under. Kachelle was gripped by her long hair and yanked up against the rock. Her son's wail made her alert. She scratched and bit, but John Joe pulled her to him and pushed her up against the rock.

'Spread them, girl! I'm going to fuck you like you've never been fucked before and if you dare open your mouth to squeal I'll kill the bastard. Drown him and you!

Kachelle smelt the drink from his breath and caught the male scent of him. Thinking quickly she raised her arms. Her magnificent creamy breasts with the large brown nipples glistened in the moonlight. Small rivulets of water made their way down the center of her breasts and gathered in large drops at her nipples.

'You think you can handle a woman like me. Try, let's see what your made of. You've a big enough tool anyway,' she coaxed huskily.

'Good girl, good girl,' he answered and placing his thin lips around her nipples he moaned with pleasure when he received her milk.

Kachelle stretched further. He thought it was to accommodate him, but she was reaching for a large, loose rock. Forcefully she brought it firmly down on his head. His legs buckled and he slid down her front until his face was covered by the green sea.

There was a deafening silence. Even the child stopped crying. Kachelle looked around. There was no one in sight. She pushed John Joe away, his blood now mingling with the sea. Quickly she grabbed her clothes, the child's clothes and sped across the strand to the bus with her son silent in her arms. She laid him on the driver's seat and dressed quickly. Wrapping her son in the small blanket, she left the bus and hurried to Biddy's.

'Jesus, Mary and Joseph!' Biddy kept repeating over and over. 'He might have killed you and the wean. There was nothing else you could have done, Alana. He was always no good. God, but bloody drink has a lot to answer for.'

'Biddy I don't know if he's alive or dead. What if I have killed him?' pleaded Kachelle.

'You were only protecting yourself and your child. Mind you, the whole bloody island will be asking why the hell you were naked in the first place. Look, if he's dead you never mention this again to anyone. As far as you're concerned you had your lesson with him and left him with the bus. If he lives, he knows to keep his mouth shut but you'll have to be wary of him. He'll be out to do you and your son harm.'

'I hope to God he's dead then. He might have killed my little one. Did I hurt him when I left him on the rock?'

'Look for yourself. He's sound asleep. There's nothing to worry about there. Go on, get yourself to bed and if anyone asks, I wasn't feeling well and you came to stay with me.'

The following morning brought no enquiries for John Joe. The women of the island were well used to their men staying out all night drinking and then lying the best part of the day in a ditch or a field in a drunken sleep.

It was the children who found him.

Just as Kachelle's generation had done, they had made their way to the large rock pool after school, only to find John Joe face down. Their squeals could be heard half way across the island. One, an altar boy, raced to the chapel at the end of the strand and began ringing the bell. In no time at all, a crowd had gathered around the pool staring in disbelief. Many made the sign of the cross and began repeating the rosary.

The Parish Priest and two others waded into the pool and pulled John Joe to the edge. A nervous laugh rose from the children and some adults because when they laid him down, there in full view was John Joe's penis standing straight and proud.

'Jesus, Mary and Joseph,' said the Parish Priest and quickly covered John Joe with his coat. He said a prayer in his ear and anointed him.

'Useless doing that, sure he's dead,' said one of the men and the priest scolded him. A black shawl was offered to carry the remains home.

'He's been taking a leak and fell in stupid drunk,' was one of the stories which quickly circulated the island.

'Why go so far down the strand just for a piss?' asked the men in the pub. The wild stories were fast and furious but no one connected John Joe's death with Kachelle. In the end it was assumed that he had gotten very drunk after Kachelle's lesson. A whiskey bottle was found near by and was produced as evidence. The bar owner confirmed that he had given him the same bottle on tick and now he would never get paid for it. No gardai were called to help with the investigation. The island people preferred to settle things themselves.

So on the morning of his funeral, the priest gave a talk on the danger of drinking and said that it was responsible for bringing about John Joe's death. His wife and four daughters stood silently by, thanking people for their condolences. The eldest one was heard to say as she placed her arm around her mother.

'It's over now, Ma. We'll look after you. At last, you'll get no more beatings and not have to stay up all night waiting for him to come home in one of his moods. You're at peace now Ma.'

The island settled back into its routine, only now the women could be heard shouting after their men, 'Don't you be drinking too much or you'll end up like John Joe.' And the children told ghost stories about John Joe walking the strand with his willie sticking out.

CHAPTER 12

Kachelle kept John Joe's Month's Mind as a mark of respect. It also gave her time to get herself gathered together. She spent her days up the mountain with her three children footing the turf. She had paid a neighbour to cut the turf and she taught her daughters to stack the small lumps of wet turf so that the sun would dry them out. At lunch time she prepared a fire and placed an old kettle on to boil to make a drop of tay. Half a dozen of fresh clean eggs were boiled in the same water. Large chunks of heavily buttered bread were offered to her neighbour and the children, and after the hard boiled eggs they all enjoyed strong sweet tea. Kachelle then lifter her son and unbuttoning her blouse set about feeding him. The girls chased butterflies and her neighbour walked a short distance off to enjoy his pipe.

Kachelle stared across the calm Atlantic Ocean. 'America is the other side,' she whispered to her son. 'I wonder what your Da is doing right now?' she asked the child. The loneliness within her heart brought tears to her eyes. She stroked the side of the child's face. He opened his pale blue eyes and smiled up at her.

'Thank God for you,' she silently prayed and kissed his forehead before returning to her work.

The first Sunday in July Kachelle inspected her bus. All her goods were neatly arranged on the shelves. Boxes of soap etc, were placed on the floor and the fish box for the sleeping child lay at the driver's feet. Kachelle took the opportunity to catch up on some chores. It was going to be difficult to get all her chores completed before setting off in the morning.

Late in the afternoon she took her three children down to the strand and watched as her daughters jumped in the ebbing tide. On her return home she found her father in law fast asleep. Her mother in law dozed on the chair, her rosary beads entangled in her right hand. She quickly fed the girls and got them to bed. In no time at all they were fast asleep.

Padraic Charlie had obviously left earlier for the pub. She was tempted to stay the night but the thought of Padraic Charlie hurting the child was too fearful. She kissed her mother in law good night and made her way to

Biddy's. She wouldn't be long away. The sun rose at 4:45am. And she wanted to have all her chores completed, the fresh meat added to her supplies and on her way for nine o'clock.

By 9:30 Kachelle's bus was slowly climbing the steep hill to Afort. Her son slept contentedly at her feet and her daughters were safe with their granny who would walk them over to Biddy's so she could get her head showered- a term the island women used to claim some peace and quiet for themselves.

Kachelle's first day went well. The women were delighted that the goods they needed were now available on their doorstep. As most of the men were busy with the salmon fishing, money was scarce. Kachelle obligingly wrote down in a small book all the goods each neighbour got and counted it up. Each woman promised to pay at the end of the salmon fishing season.

By two o'clock she was calling at John Joe's house. This small run-down thatched cottage was situated at the base of a small mountain. The garden was unkempt and there was no sign of any potatoes or vegetables growing.

Mary Ann invited her in. 'You'll take a drop of tay Kachelle?' she asked timidly.

Kachelle was shocked to see a wooden box rather like her own placed beside the hearth. A sturdy boy of one year old stared back at her with black piercing eyes and every so often he would let out a wild piercing scream for no reason.

'Mary Ann, I didn't know you had a son!' stated the surprised Kachelle.

Mary Ann simply replied, 'It's not mine. He belongs to my youngest girl. She's just fifteen years old. May God forgive me but I can't bring myself to love him, but sure what else could we do?'

'You're bound to be getting it hard,' said Kachelle comfortingly. 'I'm really sorry about John Joe's death.'

'Oh, I'm not,' Mary Ann replied sharply. 'You see, that's his!'

'What? asked Kachelle, disbelieving.

'Yes , you see I wasn't enough for him, so he took my girls. Eileen! Eileen!' she called, 'Come in here.'

A pretty, dark haired girl appeared from the small, dark room. A full grown woman of seventeen, but with the mind of a nine year old, her belly swollen with child, slowly entered the room.

'That's his too,' said Mary Ann resignedly. 'He was always a bastard. At least now we'll get some peace. I told the priest you know. He was going to send my two girls away and said he would only let them stay if I pretended the children were mine.'

'The bastard,' Kachelle's brain kept repeating again and again. Going to the van she gathered up bacon, eggs, butter, potatoes, fresh vegetables, soap and a small bag of hard boiled sweets. She placed them on the rough table.

'There, this will help you out,' and she offered the young pregnant girl a sweet.

'I can't pay you, Kachelle. We can't afford such luxuries.'

'Never mind,' Kachelle stopped her short. ' I can afford it. I'll call every week, same time to see how you're getting on. Now take care,' and she walked slowly down the dried mud path to the bus.

A few miles down the road she stopped the bus to feed her son.

'Dear Jesus, forgive me for killing John Joe, but you do work in mysterious ways,' she prayed.

Kachelle finally parked her bus, finished for the day at 9.00pm. She felt exhausted and her arms ached. Her mother in law quickly placed a meal of potatoes and buttermilk in front of her and then poured her a large sweet mug of tea. Kachelle pulled out a long cigarette, lit it and sat back, exhausted. The girls and her father in law were fast asleep. Padraic Charlie was already at the pub. A roaring turf fire was the only light in the small dark room. The tick of the clock was the only sound. Kachelle started to doze. 'Kachelle, Kachelle, love,' her mother in law gently called. 'It's almost time for his feed. You should get yourself off to Biddy's love, you're exhausted!'

Kachelle nodded in agreement and lifting her son in her arms she left for Biddy's.

When the salmon fishing came to an end, the islanders paid their bills and credit was arranged again until the end of the lobster fishing. Kachelle had made a good profit. She shared the exciting news with Biddy Joe.

'I can buy a wider range of goods now. All the Islanders are buying off me. The women are delighted. We'll have a good Christmas, Biddy Joe.

Thank God things are beginning to look up.'

'How long are you going to be able to cope Alana?' asked Biddy Joe. 'Between your chores and your business you're doing the work of a man. Something has to give. Then you're hurrying over here at night carrying himself,' and she nodded towards the child.

'It'll all work out Biddy Joe. Let's just take it one day at a time. At least himself is quiet. He never mentions the child.'

'Aye you're right love. Now get some sleep. Morning comes early.'

The following morning Kachelle was up and away before Biddy Joe woke. She was anxious to get started early. When her chores were completed, and her son settled at her feet in the bus, she drove to Chaplestrand to meet the postal boat. Some of goods were coming in. The small postal bags were thrown carelessly on to the pier.

'Here, Kachelle, throw those into the post office for me, save me the journey. I'd a feed of drink last night and my guts are aching,' moaned Phil Bann the boatman.

'Sure I will, but it serves you right. The oul drink will kill you some day,' laughed Kachelle as she flashed him a smile.

When her goods were safely packed away she lifted the two postal bags and threw them into the back of her van.

'Christ,' she cursed as she noticed a few letters had fallen out.

Climbing into the back of the van she quickly set about lifting the letters. As she stretched to lift the last one, her heart missed a beat. It was addressed to her and it had an American stamp!

'Diarmuid Charlie,' she whispered and quickly held the letter to her heart. 'Oh Diarmuid Charlie,' she whispered more softly.

She knew all the letters should go directly to the Post Office but the post mistress was a nosy old bitch and might wonder why it was addressed to her mother's. Glancing around, she quickly secreted the letter between her breasts, replaced the others in the bag and tied the top securely.

'Good morning to you, may God be with you,' called the post mistress when Kachelle pulled up in front of her. Kachelle bid her the time of the day and handed her the bags.

'At last, he's using his head and saving his feet for dancing,' she laughed and took the bags off Kachelle. 'He'll have you doing his job every day,' she warned.

'Ah sure, I don't mind. Give him time to have his breakfast,' joked Kachelle, eager to get away as her heart was pounding so loud she was sure it could be heard. Climbing into the van she drove carefully to the most isolated spot on the island and pulled the letter from her breast. Her hands shook with excitement as she opened the crinkled envelope.

'Oh God, Diarmuid, perhaps he's sending for me, we'll go to America, we will,' she whispered to her son. Her eyes scanned the page and heart sank in her chest. She shook her head as if to clear it and read it again, this time taking in every word.

My dearest Kachelle,

I hope this letter finds you in good spirits and good health. I don't know whether you are in England or back home but I'm sure your mother will see you get this. I could not write sooner my love, as I was wounded on my last tour of duty. A good mate of mine was shot down and we were ordered to retreat. God Kachelle, I could hear him crying and begging, yes begging for help. He was lying in enemy territory bleeding badly. To the day I die, I'll never forget his cries. Before I knew what I was doing I raced over to him, grabbed him up in my arms and started back to my regiment. Unfortunately I got shot several times in my left leg. I had to crawl and drag him the rest of the way. Thank God I got him to safety. The Red Cross rushed us to the hospital tent. They thought I might lose my leg but, Thank God, the doctor was able to save it. I walk with a limp but Thank God we are both still alive. Now they are rewarding me with a medal. My army career is finished but I have been advised to consider politics, as my new career. My father in law has offered me a job with his printing press and my wife is pregnant.

Please write soon Kachelle and tell me all your news. I love you my darling. You are the love of my life, my soul mate, but I have responsibilities here. I know you will understand. I carry your photo with me everywhere. Please write soon. Take care.

I love you.

Your loving Diarmuid Charlie.XXX

Kachelle sat in silence for a moment. Then the tears rolled softly and gently down her cheeks, falling on to her letter and blotching the ink.

'He has responsibilities,' she laughed softly to the sleeping child. 'I'm the love of his life,' she said to no one in particular. After a silence she whispered to herself 'He's not sending for me. It looks like it's just you and me, Kid. Damn him! He knows I'll understand,' she gulped through her tears.

Kachelle lit a long cigarette, drew in deeply and inhaled with determination. The tears had stopped, but there was an ache in her heart. Loneliness enveloped her, surrounding her like a thick blanket, making her feel claustrophobic. For over an hour she sat in silence unaware of the screeching sea gulls. If anyone had offered her a penny for her thoughts she would have had to say:

'I haven't a thought in my head.'

Dark clouds and a roar of thunder stirred Kachelle. The child awoke frightened. She lifted him to her breast, fed him, changed him then settled him quickly again at her feet. Reluctantly, she started the engine, reversed the bus and started her rounds. She greeted her neighbours and fellow Islanders with a smile, joked and laughed with the children and sympathised with those who took their time to talk about their troubles. No one could have guessed that Kachelle's heart was broken. She was determined no one would know only Biddy Joe and her mother in law, that she was crying in her heart.

On her return home, she confided with her mother in law Diarmuid Charlie's news. His mother blessed herself several times and repeated, 'Holy Mary Mother of God,' when she heard of his wounding and thanked God profusely for sparing his life.

'I'm sorry love you'll not be seeing him but I also thank God that you are here with me that I have my grandchildren. It would be a lonely life without you all. God works in mysterious ways, we are not to question them. Put all this behind you, Alana. He has his life and you have yours. Things will work out. God's good.'

Kachelle nodded quietly.

'I'll write to him later and tell him you love him and pray daily for him. And I'll tell him he has a son- two Irish children he is responsible for now.'

An awkward silence fell over the small, dark, hot kitchen. The children's laughter from the fields was the only sound.

It was late October and the changing leaves of autumn from the few trees that managed to survive the harsh island life, covered the ground with a gold, red and burnished orange carpet which shimmered in the afternoon sun.

Kachelle stood in the doorway. Her work finished, she was taking time to finish her fortieth cigarette when she saw Father Connolly hurrying across the field towards her.

'Christ what does he want now?' she asked herself.

'Good evening Father, and what can I do for you?'

'You can do as I say for a start, Kachelle Harkin.'

'Kachelle McGinley, Father, don't you remember marrying me?'

'I'll call you Mrs Kachelle McGinley when you start acting like a married woman inside and outside the home.'

'Touche, first round to you Father. Now I'm a busy woman seeing to my in laws needs, doing all my chores, feeding and clothing my children and keeping a roof over all our heads and, oh yes, coping with an alcoholic husband. Now what do you want me to do? Perhaps you're in need of a housekeeper.' And she smiled at him solicitously.

'You stop this bloody business.'

'Please, Father, your language. There are children present and a lady. Yes, here's the good woman now. Mrs McGinley, Father Connolly has paid us a visit. I'll not ask him in, he's such a busy man leading everyone's lives for them.'

'You indecent hussy! You'll stop this bloody bus business now!' he roared.

'Why? I'm providing a living for my family and a service to my fellow Islanders. What's your problem?' And she tossed her cigarette butt out across the field.

'The women on this island are good living, God fearing Catholics. They see to every need of their husbands and families. You come along with your fancy ideas of providing goods and what does this do? I'll tell you! It gives them time on their hands and the devil makes time for idle hands.'

'Well you have no authority over me father. Perhaps it would be best if you encouraged the men to drink less and work more, so that their mothers, wives and sisters won't have to work so hard. But then, you would have the publicans giving out and after all, they provide for you well, don't they father? Now I'll bid you good day, I'm a busy woman.' And she turned on her heel and entered the house, halting to light a much needed cigarette.

'You shouldn't talk to Father Connolly like that, Kachelle. You'll have bad luck. One must always show respect to a priest and do his bidding.' urged her mother in law.

'When he shows me respect, I'll respect him. Now it's probably best if I get going. Good night mother, and God bless.'

Kachelle's life fell into a daily routine. Up early every morning, chores completed for Biddy, race over to her mother in law's, help get her two daughters dressed and fed, see to the livestock and load up the bus for the day's journey. Then set off in all weathers to sell her wares. Often she didn't return home until ten o'clock. Her son would be wrapped up warmly against the cold dark December nights but herself would be chilled to the bone.

Thankfully himself would be at the pub and her father in law would be settled down for the night. This was her favourite time of the day. Her mother in law would fuss over her and the child. She would draw the chair up close to the large turf fire after supper and she would fill Kachelle in on the day's activities.

Kachelle would laugh at her daughters' sayings and doings and would feel apprehensive about the girls not getting to know their brother.

'What will you do when he starts walking and talking Kachelle? He's bound to want to stay and play with the girls instead of sitting in an old bus. The girls will be starting school soon, how will we cope?'

'One day at a time mother,' urged Kachelle. 'I can only cope with one day at a time.'

'I will start a Novena to St Jude of Hopeless Cases for you, but mind you, they say if you get your request, there is a price to pay.' offered her mother in law.

'Well it's probably best to leave it then,' whispered Kachelle and her thoughts flew to Betty and the abortion. She had prayed to St.Jude then.

Kachelle felt her eyes beginning to close. The child was fast asleep in her arms. She longed to doze in front of the fire, with the quiet steady tick of the old clock relaxing her.

'Kachelle, Kachelle,' her mother in law whispered, as she gently shook her arm.

'It's time to go, love. It's getting late and you have a fair walk ahead of you.'

'You're right mother. Will you get me my shawl and I'll be on my way.'

'Good night and God bless, Love,' whispered her mother in law as she gently flicked the holy water from the small font at the front door over Kachelle and the child.

CHAPTER 13

Arranmore in summer was a small forgotten acre of heaven. A beautiful gentle place yet wild and exciting where the sky and the sea kissed with a tremor of shimmering blue, and the hot golden rays of the sun tickled the golden sand to a bleached white. Large patches of grassland would be covered with wild flowers and all shades of purple pink heather, visited constantly by the drone of the buzzing bees who fed constantly. Cool clear water ran freely through the ancient dark bog land and the soapy, creamy salty waves rushed forth to embrace its shores.

Winter was a different story. The scene changed completely. The sun and sea parted like angry love-torn lovers. The sky was dark and threatening. The sea battered, roared and crashed against the rocks like an angry innocent prisoner begging to be released from its torment. The small fishing boats were flung against the rocks with violence; many disintegrating into driftwood which would be deposited in lands far off.

The wind was so strong and freezing cold that it cut right through you, stealing the very breath from your body.

The elements became the Islands enemy. They shook it to its very roots. Flooded fields and ditches made travelling difficult. Island and elements were in fierce competition, survival of the fittest.

Yet at times there was an eerie stillness, as if the land and sea were exhausted battling and were claiming a well deserved rest.

Such was the night, Christmas Eve 1944. Kachelle was exhausted. She had left in many tinned luxuries and goods for Christmas in November on a day when there had been a break in the weather. Delivery to her customers had been difficult but she knew an inner joy knowing that in many households Christmas would be that little bit special. Kachelle made her way to her meeting place. The large black shawl protected her and the child from the cold.

The island was silent, an eerie stillness hung like a large black fog. A hard frost crunched under her feet. On arrival she rested herself against the rock. Memories came flooding back. The hot sun shining on her up turned face. Her back comfortable against the large grey stone, Diarmuid

Charlie's arms about her waist.

'Oh God,' she groaned.

She cuddled the child closer. He awakened and fixed his steel blue eyes on her.

'Look, love, your first island Christmas,' and she held the child up.

Together they stared in wonderment. 11.30pm and every house had a candle in the window. The slow warm glow beckoned welcome.

'See, love,' she whispered softly. 'That's to let the baby Jesus know that there is room for him. Look, there's a light in Granny McGinley's. Baby Jesus is welcome there, yet there is no place for you. I'll make it up to you, I promise. Merry Christmas,' and she gently kissed the small head, which had snuggled close to her breast for shelter and warmth.

Her thoughts flew to Diarmuid Charlie, wondering what he was doing. There had been no word from him, even to his mother.

'Damn you, why can I not stay angry with you?' she called to the night above. 'I love you and I hate you and oh how I wish you were here now.'

With a heavy heart she made her way to Biddy's. On entering she put on a brave face, talking about everything and anything, but Biddy saw through her act. Rising calmly she simply embraced her and held her tight.

'Kachelle, Kachelle, Kachelle,' she said wearily, 'Put it out of your mind. It's Christmas. Enjoy what you have and make plans later.'

Christmas morning broke and a welcoming thin sun tried to shine through. Kachelle awoke to a large roasting fire and a delicious smell of fried bacon and sausage. On entering the kitchen, Biddy had set the tiny wooden table with her best china. A small colourful Christmas decoration adorned the table.

The holly and the ivy married together, gave off a sweet smell of winter and the bright red berries glistened in the firelight.

'Oh it's beautiful, Biddy,' whispered Kachelle.

'Ah, its nothing at all! Here- I've another surprise for you,' and Biddy lifted the child out of the wooden box and placed him on the chair at the head of the table. Lifting a long knotted scarf, she tied it round the back of the chair. The child was secure and squealed with delight at being able to see over everything.

'There, now he is the man of the man of the house; sitting in your father's chair,' beamed Biddy

Kachelle was delighted and beamed at her son. A thin willowy yet sturdy child of eight months with tufts of soft red hair standing on his head, his cheeks rosy and his piercing blue eyes smiled back at her.

'My blue eyed boy, happy Christmas,' and she gave him a hug and a kiss.

'The head of the table for you always my love, thank you,' and she gently kissed Biddy's wrinkled worn cheeks.

'Come on now, girl, get your breakfast down you, you have two little girls needing you this morning too,' urged Biddy.

'Oh how I wish we could all be together Biddy.'

'That day will come love, one day at a time. Come on now, eat up,'and Biddy pushed her plate forward.

Only the child's happy gurgling, the crackle of the fire and the tick of the old clock filled the room. When the meal was finished Kachelle arose and lifted the large black shawl. It was not quite eight o'clock.

'Go on, love, he will be alright with me. You see to the girls. They need you too. Perhaps you'll get over for a visit after lunch. Wish your mother in law a happy Christmas for me and maybe when she gets himself sleeping she'll get over for a visit also.'

Kachelle stole a glance at her son. He had lifted her mug and was draining the dregs of her tay.

'Looks like he's going to be fond of tay,' she laughed.

'Aye, he'll have me tortured looking his tay leaves read too,' answered Biddy and the two women fell about laughing.

Kachelle took the short cut across the fields. A magnificent view from the small hill top greeted her, as it looked over the whole west side of Arranmore and Chaplestrand bay below. Her heart swelled with pride. She loved her island home. How she wished Betty could have seen it. Betty's words rang through her head,

'It sounds beautiful, Kachelle, just like a little piece of heaven. It would be a great place to rear children.'

Blessing herself she paused and whispered back, 'May you rest in peace, Betty. May your soul and all the souls of the faithful departed, particularly my mother and father, rest in peace.'

Tightening her shawl against the bitter wind Kachelle hurried to the McGinley household. Before she could press her thumb down on the door latch, she could hear her daughters' screams of delight. Philomena was jumping up and down with excitement and Sheila was tugging at her granny's apron. Muzzily her mother in law tried to raise herself.

'I must have dozed off in front of the fire,' she confessed to Kachelle. 'I'm up from dawn as himself awoke me falling in drunk. I got him to bed and was thankful those little ones slept through the racket. Happy Christmas darlings' and she hugged her grandchildren.

'A happy Christmas to you, my daughter,' and she hugged and embraced Kachelle.

'God's blessings be with you this day, mother, Happy Christmas,' and she returned the embrace.

'Did you not bring the wee man?' asked the old woman.

'No, he is with Biddy. Perhaps we will get a walk over later. Biddy wishes you a Happy Christmas,' and Kachelle squeezed her hand.

'Shss, shss now,' pleaded both women to the excited children.

'Breakfast first,' said Granny McGinley sternly but the children's eyes would not leave the stockings hanging over the fireplace.

'To hell with tradition,' laughed Kachelle. 'Let them have their stockings. We both know they'll not eat a bite until they see what is in them.'

The children were handed their Christmas stockings and rushed forward to the table to spill out the contents. Sheila was bemused.

'Santa Claus brought them,' instructed Philomena. 'Santa Claus comes down the chimney with his big bag and left us presents. Ach, but there's nothing for Diarmuid! He's left nothing for our baby brother,' and she began to cry.

Kachelle rushed to her side.

'Don't cry, darling. Diarmuid got his present. Santa left it at Biddy's.'

'Why is he not here with us?' quizzed Philomena.

'Because poor Biddy would be all on her own and lonely on Christmas Day. Diarmuid is with her and after dinner we will all go over to Biddy's and see what Santa has left there.'

'Good, good,' shouted Philomena clapping her hands.

'Sh, sh, sh,' urged her granny. 'Let sleeping dogs lie,' and she nodded her head in the direction of the bedrooms. 'We'll all get peace. Come on up to the table for breakfast.'

When breakfast was over the children settled down to play with the precious gifts of an orange, an apple, a bright shiny penny and beautiful knitted dolls, provided by Biddy. Kachelle went to the 9.30 Mass and her mother in law to the 11.00 service. The turf fire roared up the chimney and a pot of broth simmered and bubbled alongside. The old hen which had been well past its laying days had been prepared on Christmas Eve and now cooked slowly in the large black pot on the crook. Every now and then the old woman would lift off the large black lid ceremoniously; take a large ladle and lift the hot, fat grease and pour it over the old bird. Gradually potatoes, carrots, parsnips, Brussels sprouts and turnips would be added. Before long a delicious smell filled the small household. The two men, slept on in their drunken sleep unaware of the womens' hard work to provide a warm welcoming peaceful kitchen for Christmas 1944.

'He'll have no luck for missing Mass,' whispered the old woman, nodding her head in the direction of her son's bedroom. 'Sure his father used to do the same. Aye, now, the apple doesn't fall far from the tree after all.'

'Don't fret yourself. Look,' Kachelle opened the small kitchen drawer and lifted out a small bottle filled with a golden liquid which glimmered and shone in the firelight.

'Let's have a toast for Christmas,' she offered.

'I've never touched spirits in my life,' stated the shocked elderly woman.

'Well it is about time.'

Kachelle poured a measure into two mugs, added two teaspoons of sugar, a real luxury, two cloves and then poured in a good measure of hot water from the old kettle which whistled and sang all day long at the fireplace.

'Let's toast the war being over. To absent friends and family; God only knows what lies ahead of us for 1945,' suggested Kachelle and she handed her mother in law a large mug.

The two women drank in silence. The children played quietly and the old chicken whispered and spluttered to the vegetables, while the fire slowly died down to a hot burning ember.

Kachelle viewed the little kitchen. The holly and the ivy were creatively twisted around the top of the mantel piece, the Sacred Heart picture and along the small window which gave the only daylight. The floor had been brushed thoroughly and the old wooden table had been bleached and scrubbed pure white.

The children had been bathed early on Christmas Eva and their hair twisted in ringlets. Philomena's shone a bright fiery red and Sheila's were as black as soot. Their matching dresses complemented each other. Kachelle's heart swelled with pride. She had three beautiful children and please God soon all of them would play together, under one roof. Her thoughts were disturbed by the gentle humming from her mother in law. The whiskey was starting to take effect.

'I'll take you home again, Kathleen,' sang the old woman in a hushed yet strong voice. Kachelle didn't want to interrupt her. The children gazed in wonderment.

'That was my father's song you know. He used to sing it to me every night before I went to bed. You know, he was a lonely sad man after my mother died. He used to say thank God I have you. I remember once he left me for a long time to go fishing. I was only about four and I missed him terribly. When he returned I would kick up a fuss if he went to go out the door thinking he was going away again and then he would lift me on his knee, sing me his song and say, 'I'll never leave you again love, unless God calls me!' And he never did! Did I tell you I was married a short while when he died. I came home one day and he was sitting on that chair that you're sitting on now, a look of complete horror on his handsome face. Himself was sleeping in bed. There was no doctor here, so the priest, Father O Connor, saw to everything. He said it must have been a heart attack. Ah, I just couldn't take it in. Never getting a chance to say goodbye. It was shortly after that, that he,' and she pointed to the bedroom, 'started to hit me and drink more. Diarmuid Charlie was born a few weeks later. In no time at all the two girls were next and then Padraic Charlie. He never touched me again after that. I asked him once what was wrong and he said he couldn't be sure Diarmuid Charlie was his! The girls didn't matter, all that mattered was his son Padraic Charlie! He hurt me a lot saying that, you know.' She gave out a long sigh.

'It's funny, the pain of a beating will eventually go away, but you can never forget words. Forgive yes, but once spoken they remain in your heart and head forever. That pain always stays. But sure, our good Lord only asked us to forgive, he never mentioned forgetting. Ah child dear, if only we could turn back the hands of time..' Slowly her head lowered onto her chest and she quietly dozed. Kachelle eased the mug, its contents dry, from her worn thin fingers.

Kachelle set about setting the small kitchen table. The fire was built up and the two men slept soundly. Gently she awakened the old woman and the three generations of women sat down to enjoy their Christmas dinner. They clasped their hands and said grace.

'Do you think we should waken them for dinner?' asked Kachelle nodding in the men's direction.

'Na girl, let them lie. Many's a time my Christmas dinner was spoilt waiting for himself to join us only to start an argument and clear the table with his fists. Let them lie, it's not food they'll be looking.'

The dinner was enjoyed, the children gulping their food so that they could get to Biddy's sooner. After the dishes were washed and the fire banked down with small dark wet pieces of turf, the women and children wrapped up warm, and left for Biddy's

'Come on, come in, you're all welcome,' greeted Biddy. A roaring fire and Tilley oil lamp gave a welcoming glow and the child squealed with delight on seeing his mother and sisters.

'God but he's bonny,' stated his granny, lifting him up. 'My blue eyed boy,' she proudly stated sitting him on her knee.

'What did Santa bring him?' quizzed the girls.

'Oh Santa came here too,' replied Biddy and handed the girls a small stocking each, placing one also before the child. The children quickly fell about opening their stockings. Philomena's revealed a small brightly coloured top with a pointed metal end and a small stick, with a piece of string attached, Biddy demonstrated by winding the string around the top tightly and then flicking the top across the stone kitchen floor. The small top skipped and twirled while Biddy whipped it to keep it going. The girls squealed with delight.

Sheila's parcel produced a length of blue fishing rope attached to small wooden handles.

'Now, I'm not demonstrating this,' Biddy laughed, 'Your mother is younger and fitter than me.'

Kachelle took the rope and gave a few skips. Sheila eagerly grasped it from her mother's hands and set about jumping. Diarmuid Charlie's parcel produced a bright red ball.

The excitement in the small household was electrifying. Biddy produced three mugs and set about making three hot whiskeys.

'Oh dear God,' laughed Mrs McGinley. 'I'll be as drunk as himself if I keep this up'

'Well now, you see, that's were we women go wrong. Every time they go to the pub we should go with them. If they fall in drunk, we should fall in with them. After all, what's good for the goose is good for the gander,' mused Biddy. The three women fell about laughing. Stories were exchanged about Christmases past; loved ones were remembered and Kachelle was called on for a song. Silent Night was followed by a Christmas carol, Jingle Bells and finally I'll Take You Home Again, Kathleen. Granny McGinley wiped the tears from her eyes and thanked everyone for a beautiful Christmas.

A strong wind had whipped up and whistled around the little house. Large drops of rain started to fall.

'You needn't take the children home in that weather,' advised Biddy. 'Leave them here with me, sure their eyes are closing in their heads. They'll sleep until morning.'

Kachelle looked at her three children, they were worn out.

'OK, I'll just see mother home and then I'll return.'

'Good night, Biddy and may God bless you. Thank you for a wonderful Christmas!' and Granny McGinley embraced Biddy.

Kachelle and her mother in law linked arms and with bent heads against the icy cold wind they picked their steps across the damp scattered fields of Arranmore. Kachelle shouted to her mother in law to lean on her, but her voice was caught on the iodine scented wind being blown in from the Atlantic Ocean. Biddy watched them from her front door. A shiver ran down her back- not from the cold but from a bad feeling. She quickly blessed herself.

'Something is wrong,' she thought to herself. 'There'll be changes before morning. Oh God keep them safe.'

The two women entered the dark warm house. Men's voices could be heard from the back bedroom. Kachelle quickly filled the kettle and her mother in law settled herself in her chair, taking up her rosary beads.

Padraic Charlie entered the kitchen.

'He's wanting to go to the pub,' and he inclined his head towards his father's bedroom.

His mother answered in a clear voice,

'Well this is one Christmas he'll be disappointed, unless you carry him on your back!'

'Where are my daughters?' he asked Kachelle.

'They're at Biddy's. They were worn out. Besides it's pouring out. They would have got soaked through.'

'Their place is here, not at that old witch's house. You go and get them right now!' he demanded.

'Why?' asked Kachelle, 'So you can play the role of the drunken father? You should have been up this morning to wish them a happy Christmas and spend the day with them. It's a bit late now to show your loving, caring father side.'

'You bitch, you whoring bitch,' he roared and with one swipe cleared the little table of its Christmas decorations and crockery.

'Like father, like son,' whispered his mother softly, as large tears started to fall down her worn cheeks.

'Son! son!' called his father, 'To hell with the two of them. Come on, get me out of this fucking bed and we'll go for a jar.'

'Da, you can't. I couldn't carry you. I would never get you as far as the pub.'

'Fuck these fucking useless legs,' roared the old man as he beat upon them wildly.

'At least get me a bottle,' he pleaded.

'I don't have any whiskey Da, but I do have a bottle of poteen that Jimmy Joe gave me. You can have that,' and he left the room.

'That will do, son. Thank God for you. It's as well I'm not depending on those two bitches. Two whores that's what you are. Two fucking whores!' and he fired a large empty mug at the wall.

Kachelle's heart went out to her mother in law. She was on her hands and knees trying to gather up broken bits and pieces of crockery off the floor. The holly and the ivy, torn apart, lay scattered about. The old woman tried desperately to arrange the small pieces of Christmas decoration on the table. Kachelle gently held her for a while then eased her back on to her chair.

Taking command, she lifted the broken crockery and set it aside on the dresser. Then, sadly, she removed all the holly and the ivy and tossed it on to the fire.

'Oh, Kachelle, it's bad luck to take the decorations down early,' stated her astonished mother in law.

'Christmas is over for us, mother. It was beautiful while it lasted. Our bad luck is in the next room; it has nothing to do with decorations.'

Padraic Charlie entered the room with a large whiskey bottle of poteen.

'Please, son,' begged his mother, 'don't give your father that. That's worse than whiskey. That stuff of Jimmy Joe's could kill him.'

Her son hesitated for a second.

'Padraic Charlie, where are you, son?' roared his father.

'Here, Da, here,' called Padraic Charlie as he entered the small bedroom and handed his father the bottle.

'You're a good son, a man after my own heart! Now you listen to your Da. Never let a woman get you under her thumb. Show her who is boss. Always stay master of your home. If you don't, you won't have the life of a dog. Now do you hear me son?'

'I do, Da. I'll be off. See you in the morning,' and he closed the bedroom door after him.

Kachelle stood with her back to the door, her arms folded tightly about her. His mother sat in the chair, her rosary beads on her lap.

'Please, son,' she begged as she looked him directly in the eyes, 'I love you, son. You're my baby. Don't listen to your father. He has got it all wrong. We can't force people to love us. Love can grow out of caring, sharing and showing respect, not out of violence.

'Don't make me laugh,' he sneered. 'You never loved me. That bastard Diarmuid Charlie was always your favourite. My Da told me all about you. You're only a whore.'

'Padraic Charlie,' intervened Kachelle, but her mother in law bade her be silent.

'Diarmuid Charlie is no bastard, son; he's your brother. His father is in the next room. Your father has a sick, poisoned mind, and he has turned you the same. You're a grown man now. Think for yourself son. None of my children are bastards.'

'To hell with the lot of you,' answered Padraic Charlie as he lifted his coat and tore out of the small household,

For a long time the two women sat in silence. Kachelle's thoughts were of her own happy childhood and family. Granny McGinleys were of her father.

After a while Granny McGinley broke the silence by whispering to Kachelle, 'You'd better go, love. Biddy Joe will be wondering what is keeping you. The children will need you when they waken.'

'What about you?' asked Kachelle, gently reaching for the old woman's hand.

'I'll be fine. He'll eventually fall asleep. Besides he can't get out of bed so I have no fear of him now. You get along, love, and wrap up well.'

Kachelle reached for her large black shawl and wrapped it up and over head and shoulders. Granny McGinley kissed her on the forehead.

'God be with you, love, and safe journey.'

Reaching for the Holy Water she blessed herself and sprinkled some over Kachelle.

Settling down for the night, she prayed that himself would soon fall into a drunken sleep and she would get some peace and quiet. Alas, this was not to be. Within an hour she was awakened from her slumber. He roared through the small household.

'Come here, bitch, and get me more drink.'

Granny McGinley quietly opened the bedroom door and stepped timidly inside.

'Get me another bottle of poteen,' he demanded.

'There's no drink left. Settle down and try to get some sleep. Padraic Charlie will not be home until morning.'

'Get me another bottle,' he hissed and lifting the empty one he fired it at her.

The bottle bounced off the back wall, missing her by inches.

'Why do you hate me so? You used to tell me you loved me,'

'Love you? I never loved you! Hated you, yes, because you had everything that I wanted!!'

'I don't understand you, it's the drink making you talk this way. 'Well for your information your great Da was my Da too,'! He roared angrily.

'I don't understand. What are you talking about? The poteen is sending you raving.'

'Miss High an Mighty with the perfect family life and father! Don't make me laugh- he was no different from the rest of the men. He enjoyed his drink and women.'

'You evil, evil man! May God forgive you for talking ill of the dead.'

'You really didn't know? Oh what happiness that I have the pleasure of telling you: You talk often enough of the time your father left you to go fishing and and oh you were so lonely! Well, his fishing boat stopped off at my island for a week due to a bad storm and lo and behold he met my mother. Took her down, he did, and then left her! Left her to come back to your mother. Tell me, did you ever wonder why a younger man like myself was interested in you? He protected you like the Vestal virgin, and then started to worry because nobody would look at you!

'All my life I heard about the great man and his fine fishing boat and the land he owned on Arranmore. My poor mother had to go to England to have me and return pretending she was a widow. Everyone knew. They scorned her and me. All I was called was the Bastard McGinley.'

'May God forgive you for your lies: the drink has wrecked your brain. You're an evil man,' she answered angrily.

'Evil man- yes! And I am enjoying it. I came to this island just to get a look at him but when I saw this fine house and garden and his fishing boat which I knew should be mine I was determined to own all. Then there was you. He hadn't a clue who I was. God did that hurt! You would think a father would know his only son. I thought about confronting him but I wanted him to suffer so I courted you and you, you silly bitch fell for it and so did your Da.'

Granny McGinley was speechless. Her brain was trying to take all in.

'I told him you know! He had the cheek to tell me that I should be working and earning to provide for you. Ha Ha Ha! I told him I would never need to work, hadn't I the fine house and boat which was rightfully mine. I fired the whole story at him. All he could say was 'NO! Then you're my princess's half brother? NO No!' I pushed him down on the chair and said, 'It's been a pleasure knowing you, father. Tell anyone and I'll kill her and you. After all I only wanted the house, land and boat.' He was found dead on the chair later.'

Granny McGinley recalled the shocked look on her beloved father's face, the way her husband started to beat her even though she was pregnant and the way he only touched her when he was drunk.

Years of dormant temper rose in her.

'Get me another bottle now,' her husband demanded and reaching to the bedside table he flung the large statue of Our Lady at her but it fell to the bottom of the bed.

Slowly turns the worm - in this case the worm somersaulted. Lifting the statue she unexpectedly brought it down on her husband's head again and again. There was no way he was going to tell his filthy lies to Kachelle or her children. He had a sickened poisoned mind and he must be stopped.

He flung himself at her, catching her by the elbow. The old woman had no idea where her strength came from but with all her might she flung him from her, causing him to fall backwards out of the bed. His head hit the stone floor and without any effort his useless legs followed.

Silence penetrated the house. Granny McGinley stood breathing heavily. Eventually she walked to the side of the bed and stared down. He lay gazing up, his eyes a deathly stare. Dark blood flowed slowly from the back of his head. The dark scarlet and bubbling blood escaped as his last breath followed it.

'Leave the bastard where he is,' her brain screamed, but years of Catholic belief could not bring her to do so.

Moving slowly around the bed, she timidly said an Act of Contrition into his ear and then stiffly standing she placed her fingers into the Holy Water font and sprinkled him with the Holy Water. Then she quietly left the room and settled her self on the old bed settee.

Her brain was in turmoil. What was she going to do? Run to get help? She didn't want to get him help. May God forgive her! No, he could lie there. She would pretend that she was sleeping. If anybody asked, she would say that he must have fallen out of bed looking for more drink.

Her mind boiled with fear and doubt and disbelief. Oh, he was an evil man, to tell lies like that on the dead. Confusion continued to eat her thoughts. Was it true? Her father HAD left the island. There had been a look of horror on his dead face. The beatings and verbal abuse began after her father's death, but surely she couldn't have married her half brother? Oh God help me please, her heart and brain screamed.

'Oh Sacred Heart of Jesus, I place all my trust in you,' she prayed and then with a sigh the words 'What will be, will be,' gently echoed throughout the small house and Granny McGinley fell into a deep sleep, sleep that had been denied her for almost thirty years.

At five thirty the next morning Padraic Charlie stumbled into the humble house. The house was in darkness, the fire spluttering, calling to be fed. Unconcerned about his father and mother he found his bed and collapsed fully clothed on to it. By seven thirty he was being urgently called by Kachelle.

'The priest! Quick, run and get the priest. Your father has fallen out of bed! Hurry Padraic Charlie he's hurt bad.'

Padraic Charlie quickly jumped from the bed and hastily blessed himself as he stumbled out the door, Kachelle took a deep breath and surveyed the scene. Granny McGinley was fast asleep on the couch. The long day yesterday and the whiskey has worn her out thought Kachelle.

Hurrying into the bedroom she stared at her father in law lying on the floor. He was obviously dead. His eyes wide open, glazed, stared angrily at her.

'He must have been reaching for his drink,' she whispered to herself but then her eyes caught the large statue lying at the bottom of the bed. Oh God! her mind screamed.

There must have been a row, but that means…….. she muttered to herself. Running to Granny McGinley she urgently shook her. To her amazement she wasn't sleeping.

'Granny McGinley, Granny what has happened? You must tell me before they get back.'

No sound came forth. Granny's mouth was slightly twisted to one side.

She became very agitated, her eyes begging and pleading with Kachelle to understand. Kachelle stared at the bedroom and then Granny McGinley. Something had happened- but what?

Granny had begun whimpering like a puppy trying her best to communicate with Kachelle.

'There there, love, it's alright. I'll see to everything,' she assured her. Granny McGinley's eyes softened and filled with tears.

'Sssh, sssh, now, you lie there. I'll fix things. He's hurt you for the last time,' and she hurried back to the bedroom.

Lifting the large statue she wiped it clean with her skirt and placed it in its original position. Running to the kitchen she grabbed the broom and hurried back to the bedroom and swept the broken glass under the bed. She would remove it later.

Looking at the old man she hissed at him, 'You bastard! What did you do to her? Hell will not be full until you're in it!'

Kachelle had just replaced the broom when the door burst open and Padraic Charlie and the priest entered.

'He must have fallen out of bed, Father, I found him when I returned this morning,' explained Kachelle.

Father Connolly hurried to the bedroom and knelt at the old man's side. Within a few seconds he was pronouncing the old man dead and promptly set about blessing him. Padraic Charlie sat in the first available chair, his head in his hands. Kachelle helped Granny McGinley into a chair, talking quietly to her explaining.

'He's fallen out of bed, Granny, must have been reaching for the poteen.' Granny McGinley squeezed her hand in gratitude. Kachelle sat about busying herself with the fire.

'Padraic Charlie,' roared the priest. 'Come here and help me lift your father on to the bed.' Padraic Charlie froze.

'Go on,' urged Kachelle, 'you can't leave him lying on the floor,' and she gently pushed him towards the bedroom

'Kachelle, get in here and give us a hand,' roared the priest again.

As the three of them struggled to lift the dead man off the floor the priest fired questions at them, answering them himself. 'Where were you when this happened, Padraic Charlie? At the pub, no doubt! And as for you, I suppose you were sleeping at old Biddy Joe's. This is your home, girl! If the two of you had been here, this man would not be dead. Who gave him the bloody poteen any way?' he demanded.

Padraic Charlie paled instantly and turned his head to avoid the priest's stare, frightened of him.

'I gave it to him, if you must know,' answered Kachelle assertively. 'He was threatening to crawl out of bed and go to the pub! You have known for years that he had a drink problem so don't bother concerning yourself now, Father. There's an old woman in there, you should concern yourself with the living.'

'You mind that tongue of yours, girl. One day it will get you into serious trouble,' and with that he left the room.

Padraic Charlie was the first to speak. In a timid voice he simply said, 'Thanks Kachelle.' and he nodded his head.

Kachelle's heart softened to him.

'Everything will be alright Padraic Charlie. You're the man of the house now. You have responsibilities. If you don't live up to them now you'll end up like him, craving drink and dying alone.'

Three days later, Charlie Hughie McGinley was led to rest. There was a low turn out to the funeral. Padraic Charlie said it was due to the bad weather.

Biddy Joe simply stated, 'He was a blow in, not one of us, and sure nobody liked him.'

After the burial service, Padraic Charlie and the island men retreated to the pub and the women returned to the house. Kachelle hurried to the old man's bedroom, and opened as wide as possible the small bedroom window and the front door to release his spirit. Then the women sat about the fire, huddled out of the draught awaiting eagerly a strong cup of tea. After a few minutes, Biddy Joe shouted to Kachelle, 'You can close them now. His spirit is well gone. See now to your mother in law,' and she patted the old woman's head.

Granny McGinley had not attended the funeral service. She didn't particularly want to hear about it, but had no choice only to listen to the women sing his praises. The fine handsome man that he had been, sure half the women on the island fancied him when he had first come to live among them.

'Now let's not get carried away girls,' stated Biddy Joe. 'He was a drunk, and a vicious beast like most of the men, but then sure that's the only beautiful thing about death. It can turn a rogue into a saint.'

Granny McGinley reached over and squeezed Biddy Joe's hand. The gesture did not go unnoticed.

After the women had left and the dishes washed and the fire backed up Granny McGinley dozed in her chair.

'What now, Alana?' asked Biddy Joe, 'How are you going to manage? The old woman will be a handful for a while and you have a business to run and three children to rear. You and himself need to talk.'

'I don't know how I am going to manage, Biddy Joe. Padraic Charlie might stop drinking and he might drink more. One of us has to be strong. I don't know if he's man enough to forgive everything and start anew.'

'What about you, can you start anew, in every way, even sharing his bed?'

'I believe I could, Biddy Joe. I love him. I always have loved or strongly liked him- call it what ever you want, but I am not 'in love' with him. If he was prepared to stop drinking and get back to work and accept my son, I would be willing to have another go at it.'

'I tell you what. Make a pot of tea and I'll see what the tea leaves say for you. It's been a while from you had a wee reading.'

Half an hour later and Kachelle was draining the last dregs of tea from her cup. Biddy Joe studied her cup for a while and then spoke;

'There's sill a bit of rough road ahead, Kachelle. He'll not settle down for a while but when he does there will be conditions. You'll have to accept them in order to move on with your life. You have your son but not under the same roof for a while. I only see you, him and the girls. Granny is leaving here never to return.'

'Oh God, she's not dying too,' cried Kachelle.

'Not for a while, but something has happened. She will tell you in her own good time. She loves you and young Diarmuid Charlie and his father. Fate has played her a cruel blow, but she will put everything right. You must listen to her and carry out her wishes. I see more children for you- at least three but only one will survive. A dark haired son. When Padraic Charlie gets his son he'll settle down. Then you'll get life a little easier.'

Kachelle sighed, 'Makes you wonder why we are born.'

'Don't worry, Alana, God makes the back to carry the burden. We all have our crosses to bear in life. Now let's get things organised. How are you going to manage? The child is fine with me. Why don't I take Granny to live with me? The light stroke, if that is what it is may pass, and again it may not.'

'Has she had a stroke Biddy Joe?' asked Kachelle.

'I don't think so. She has certainly had a shock and it's as if she has curled herself up tightly into a ball for protection. I believe she will be well again. Time is a great healer. Did you notice anything different when you returned that morning?' quizzed Biddy Joe.

Kachelle confided in her friend about the statue with blood stains and the broken bottle.

'He must have attacked her and she defended herself,' offered Biddy Joe.

'Do you think he hit her? He was a filthy dirty old man. I couldn't stand near him but he would be touching me, trying to grab my breasts, always leering with those angry evil eyes,' and Kachelle shuddered, pulling her shawl tightly round her.

'Sure the drink puts them mad. He probably got her to hand him the bottle and then lunged at her,' offered Biddy Joe.

'But she is an old woman, Biddy Joe. Surely he wouldn't have wanted to........?'

Kachelle allowed the last sentence to hang in mid air.

'A standing cock has no conscience,' answered Biddy Joe gently. 'Something sure has happened and at her time in life and she didn't need it.'

Both women gazed at the sleeping granny and silence fell between them. A short while later, much to their surprise, a drunken Padraic Charlie, returned home. Instead of finding his bed, he pulled a chair towards the fire and sat rubbing his hands.

Before long the tears were running down his face.

'Make a strong sweet cup of tea,' advised Biddy Joe to Kachelle.

'Let it all out, son. Your Da's gone and you'll miss him. You'll have to be strong now and carry on.'

Padraic Charlie accepted Biddy Joe's sympathy by nodding his head.

'Your poor mother is unwell, son. She needs looking after. I'll take her home with me until she gets better. You and Kachelle will have the house to yourselves. You two are the next generation. The better you two do the better for yourselves and your children.'

'My house, my land now,' pronounced Padraic Charlie. 'That bastard in America will never get his hands on it and neither will his bastard son. You keep him with you too, Biddy Joe,' sneered Padraic Charlie.

Kachelle's heart froze. She was about to retaliate only Biddy Joe urged her not to.

'Put the past behind you, son. It's no good looking back. Treat her well and you will have a son of your own. There would be something to work for then, wouldn't there? You do have two beautiful daughters- perhaps even grandsons some day,' invited Biddy Joe.

'I'll be going, Kachelle, I'll make arrangements with Tony Joe, to collect herself tomorrow and the few things she'll need on his tractor. Try and get a good night's sleep both of you,' and Biddy Joe quietly let herself out.

Kachelle made Granny McGinley comfortable. She thought of Biddy Joe's reading. Surely this could not be the last night for her in the home she grew up in? She glanced at Padraic Charlie. He was falling asleep in the chair. Let sleeping dogs lie, Biddy Joe would say, she thought to herself.

'My land, my house,' he would mutter to himself. Kachelle fell into bed, worried sick about his words to Biddy Joe. 'You keep him with you too.'

Oh, please God, she prayed, let his heart soften and allow me to bring my son here.

A few minutes later and herself and Padraic Charlie had fallen asleep. Only the old woman stirred.

She had heard every word of Biddy Joe's invitation to live with her. She prayed to God also, for the child to stay with her and Biddy Joe.

She loved him and didn't want to be parted from him. Easing herself quietly out of the chair Granny McGinley made her way to the old man's bedroom. With great difficulty she pushed the mattress a little to one side and placed her hand under it. Feeling around for quite a while she found what she was looking for, a large knob which she twisted to the side. A small drawer shot out of the wooden base, and there it was. His money. Money denied to her over the years. She collected it all, not knowing how much there was. Looking about the room, she hesitated where to hide it. Suddenly remembering that she was to leave this house tomorrow never to return she sat about hiding the money in her bosom and across her belly which was protected by thick fleecy knickers with tight elastic at the knees.

Returning quietly to her seat she wondered if she should give the money to her son. Glancing at him she thought NO! He'll only drink it. Perhaps Kachelle could use it. Kachelle was young and strong and had a business. The person who would need it was her grandson Diarmuid, Diarmuid McGinley. She would leave it all for Diarmuid. When he was old enough she would give it to him, God spare him.

Two o'clock the next day and Granny McGinley took her farewell of her home and sat quietly on the back of the tractor. Kachelle reached into the water font, blessed herself and the old woman, saying, 'God be with you.'

Padraic Charlie did not come out of the bedroom to see his mother leave. Kachelle quickly prepared him a meal. It was strange, only the two of them alone in the house.

'I'll have to be going soon to get the children from Biddy Joe's. It was best they didn't see your father laid out.'

'You're not to bring him back here,' he quietly stated. 'Your place is here now. You can see him at Biddy Joe's every day. Besides you can't look after him and run your business.'

'You could take over the business. I'll do the books and see to the house and livestock.'

'I'm a fisherman,' he roared, 'not a bloody greengrocer. 'If you insist on having him here he can sleep in the barn,' and he abruptly left the table.

Biddy Joe helped wrap the girls against the bitter December weather. The child was asleep in Granny's arms.

'Leave him for a while, Kachelle. Right now she needs him more than you do,' offered Biddy Joe.

'But he is my son,' wept Kachelle.

'Aye, and we suffer in the coming and going. Things will change, Alana, one day at a time.'

CHAPTER 14

For the next three years Kachelle continued to be the breadwinner of the family and young Diarmuid was growing into a fine boy with curly red hair. Granny McGinley had called him D.D. when her speech began to improve and now the girls simply called him D.D.McGinley.

Kachelle, on Biddy Joe's advice, urged the girls to call him Diarmuid Padraic but the name never caught on. D.D. he was constantly called and in the end everyone accepted it. Perhaps never hearing the name Diarmuid had helped. Padraic Charlie took periods of not drinking and at times Kachelle and he were a little closer. Kachelle had miscarried her forth child and the fifth. The wee pet had been badly deformed. Padraic Charlie had been drinking heavily ever since. The two girls were growing up fast and D.D. was starting to ask questions. It broke Kachelle's heart to hear him ask,

'Why can't I stay with you, ma, and the girls?'

She tried to explain that Granny and Biddy Joe needed him. They would be very lonely without him, but he would get angry, stamp his foot and say, 'Let one of the girls stay.'

Kachelle realised the old women were spoiling him rotten but what could she do? Granny McGinley's health had improved and herself and Biddy Joe were contented.

Child number six was produced the following year. A dark haired daughter, the image of her father. Padraic Charlie was delighted but also disappointed that he did not have a son. As the months went on it was quickly realised that there was something wrong with the child. The old folk would have said 'a child of the fairies,' others more cruel 'not the full shilling.'

Her two sisters doted on her and did everything for her. D.D. was passionately jealous and would fly into a rage if Kachelle even held her. Again Padraic Charlie took to the drinking severely, until the following year when he stumbled home from the pub after a heavy night drinking of whiskey. Kachelle had the two girls ready for school, deliberately dressing them in worn summer clothes against the bitter winter weather.

The publican's children called for them for school. Padraic Charlie roared through his drunkenness at the fine coats, hats and shoes on the other children and then at his own girls shivering, in their rags.

'Get them children dressed,' he demanded.

'I can't,' Kachelle simply said, 'Business has been slow for a while and I can't afford to buy clothes.'

'Look at them ones with their fine hats and scarves,' he pointed out. 'Yes, and who put them there? You did. Sure every penny you get you spend it in their Da's pub. That's why they're dressed well!'

Padraic Charlie spoke not a word but made his way to the bedroom. Kachelle lifted the coats from behind the door, put them on the children and hurried them off to school before starting her day's calls.

Padraic Charlie lay in bed, his mind in turmoil. He loved his girls and he loved Kachelle. Why oh why could she not love him in the same way? As for his Da, he had always promised him that there was money for him but the old bastard had not said where he had hidden it.

'Enough to buy you a fine fishing boat,' he had promised, but he had stripped and decorated the house looking for it, unnoticed by Kachelle.

He had even taken to digging the garden. Kachelle had been delighted that he had taken an interest in the house while all along he was desperately seeking his fortune. As always, when disappointed he needed a drink.

Kachelle's statement had hurt and shamed him. He knew she was trying to give him a son and when he had her in his arms and was allowed to touch her he was ever so grateful. Perhaps he should try and drive the bloody van and pull his weight more. It wasn't fair to his daughters

When Kachelle returned home that evening she was surprised to find the fire roaring up the chimney and the potatoes boiled. The girls and she were frozen so they welcomed the sight.

'Thanks, Padraic Charlie, it is much appreciated,' offered Kachelle and lowered the youngest child, Elizabeth, on to the floor. When the meal was over Padraic Charlie, embarrassed said he would try to do better.

'I have an idea,' offered Kachelle. 'You want to fish. I'll go and see the bank manager in Dungloe and see if I can get a loan for a fishing boat. That way you can return to work and it will take your mind off the drink.'

'Did you find any money in this house?' he demanded.

'No I did not,' answered Kachelle quietly. 'I know you believe your father left you money but surely you would have found it by now. If there had been any money your mother would have told you where it was: Do you want me to try the bank or not?'

The thought of owning a fishing boat delighted Padraic Charlie, so he urged 'yes.'

The following month when there was a suitable break in the bad weather Kachelle made her way to the bank in Dungloe. She had a quite substantial amount to deposit. Almost a thousand American dollars.

Diarmuid Charlie had been sending regular payments for D.D. and Philomena and she had been hiding them away. Now was a good chance to deposit them safely until D.D. was old enough to use them. She had to hide this money from Padraic Charlie.

The bank manager admired the attractive red haired island woman, and listened intently to her business plan. He knew immediately that she had a good head for business and carefully studied her plans for paying off the bank loan. He didn't ask any questions concerning her deposit of $1,000 and believed her when she said there would be regular payments. The loan and the savings were secured and they both shook hands.

After purchasing a few items in Dungloe, she walked to Burtonport to catch the boat returning to the island.

The dark sea tossed and turned the small boat, splashing the icy cold waves over its occupants. Everybody on board silently prayed for a safe journey, mindful of the stories they had heard about the Arranmore disaster in the late 1920's. A few of the younger passengers quizzed the older ones on board asking, is it true it was a calm night? Did the Devil really travel with them? Was it not true that one of the passengers had a cloven foot? Was it because there was a red haired woman on board? And they glanced frightened looks at Kachelle.

'The priest said it was God's way of punishing them because they planned to dance at the cross roads next day which was a Sunday; dancing on the slabs of hell,' is what he said.' reported a timid blonde girl of about fourteen. The conversation went back and forth, Kachelle took no notice; her mind was occupied with thoughts of her own.

Kachelle was thankful to return home to find the fire burning brightly up the chimney and the three girls enjoying hot tea and toast.

'Did you get the loan?' asked Padraic Charlie eagerly.

'I did. You can get the boat you have always wanted. But mind now, if you don't pull your weight and make it pay, you lose it.'

'I won't, I won't. I promise to work hard. You know the fishing is in my blood. Thank you, Kachelle,' and he quickly gave her a hug. The girls, unaccustomed to shows of affection, giggled loud and the baby banged her spoon on the table.

'I'm delighted things seem to be working out,' offered Biddy Joe. 'Perhaps returning to fishing will help him.'

'And I'm going to cut down on my travels.' Biddy Joe stared at Kachelle, not understanding.

'I'm going to get an extension to the house, like a small shop and store. People can come to me Monday to Thursday and on Fridays and Saturdays I'll travel to the far end of the island. I'll be home more, able to look after the girls and most of all Diarmuid can come and stay when himself is away fishing.'

'Will that be fair on the child?' questioned Biddy Joe.

'Yes it will, Biddy Joe,' declared Kachelle. 'He'll have the best of both worlds, my home and you and Granny McGinley.

'What about when himself is at home during the bad weather?'

'Ah, Biddy Joe, one day at a time. Right now I can't wait to spend all day, every day with him. God will work something out.'

'Aye, Alana, no doubt he will. What's allotted can't be blotted. It's good to see you happy,' and Biddy Joe gently kissed Kachelle's cheeks.

By Easter morning, 'The Queen Of The Ocean,' bobbed gently up and down at the quiet blue sea pier at Leabgarrow. Father Connelly was in full charge of the Blessing of the Boats service and owners and family members waited patiently to leave religious objects and, most important of all, a small container of Holy Water, aboard for protection.

Granny McGinley and Biddy Joe linked Kachelle's arms and the children quickly scrambled on board. Young D.D. was in his element. Almost five years of age, of light build with a head of unruly red curls like his mother, piercing blue eyes and a cheeky grin, he was in full command of 'da's boat.'

'Da's boat. Me and da go out fishing,' he would shout excitedly.

'Us too,' would chirp the girls.

'No,' he cried fiercely, 'girls don't fish. Me and da's boat.'

Kachelle's eye caught Padraic Charlie strolling across the strand towards the boats and quickly pulled the children to her side. The men prepared to venture out to sea for the first fishing season. The women called out individual saints names to protect them and all the children fell silent as the boats slipped away.

Childhood memories came flooding back to Kachelle of Padraic Charlie, herself and Diarmuid Charlie playing along the pier and waving until they could no longer see the boats. The boys would start to argue who would have the biggest fishing boat in all the island. Padraic Charlie always won the argument.

'Well, he has got his fishing boat now, here's hoping he will make a success of it,' prayed Kachelle.

That evening, Kachelle sat in the doorway and enjoyed her four children romping and playing. Padraic Charlie would be away for two or three nights so her son could sleep under her roof. Supper time was hilarious with all the children excited and exhausted but all too soon they had settled down for the night. The two girls now slept in the old man's bed and the baby was in her cot beside the large statue.

Young Diarmuid Charlie was curled up on Kachelle's bed, fast asleep. Kachelle slipped her arms about him and his head settled on her left breast. She stroked his cheek and played with his curls.

'Oh how I love you, my son. Hopefully soon you can stay here all the time,' she whispered into his ear before falling asleep herself.

On 17th April 1950, a vibrant spring sun shone down on Arranmore Island. The McGinley household was in a state of excitement. A birthday party was planned for two o clock with many of the island children attending. D.D.McGinley was celebrating his sixth birthday. Padraic Charlie was away fishing and Kachelle had spent the past two days baking and scrubbing the entire house for the grand event.

Birthday parties were unusual among this tiny community so talk of cakes, lemonade, sweets etc....had caused much stir, not only among the island children but also the adults who were invited to attend.

Kachelle had arranged for old Brendan Paul to play his fiddle and she had a good supply of whiskey at hand. She stood back and viewed her home with pride. A large turf fire burned brightly, its flames climbing the chimney fiercely. The table was set with all kinds of goodies, which many of the island children and adults had never seen.

The extension to the house which now served as 'the shop' was well stocked and the island women enjoyed travelling to Chaplestrand to buy because now they got a chance to meet each other, share news and exchange old cures for various health problems. Kachelle always kept a pot of tea ready, as she knew this was the only outing that many of the women had. Of course Father Connolly had given out to her for providing such a service claiming that half a morning or afternoon was wasted and the women would be better off in their homes. As usual, Kachelle had turned a deaf ear and continued with her business. The loan on the bank was paid regularly and Padraic Charlie's time was taken up with fishing.

'Life is good now, thank you, God,' she whispered to the Sacred Heart picture and quickly set about welcoming the children.

D.D.McGinley was tall and thin for his age. 'He'll be a fine man when he fills out,' was a constant statement of Granny McGinleys. D.D. was an astute, intelligent boy, but he was worried. He couldn't understand why he only got to stay with Ma and his sisters when Da went fishing. Lately he had got to thinking that his Da didn't love him. All the other boys got to help their Das with the boat and fishing nets and talked constantly about going to be fishing men when they grew up. His Granny McGinley talked constantly about his Uncle Diarmuid Charlie in America. How handsome and kind he was, the fine man he was, the great soldier he had been. His Da's name was never mentioned. Biddy Joe usually avoided his questions by telling him children should be seen and not heard.

He loved his Granny and Biddy Joe and on winter nights when he would settle back in the small chair close to the fire he enjoyed listening to the two old women telling stories about island life when they were young. Many called to visit, men and women. He would listen closely to Biddy reading their cups. Often the old women referred to him 'clocking in the corner,' or 'like an old clocking hen,' but they would soon receive the sharp edge of Biddy Joe's and Granny's tongues.

'D.D!' his mother called. 'Come on, son, your party is about to begin,'

'Is Da home yet?' he asked. 'No, son, he's away fishing. Now come on, there are lots of surprises for you. There is a large box from America. Come and see what Diarmuid Charlie has sent you.'

The young boy tossed his head of red curls and shrugged his thin shoulders,

'It would be nice to have Da here,' and he slowly made his way towards the house. Squeals of delighted children echoed throughout Chaplestrand. Old Brendan Paul's fiddle set adults and children's feet tapping and Kachelle was kept busy serving everyone.

Within an hour D.D was blowing the candles out on his cake and everyone was singing Happy Birthday.' Small birthday presents were given to D.D. and a silence fell over the table when the box from America was produced. D.D, with help from his sisters, tore open the wrapping and he reached down inside. A magnificent red sailing boat was brought out, its creamy white sails stood tall and proud.

'Ohh,' whispered the island children.

'Beautiful,' said the adults.

The boat was two feet long, bright red in colour with a sand coloured deck and brown fittings. Its sails were a thick creamy coloured canvas with a small American flag displayed on the highest mast.

'Have a wonderful birthday, from Diarmuid Charlie' was penned on a small card inside the box.

'Let's go and sail it now,' roared the children.

'We'll go to the rock pool' encouraged one.

'Be careful John Joe McCafferty doesn't get you,' laughed one of the old women. Then she quietly blessed herself saying 'May God rest him.'

Kachelle paled at the mention of John Joe's name and quickly hurried the children out.

'Ah, give us a go,' pleaded the young boys while the girls paddled in the rock pool seeking out small crabs and shells.

'No, it's my boat,' said a determined D.D. 'There is only one boat on the island like this and I have it,' he said proudly.

'Well if you're not going to let us play with it too, we're going home. You can keep your boat. Besides, we get to play on a real boat when our Da's come home. You're not allowed on your Da's boat, so there!'

With that the young boys walked away from the rock pool leaving D.D with his sisters.

'Come on, D.D, it's getting late. Never mind them they're just jealous.'

D.D lifted the boat out of the water. All joy in his heart was gone. His shoulders drooped and his pale freckled face was a picture of complete sadness.

'Wait till Da sees it, D.D. It's the finest sailboat ever. Da has the best fishing boat and you have the best sailing boat. Never mind those boys. Hurry on now, it's time we were home,' comforted Philomena.

The children entered the warm, bright household. Only old Brendan Paul, Granny McGinley, Biddy Joe and their mother were present. The table had been cleared and the three elders were deep in conversation, reminiscing. D.D settled down to dry his boat.

'Philomena, put your sisters to bed for me,' urged his mother. 'D.D it's time to go now with Granny. I've packed up some goodies for you and you can take your boat.'

'Why,' asked D.D his voice crisp, sharp and clear. 'Da is coming home isn't he? I want to stay here and show him my boat.'

'No, darling, you can show him tomorrow. You must go with Granny and Biddy Joe now.'

'Come on, son,' urged Granny McGinley, 'Give me your arm and help your old Granny home. Brendan Paul, you come too and we'll finish the party at Biddy Joe's.'

An angry six year old picked up his boat reluctantly and headed for the door. His mother caught him clasping him to her breast.

'I love you darling. We'll be together soon. Mummy will make this all up to you, I promise.' D.D did not understand his mother's words and with a heavy heart he left.

Next day, D.D hurried over to Chaplestand. His mother was busy packing up the van to collect her goods from the port. His sisters were already settled in the front seat.

'No, don't go in, son. Your Da's sleeping. He's tired after his fishing!'

'I'll go down to the boat then,' he answered cheerfully, 'the other boys will be there.'

'   'No, you know you are not allowed on the boat. Now either come with me or go back to Granny and later you can sail your boat.'

'I don't want to sail the bloody boat,' shouted the angry young boy. The girls gasped at the use of the bad language. Kachelle lifted her right hand and brought it across his backside.

'Never you use that bad language again, young man. Now get home to Granny.'

A startled D.D fought back tears. He had never been hit before. His Mammy had shouted and hit him!

'I hate you! I hate you!' he screamed while backing off.

'Come here, son,' urged Kachelle, but he was quickly hurrying across the fields.

Kachelle drove the van. Her mind was in turmoil, her heart breaking in two. Her beloved son said he hated her. She had hit him. Oh God, what was she going to do?

'Mammy, wouldn't it be better if D.D lived with us? I'm sure Granny and Biddy wouldn't mind. I'll stay with them if you like,' urged Philomena.

Kachelle patted Philomena's hair into place. 'It's alright love, something will be sorted out,' and with a heavy heart she continued her day's work.

D.D busied himself with the boat. All the other boys would be down the strand at their Da's boats. He felt very alone and angry. Young John Paul McCauley approached.

'I'll let you see my comics if you let me play with your boat,' he offered. 'My comics come all the way from America,' and he showed them to D.D. Although unable to read D.D found the pictures fascinating.

'That's Superman,' explained a delighted John Paul. 'Here, you can look at them and I will play with the boat.'

'No, it's my boat! You're not touching it!'

'Suit yourself!' and John Paul started to walk away.

'My mummy will get me comics, just you see' D.D shouted after him. That evening when Kachelle called at Biddy Joe's she found a reluctant D.D when she opened her arms for a hug.

'He's been in a foul mood all day,' stated Biddy Joe. 'Leave him. He'll come out of it as quick as he went into it.'

'Don't you worry about a boat, son,' coaxed Granny McGinley, 'When you're big enough I'll buy you the biggest and finest boat ever to be seen on this island. Even better than Padraic Charlie's.'

Kachelle finally got her son to take a walk with her.

'I'm sorry about this morning D.D. But you're really not allowed to say bad words. Suppose Father Connolly heard you? He wouldn't let you make your Communion next year and just you wait till you see the fine suit I'll get you. We'll go to Dublin, just you and me, and get the finest suit and shoes. I promise.'

'Will the girls go too?' asked D.D. quietly.

'No, just you and me on the big train. We'll stay in a fine hotel and gets loads of nice things. Mummy loves you so much, I would do anything for you.'

'I want comics from America, Superman ones,' demanded D.D.

'OK. I'll write to Diarmuid Charlie and he'll send them to you.'

'No, I want them now.' John Paul has comics from America I want his!'

Kachelle fell silent trying to take all in.

'You promised. You can get me John Paul's, can't you Mammy?' And he slid his thin arms around her neck and hugged her.

'Yes of course I can. Now let's get you in for tea.'

Within an hour Kachelle had returned with the comics. The offer of a large £5 note was too much for John Paul's mother to resist and the promise of one every month in exchange for the unopened comics was even harder to resist.

D.D. lay in bed, his comics beside him. His boat was proudly displayed on the window sill.

'Serves John Paul right,' he said. 'I'll show them, I'll show them all.'

And so that summer D.D. isolated himself more and more from his young friends. When they wouldn't allow him to play football, he would appear a few days later with a brand new leather ball, which left all the other boys envious. When the season turned to hurling, he had the finest hurling stick. When no one had a tennis racket, he had two and so the young boy had power over who he would let play his games.

'You're ruining him,' stated Biddy Joe. ' He needs a firmer hand.'

'Leave the boy alone,' urged Granny McGinley.

Kachelle listened to the two women arguing over her son. She had to admit to herself that he was rather spoilt. More so than the girls but then they had a home and family. It wasn't his fault he was left with two old women.

'Maybe I should just move him in regardless of what Padraic Charlie says,'

'No, please don't,' urged Granny McGinley. 'Please, Kachelle, I'm an old woman and he's all I have left. I love him just like you do. God only knows how long I have left. Don't take him away please,' and she clutched Kachelle's two hands. Biddy Joe was silent.

'OK.' said Kachelle, 'Maybe when Padraic Charlie gets more scttled at the fishing. Don't fret yourself.'

Unknown to the three women young D.D had heard the conversation. Lying in bed later he pondered over the conversation. He loved his Granny and Biddy Joe but something was stopping him from staying at Chaplestand. He would have to find out what.

CHAPTER 15

It would be three years later before D.D heard yet another conversation. Now nine years old 'a spoilt brat,' is how the Islanders described him. D.D had turned into a clever manipulator. He could get his mother and Granny to do anything for him and lately even his sisters could be made to do his bidding. If he got into trouble at school or with a neighbour his mother always came to his rescue.

When all the other children had to carry a sod of turf each, to school each day for the school classroom fire, his mother had arranged a cart of turf to be delivered on his behalf. His sisters, in the older class carried their sod each day for their classroom.   When money was being raised for the Black Babies the other children brought in pennies and halfpennies. D.D arrived with a £5 pound note, so he always won the prize. It didn't worry him that other children scorned him. He could easily win them around with sweets, comics, even money.

In 1953, the island suffered one of the hardest winters for many a year. Many people were ill with flu. The school was closed because the teachers had fallen ill. Many of the old did not survive. Granny McGinley was one of them. D.D had been asleep when he was awakened by his Granny standing at the bottom of his bed. Her large black shawl was up and over her head. Sitting up sleepily he rubbed his eyes.

'What's wrong, Granny?' he asked, still rubbing his eyes.

'Nothing, son. Just you always remember, Granny loves you, and everything Granny has is for you.'

D.D lay back down in bed and fell fast asleep. Next morning his mother woke him. She hugged him tight.

'Oh darling, listen to Mammy. Granny is gone, gone to heaven, she died last night.'

'No, she didn't,' answered the boy, 'Granny was here. She had her black shawl on. She told me she loved me and everything she had was mine.'

'No, darling, no. Biddy and I have been with Granny all night. Granny never left her bed.'

'She did! She did!' he shouted. 'Just you ask her,' and he raced towards his Granny's room. He halted in the doorway. His granny lay stiffly in the bed with two large pennies on top of her eyes.

'Granny,' he whispered and reached out and touched her hand, withdrawing his quickly because she felt so cold.

'She did come to see me,' he cried over and over again to Biddy Joe. Kachelle stood quietly in the doorway.

'Maybe she did, son. I do believe her spirit couldn't have left this world without saying goodbye. She loved you, always remember that. Now go and get dressed. We have to prepare the wake house,' sighed Biddy Joe.

Biddy Joe's little home was bulging at the sides with islanders who came to pay their respects. Kachelle wanted to bring her mother in law to Chaplestrand but Biddy Joe advised her to leave the remains where they were. D.D sat quietly in the corner listening intently to island tales- stories about his Grandad's fine boat, the war in Great Britain and mostly about the Irish troubles and the 1916 Rising. His Granny had been a great admirer of Michael Collins, the Irish freedom fighter. He knew Michael Collins had been shot, but now he was learning how the traitor Eamon DeValera had played a part in his killing.

'DeValera hadn't the guts to go to England. He knew Michael Collins couldn't win,' argued an old man.

'He alone is responsible for setting the Irish against the Irish. If he had signed the treaty there would have been no civil war,' advised another.

'It's those poor Catholics in the North isolated from the rest of us that I worry about,' contributed old Brandon Paul. 'The poor creatures daren't open their mouths or the B Specials will shoot them,' And the conversation went back and forth with the young boy taking all in.

'He'll have to move in with you, Kachelle, I'm too old to be coping with him. I never did spoil him and now with his Granny gone it's constant rows. Did you know he goes out every evening, running the island mad and doesn't come back till all hours? There I was thinking he was in bed sleeping. He goes to the pub, listening to the aul fellows. Sure they'll fill his head with rubbish and if you're not careful he'll be drinking before long,' complained Biddy Joe.

'Hopefully this time it will be a boy,' said Kachelle, patting her stomach. 'Then Padraic Charlie will relent. I've been a good wife to him, Biddy Joe.

He has his fine boat, fine house, beautiful daughters and I have a successful business. All I ask is that I get to have my son under my roof before he gets much older. I don't think that is too much to ask.'

'Well, you will have to talk to Padraic Charlie. I'm too old, Kachelle, for caring for a boisterous spoilt lad of ten!'

Kachelle had sent the girls over to the chapel to light candles for the new baby that was to be born. Padraic Charlie had risen earlier and was now enjoying a cup of tea and listening to the weather forecast on the radio.

'There'll be no fishing for the next couple of days,' he said. 'There's a storm heading our way. I'll go down later and check the boat.'

Kachelle, not knowing that D.D had just arrived at the door blurted out, 'I need to have D.D living here. He's too much for old Biddy Joe.'

'No, I said he would never sleep under my roof,' shouted Padraic Charlie. 'I want nothing to do with him.'

'If he can't come and live with me I'll swear if this baby is a girl, I'll never try again to give you a son and your fine boat and house and land will come to my son anyway,' answered Kachelle confidently.

'This is not your roof until Diarmuid Charlie says so. After all he is the eldest son and by right this house and land belongs to him. Your mother left word that everything she owns was to go to Diarmuid Charlie. If he doesn't put it in writing, giving this house and land to you, you have no right to it!'

'Shut your bloody mouth,' roared Padraic Charlie, 'It has always been you and Diarmuid Charlie and your bastard son! I'm the one who has stayed on the island, rearing my family here. I have a better right to all this. I tell you now, if I thought it would come to that bastard of yours I'd drown him!'

Kachelle gasped. Taking a deep breath and trying to cool the situation she urged her furious husband to calm down. She knew he meant what he said, he was capable of killing her son.

'What if I write to America and get himself to hand over all rights of this house and land to you, and then if this is a son and she patted her stomach, you can leave it all to him?'

Young D.D was rooted to the spot. He wanted to run but his legs wouldn't move. His Da wasn't his Da! He couldn't understand what was happening. His mother moved towards the other door and he took flight. Running with all his might he raced over the fields his heart pounding in his chest, tears stinging his eyes while all the time his head screamed:

'My Da is not my Da! My Da is not my Da!

His feet carried him to the very spot of his conception. His mother and father's meeting place.

Resting against the very rock that had supported his mother in her joy and sorrow he tried to catch his breath, gulping in the salty iodine spray of the Atlantic ocean.

'I live with Biddy Joe because my Da doesn't love me. No he is not my Da - that's why he doesn't love me. Your bastard son, what did that mean? His brain screamed. He had heard the word bastard before. Old John Joe always shouted it at his cattle, 'Ah, you aul bastards move on, now, move on,' he would shout as he brought his stick down on their backs. He knew 'bastard' was a bad word. He wasn't a bad boy. Why then was he called a bastard? His young mind was in turmoil.

Lifting some stones he started firing them at some nesting gulls shouting as he did so, 'Bastard, Bastard.'

'Whoa, but you have some temper today,' shouted John Paddy, an old bachelor, who had climbed the hill looking for his sheep. 'You'll knock those poor birds right out of the nest if you're not careful, son. You're young D.D., Kachelle Harkin's boy. I would know you anywhere with that red hair. What on earth has put you in such a temper?'

D.D fell silent. He knew John Paddy to see but this was the first time they had spoken.

'Here, take a pull,' and D.D. was offered a cigarette. He stared in amazement.

'Well if you're capable of such a bad temper you're capable of pulling on a cigarette. It'll do you no harm. Come on, leave them aul birds alone, sit with me and enjoy a smoke.'

D.D accepted the cigarette, feeling all grown up. John Paddy showed him how to light and inhale. After the first pull he choked and spluttered, coughing hard. John Paddy laughed.

'There now, that will take your mind off your temper.'

The old man and young boy sat for a while in silence.

'Are you married?' asked D.D.

'No I'm not. I had a lucky escape. Women are no good. You stay clear of them, son. They are all a pack of aul whores. They're only out to use you. Use them and lose them is my motto. Now, do you want to tell me why you are so angry?'

D.D was silent.

'That's okay. You don't have to tell me, son, but can I give you a wee bit of advice?'

D.D pulled hard on the cigarette and nodded.

'Don't get mad, son, get even! It's a clever man that holds his cards close to his chest. Whatever put you in such a state today you keep to yourself, but you know you can play the person who hurt you like a cat plays with a mouse and believe me you will get more information and satisfaction watching them squirm. I'm off now to look for those bloody sheep, call and see me anytime you wish and remember what I told you. Here, keep the rest of these, but mind- don't tell your mother,' and he tossed D.D the packet of cigarettes and matches.

D.D ran his fingers over the glossy packet. The photo of a ship's captain was on the front, 'The real cigarette for the real man,' was printed around the sea captain's head. Taking the matches he lit another cigarette and held it between his fingers just like John Paul had done.

'Don't get mad, get even,' he repeated again and again and by the time he had finished the cigarette his heart had stopped pounding, although the pain in it was still there. His mother had lied to him. Biddy Joe had lied. Even Granny McGinley lied. John Paul was right. Women were no good. What had he said? 'Use them and lose them'. Well, that's what he would do. Putting the cigarettes in one pocket and the matches in another he started to descend the hill.

He was glad he met John Paddy. He liked him and would visit him.

Kachelle did not notice the change in her son. Her mind was taken up with the forthcoming birth and writing to Diarmuid Charlie in America. She did not want him to sign the house and land to Padraic Charlie, she wanted it all for D.D but how was she going to compromise?

Only Biddy Joe watched the change in D.D. The boisterous ten year old was gone. A silent, suspicious, devious character seemed to be setting in. He was smoking too. She had smelt the tobacco in his bedroom. On questioning him he had simply stated that John Paddy had given him a cigarette and he enjoyed it and would continue smoking, raising an eyebrow at her as if to say, 'You can't do anything about it.' Biddy Joe couldn't understand the change in him. Kachelle certainly had not mentioned anything. Perhaps he was just growing up.

On a Sunday night at seven o'clock, Kachelle went into labour, praying that this baby would survive and be a boy. Padraic Charlie busied himself at the boat praying for the same favour. On impulse, he placed his forefinger into the little Holy Water font his mother had placed on the boat and on blessing himself promised never to drink again if the baby was healthy and a boy.

Their prayers were answered. On Monday at midday Kachelle finally pushed into the world a strong, black haired, healthy boy. She held him close to her breast. 'Thank God for you,' she whispered to him. It was finally over. There would be no more children. Padraic Charlie entered the bedroom nervously.

'Come and hold your son,' she whispered and handed the baby to him.

'You were right, Biddy. I have a son,' and he stared down in amazement.

The child clasped his father's large forefinger and held it tight. The forefinger that Padraic Charlie had placed in the Holy Water when he'd made a promise. A promise he would keep.

'I'll never drink again,' he stated firmly. 'Thank you, Kachelle.' He handed the child back and silently left the room, his spirits high.

Kachelle sighed a contented sigh. At last, things were starting to settle down. Once she got the letter off to Diarmuid Charlie everything would be sorted. She stared down at Padraic Charlie's son! Her heart filled with pride. She loved her two sons so she would ask Padraic Charlie to sign everything over to them equally. With a marvellous feeling of contentment she slipped into a much deserved sleep.

Biddy Joe eased the blanket up and over her shoulders. Kachelle had what she wanted. Padraic Charlie was content also. The love of his life lay beside the woman he always loved. But what about D.D? He was only a child with a host of adult problems, what lay ahead for him?

D.D studied the comfortable scene. His mother lay in her bed, her beautiful red hair glimmering in the light, his new brother in her arms. His

'Da', his face beaming with delight sat in an old armchair, which was pushed tight against the bed, holding his sisters on his knee while they all laughed and played with the baby.

'They all love the baby,' he thought to himself . Not able to bear looking any longer, he tore himself from the window and raced to the barn where he threw himself on the hay sobbing his heart out saying over and over again, 'Nobody loves me.'

Unknown to D.D a small baby girl had just been born in Northern Ireland who would love him with all her heart and soul.

Padraic Charlie kept his word and no drink crossed his lips. He would busy himself with the boat then hurry home to nurse his son.

'You'll spoil him,' stated Kachelle. 'Then when you are off fishing I can't get him settled. I can't be nursing him all day.

'I'm not going back to the fishing!'

'What?' exclaimed Kachelle, 'But you love the boat. It's your life!'

'No, it's not,' Padraic Charlie simply stated. 'He is; my son, Padraic Charlie is. I've decided to rent the boat to John Paddy and his two brothers. I'll work in the shop, you're place is in the home!'

'No way,' shouted Kachelle, shocked at his plans. The shop is mine. I enjoy working and my home and children are not neglected. You can rent the boat out as long as the payments are made with the bank and you have some left, but I'll decide what to do with the shop. Besides, I thought you loved fishing.'

Stretching up out of the chair, he placed his son on his shoulder and patted his back.

'The long spells of fishing will keep me away from him,' and he kissed the top of his son's head. 'I want to be at home everyday so I can be with him.'

'Now you know how I feel about D.D'

Padraic Charlie ignored her.

'When he is off the breast, I'll take him to my room. He'll share with me!'

'What about D.D? Isn't it time I took him home and we try and be a family together?' Kachelle grasped Padraic Charlie's large rough hand. 'Look, we have the girls and the boys, let's work together for their sakes.'

Stroking the baby's head she kept Padraic Charlie's attention.

'Diarmuid Charlie is in America, never to return. It's only you and me now. The old ones are gone. Let's work together to give our children, our sons, a good start in life before we are the old ones. You know how disappointed you were when your Da did not leave you any money, money you could have put to good use. Let's not break promises to our children.'

Padraic Charlie considered her proposal.

'I want the finest fishing boat money can buy and I want him to go to college. The fishing is changing. I want him to be a proper captain, educated, with letters after his name. I want him to have a fine house on the island and I never want him to leave the island!'

'He is my son also. I only want these things for him too. But we have to work together and keep the family united!'

After much silence between them he spoke.

'OK. I agree with that, but I want to work at something that will keep me here near to him.'

'Leave it with me. I'll sort it out. Now I'm going to get D.D!'   Padraic Charlie gave a slight nod of his head in agreement.

Kachelle skipped like a school girl to Biddy's, unable to contain her excitement.

'Biddy Joe, oh Biddy Joe, D.D is coming home! Everything is going to work out. Oh thank God everything is settled. Where is he?'

'He's not here, love. You'll probably find him with John Paddy. He's taken to staying a lot with him.'

'God, that's a coincidence, Padraic Charlie is talking of renting the boat to him and his brothers. I'm off Biddy. Catch you later! I can't wait for D.D to come home.'

Kachelle entered John Paddy's home, calling out the usual salutation, 'God bless all here.'

She heard no reply but caught voices from the back field. John Paddy and his brothers were making lobster pots and there in the middle of the commotion was D.D.

'Good afternoon to you Ma'am,' and John Paddy raised his cap to her. 'I take it you're looking for this young fellow.'

'I am indeed. I hope he hasn't been a nuisance.'

'Not at all. In fact he'll make a grand fisherman. Tell me now, has that man of yours decided what he's doing about the boat?'

John Paddy asked slyly, knowing full well that the final decision would be Kachelle's.

'Yes, he has. He'll be renting it to yourself. Sure the whole island knows that your family are the best fishermen around. Padraic Charlie will discuss terms with you!'

D.D squealed with excitement.

'You'll take me fishing, won't you, John Paddy. Please, oh please say yes! I can go ma can't I?'

Kachelle hesitated and John Paddy sensed her hesitation.

'Well, if he's going to make a living here it would be best if he had gained knowledge of the fishing trade- and you did say myself and my brothers are the best!'

'OK, OK.' laughed Kachelle. 'You can go fishing with John Paddy.'

An excited D.D raced towards Kachelle, but turned left to hug John Paddy, thanking him over and over again. Kachelle felt a pang of jealousy.

'Go on with you now,' and John Paddy rubbed the top of his head. 'You know I'll take great care of him. I have no family, so he's like my own son. Never fear, I'll make him the finest fisherman that ever walked this island!'

Kachelle merely nodded. She had other plans for her son, but for now he looked too happy to refuse.

Calling goodbye she clasped her son's hand.

'You know you have got a little baby brother now and he'll look up to you to help him with many things. How does it feel to be a big brother?' she asked.

D.D shrugged his shoulders.

Kachelle continued, 'You have to leave Biddy Joe's now and come home to help with your little brother.'

D.D was shocked. Staying at home meant he would have to hide his cigarettes. It would be difficult to slip out at night to go to the pub and sit and hear the old stories.

'I don't want to come home,' he stated flatly remembering the words 'your bastard son.'

'But your little brother needs you and by the time he starts school you'll probably be going to college.'

'What age do you go to college?' he enquired

'About fourteen I think, but....

Kachelle did not get to finish.

'I'm not going to college, I'm going to America,' And he slyly looked at his mother out of the corner of his eye.

'America?' She asked astonished. 'Now why would you want to go to America?'

'To live with my uncle, of course,' he answered cheekily while all the time keeping his eye on his mother.

'So you see, by the time the baby is four I'll be away.'

Kachelle paled and was lost for words. The young boy did not fail to notice.

'Don't get mad, get even' rang out in his head. For the first time in his life he felt power, felt in control, and he liked it.

CHAPTER 16

Days ran into weeks, and weeks into months. John Paddy was now responsible for the boat and Padraic Charlie seemed to be constantly under Kachelle's feet. The baby was now off the breast and taking solids. Padraic Charlie had been true to his word and not touched a drop of drink; he didn't even visit the pub any more. He had simply walked across to Kachelle a few nights past, lifted the baby from her knee and announced that the little one would be sleeping in his bed from now on.

Kachelle quietly handed the baby over and stated that she was hoping to get an appointment with the bank manager in a few days and would he mind all the children?

'Now what about these plans for the future?' Biddy Joe had asked Kachelle.

'I've been thinking. I read an article in the Sunday Press that the government is willing to finance Irish speaking schools, summer schools, so that young ones can either learn or strengthen their skill of the Irish language.'

'Would you not have to be a teacher for that?' asked Biddy Joe.

'No, the way it works is this- the young ones stay with families who can speak the Irish language fluently. They will live with the families for three weeks, constantly speaking Irish. This will enable them to do better at school and pass their Irish exams. All of this Island has fluent Irish. I'll get a few more women interested. The families of the children pay a set rate to the host families and the government provides the teachers and school. I'm going to write to the Gaelteacht in Dublin with my idea of setting up an Irish speaking college right here on Arranmore. Parents from all over Ireland will send their children here. It will be a great boost for the island women, a chance to earn a few pounds.'

'Himself will hardly agree to strangers sleeping under the same roof as his family, you know how odd he is,' threw back Biddy Joe.

'I know, and I think I have solved the problem. I'll build a chalet bungalow with four rooms and buy those bunk beds, enabling me to accommodate sixteen.'

'Jesus, Mary and Joseph,' whispered Biddy. 'Sixteen? With your own family to look after and your shop! You'll never do it, Kachelle,' she answered shaking her head.

'I will, Biddy Joe, because I'll give him the responsibility of running the shop. I will teach him to drive. He can do the rounds with the goods. Go to the mainland for the stock etc...He needs to work at something and this way he will be at home for his son every evening. I have to see the bank manager and persuade him to lend me the money to build. Here give us a wee reading before I go,' and she pushed her cup towards Biddy Joe.

'Mmm,' followed by a deep sigh eased from Biddy Joe as she turned Kachelle's cup in her hand.

'My, oh my,' and quietly she studied the tea leaves.

'Ah, come on,' laughed Kachelle, 'the silence is killing me. Do you see me building or not?

'I see you more than building. There is a man coming into your life very soon. He will end up adoring you and you're going to go with him.'

'Ah, Biddy, have I not enough trouble without another man in my life? I don't believe you. Sure there's not a decent looking man left on this island!'

'He's not from the island, love, he's from the mainland. Dare I say, you'll fall in love with him so much you could well turn your back on the island and make a new life a different life? Though you can never marry him. He is already married with a family.'

'Oh, honestly, Biddy Joe, I think you're reading someone else's cup. I can't imagine that ever happening,' replied an astonished Kachelle.

'Well the tea leaves never lie. I even see the initials F.F. He will turn your life around. The children are fine, the girls will never give you any problems, neither will the baby, he's his father's son. But D.D, well D.D will break your heart. You will spend many a night on your knees praying for him!'

With that Biddy Joe rose and washed the cup in the large bucket of water.

'D.D is fine. He's just a little cheeky and playing at being all grown up. He seems to have settled fine with us all,' explained Kachelle.

'D.D is turning into a malicious little monster because you spoil him rotten, Kachelle. Do you now he is still going to the pubs late at night listening to the old ones talking? Sitting like a clocking hen taking all in.

157

They'll twist his mind. Sure John Paddy has some weird ways of acting. He turned very bitter when McCauley's daughter refused to marry him years ago and has spent his life thinking ill of women. God alone knows what he'll teach D.D. I love him too, Kachelle, and want only the best for him. You're going to have to spend more time with him. You'll certainly not be able to do that if you start looking after other children in the summer.'

'I'm only doing it so I can give all my children the very best in life,' stammered Kachelle. She did not like to hear anything bad about D.D

'Time is what children need, Kachelle, not money! Time to listen to them. Time to let them talk. In the rush to make money you'll lose sight of them.'

'Ah, Biddy Joe, I'm away,' said Kachelle angrily, 'I'll let you know how I got on,' and she hurried out the door, forgetting to give Biddy Joe her usual kiss on the cheek.

'Honest to God, she's losing her wits,' muttered Kachelle to herself as she strode out across the fields to home. 'Me and another man!! Me going to leave my children, after all I've gone through to get them all under the one roof. D.D break my heart! Really Biddy Joe has definitely lost her marbles.'

Kachelle bustled in and quickly set about preparing the evening meal. Padraic Charlie sat in the chair by the fire dozing, the baby fast asleep in his arms. Kachelle shook her head in dismay.

'Here you,' she called to Padraic Charlie. 'Padraic Charlie, wake up and listen to my plans.'

A startled Padraic Charlie stirred and immediately rocked the baby gently in his arms in case he would wake.

'I'm going to teach you to drive the van and you can run the shop. I'm going to build a chalet bungalow and start an Irish speaking college to run during the summer months. You can take the baby with you, the way I used to do with D.D, and maybe you'll see just hard I worked to keep a roof over our heads while you were busy drinking!'

'Sh, sh, you'll wake the baby. Look, that is all in the past now. I've kept my word. I haven't touched a drop, and it hasn't been easy for me. So I'll run the shop and you do what you have to do. You always did anyway!'

Padraic Charlie leaned back in his chair and closed his eyes. Kachelle knew there would be no point arguing with him.

'I'll go to the mainland tomorrow. It will take me a few days to get an appointment with the bank manager and I'll need something to wear, after all my mother, God rest her, used to say, 'presentation is everything,' so you can mind all the children.'

Later that evening Kachelle called D.D from play to her side.

'D.D I have to go away for a few days so I want you to be good.'

'I'm always good,' he answered cheekily.

'By good, I mean no running off to John Paddy's or the pub at night. You have to go to school, help with the chores and stay in at night.'

'Can I come with you?' he asked, looking her straight in the eye.

'No, I have to go alone. I'm hoping to build over there,' and she pointed across the road, 'and next summer you'll have lots of boys from the mainland to play with.'

'Mainlanders are only tramps,' he stated.

'D.D!' she exclaimed, 'where did you hear that?'

'John Paddy calls them all tramps.'

'Well my mother, your Granny, was a mainlander and she was certainly no tramp. I'll have to have a word with John Paddy or else I'll have to forbid you to visit.'

'Don't care anyway,' the young boy stated flatly. 'Sure I'm going to live with a tramp. My uncle in America, he's on the mainland now so that makes him a tramp,' and he stamped his foot.

Kachelle felt the urge to hit him but controlled himself.

'Listen, if you be good when I'm away I'll bring you home something nice. Promise me you'll be good and stop this nonsense talk about America. And Diarmuid Charlie is no tramp!'

'I'll promise if you bring me a new fishing rod. Not a wee boy's one, a proper fishing rod and I AM going to America.'

'OK. I promise. Now will you be good for me?'

'Sure I'm always good,' and he shrugged his shoulders and swaggered away.

Kachelle packed a few belongings and hurried off to catch the boat to the mainland. The heavy rain did not dismay her as she was booking into

Dungloe Arms hotel for a few days. The break away from everything had already started to do her good. She felt excited and light hearted. Stepping off the boat onto the pier at Burtonport she did not realise she was turning not only mens heads but the local womens also.

The rain had made her long ginger hair more curly and brighter looking and her face was flustered with the ocean spray. She had quickly returned to her figure which had improved with childbirth. Her breasts were now fuller, her waist narrow and her long sleek legs seemed never ending.

A dark bruise in the sky signalled more heavy rain and Kachelle hurried to the old bus which would travel to Dungloe. There were not many passengers. An old couple sat huddled together for warmth. Kachelle noticed they held hands, and a loneliness enveloped her. The old bus eased forward, halted, gave a hoarse smoky cough and slowly crept forward. The driver seemed to hit every pothole in the road and jerked the bus constantly. The younger passengers complained but the old man replied by saying;

'Hold your tongues and be thankful to be in out of the rain. In our day we had to walk this road, into Dungloe and out. Yous are spoilt, have no stamina, get life too easy.' His wife simply patted his hand and nodded in agreement.

Kachelle pushed open the door of the hotel and approached the desk.

'Hello, I require a room for a few days.'

'We only have a double room available as we are decorating,' explained a nervous receptionist.

'Don't worry. That will do,' and Kachelle signed the book.

'Breakfast is served until 10.00am. Do you require an evening meal?'

'Yes, that will be fine,' nodded Kachelle and a young boy was called forward to carry her bag.

Her room was warm, bright and colourful. She felt free and reckless. Biddy was wrong. Money did make a difference. If she had not had the money she would not be staying in this beautiful hotel and not be able to go shopping for new clothes. Life on the island would be very dull indeed if one could not afford a few little luxuries.

Kachelle booked into the hotel until Saturday. It was only noon on Wednesday so Kachelle decided to shop in Dungloe.

Her first purchase was a fishing rod and reel with all the necessary trimmings. This was followed by a new dress each for the girls, new boots for Padraic Charlie and a water proof jacket. To these she added some new clothes for baby and, of course, some toffees for all the children and snuff for Biddy Joe. Kachelle purchased a few magazines and an evening paper for herself.

Hurrying back to her hotel she laid all her purchases out on the bed, making sure she had forgotten no one. Satisfied that she had everything, she wrapped them all tightly together for her journey home.

Stretching out on the bed she glanced through the magazines, reading nothing in particular. She was on her third page of the newspaper when an advertisement caught her eye. The tweed shop in Donegal town had advertised a massive sale. The model was dressed in a three piece suit, jacket skirt and trousers. The woman was wearing trousers and she looked marvellous. Obviously the Parish Priest would have something to say, but Kachelle longed for that suit.

'I'll go to Donegal town tomorrow,' she said aloud, 'After all I've nothing else to do and I'll buy myself that suit. I will, I will!' and she fell back on the bed laughing to herself.

Kachelle dressed for dinner, a modest white blouse and dark green straight skirt and black stilettos, with fine tan stockings. Her hair was brushed thoroughly and a little pink lipstick completed the picture.

Kachelle walked tall and confidently into the dining room, unaware of the commotion she was causing. She ate alone. Afterwards she settled herself in the lounge and called for a brandy and ginger ale. She had never done this before, but was enjoying the feeling of being in command.

A small gentleman asked if he might join her and on Kachelle's invitation sat down. They soon got talking about his work, selling insurance and about Kachelle's plans for the college. A few couples joined them and in no time at all Kachelle had a sing song going. Everyone had a pleasant evening and a very flushed Kachelle made her way to her room.

Collapsing on to her bed, she admitted life was good. Life had turned good. No more of Padraic Charlie's advances. No more babies. She would take more of these trips to Dungloe. She deserved it. If she was going to make lots of money she should also enjoy spending it. Before drifting off to sleep, the image came to her of the old couple holding hands.

So much in love after all the years. 'Lucky them,' she whispered before falling fast asleep.

Next morning, Kachelle was up and dressed by 7.00am. She breakfasted alone and was on time to catch the 8.30am bus to Donegal town. Kachelle stared out the bus window. The sky was deep blue and slightly streaked with clouds that might just come together to bring more rain. But she was off on an adventure to Donegal town on her own for the first time, and it felt good.

Her purse was well stocked, at least three hundred pounds, and again she reflected that one could easily travel the world if one had money. By eleven o'clock she was enjoying a cup of tea and some fresh scones in a small clean tea shop in Donegal town. Her mind was taking in everything, the table cloths, crockery, decoration- just in case she might decide to open such a business on the island during the summer months for the tourists.

The Angelus bell had just finished ringing at noon as Kachelle pushed open the smart, expensive-looking shop door. Large rolls of various coloured materials were on display. Aran knitted sweaters and hats for men, women and children caught her eye, as did the price! She knew many women on the island who could produce excellent garments without using complicated printed patterns and would be delighted to earn some extra money. On impulse she decided to speak to the manager before she left.

'May I help you madam?' a polite voice asked.

Kachelle turned around to see a small, attractive woman in her mid-forties, neatly dressed, facing her..

'Yes I'm interested in the three piece suit as advertised in the 'Donegal Chronicle.'

'We have only the one madam, if you would care to walk this way.'

Kachelle followed the sales assistant to a rack at the side of the window.

'We have had many enquiries about this suit but I'm afraid the ladies interested are not wishing to purchase the three piece and the owner will not separate the items,' explained the quietly spoken woman.

'I suppose they are all afraid of their Parish Priest giving out to them for wearing trousers,' laughed Kachelle.

'I take it you are not afraid?' queried the shop assistant.

'No,' stated Kachelle confidently. 'It was the trousers that caught my eye.

Please may I try it on?'

Alone in the small cubicle Kachelle ran her rough hands over the tweed material and pressed it to her face. She could smell the richness of the wool and delighted in the vibrant colours. The trousers were quickly pulled on, followed by the jacket. The transformation was unbelievable. The trousers seemed to make Kachelle's legs seem even longer but they were too big in the waist. The jacket give the appearance of broad shoulders, and narrow waist. Unknown to Kachelle a gentleman had entered the shop and approached as she emerged from the fitting room.

'Good afternoon, Mr McAlinden,' said the shop assistant nervously. 'This lady is interested in the suit!

He did not need to be told. He was speechless. This lady was like one of those Hollywood movie stars. That red hair, the figure, those eyes and her smile, she was just what he was looking for.

'Indeed,' he said coughing slightly. 'The suit does suit you but, may I say, just a little too big in the waist?'

He moved quickly forward and without hesitation lifted the back of the jacket and gently tightened in the waist of the trousers.

'See the difference that makes. We could easily have that altered for you. Miss Hagan, go to the store and bring me the new Donegal tweed waistcoat. Would you try it on for me with this suit please?' he begged.

'You see,' he explained, 'I designed the suit, and you are the first brave woman to come through that door to try it on.'

Kachelle warmed to him instantly. 'Tell me,' she said with a quick nod of her head for him to follow her to a quiet corner of the shop.

'Do you own this shop?'

'Yes, it was my father's and my grandfather's before that. I'm afraid they kept it very old fashioned. Plenty of tweed suits and hats for men, the odd costume suit for the spinster lady, I'm trying to sell to the younger woman, hence this suit.'

'Well, you certainly have convinced me, and I'll try it on with the waistcoat provided we can talk privately afterward about a little deal concerning your Aran sweaters.'

'May I take you to lunch?' he begged. 'We have one of the finest hotels right here in Donegal town.'

'Yes, I'd like that,' and she smiled sweetly at him as she accepted the waistcoat.

Earlier that morning Kachelle had worn a white blouse with a small pointed collar. Now she buttoned up the waistcoat and replaced the jacket. When she stepped out of the cubicle, Mr McAlinden clapped his hands in appreciation.

'Wonderful, wonderful!' he cried. 'Miss Hagan, the boots, the boots.'

Miss Hagan appeared with a strange yet beautiful pair of dark brown boots. An ankle boot with a strap and small shiny buckle, pointed toe and two inch heel!

'They are a size six, would they fit?' he asked.

'I believe they just might,' laughed Kachelle.

The soft pure leather clung to her foot with a softness she had never experienced before. They completed the lower half of her outfit. As she twirled around the sight was incredible. Mr McAlinden and Miss Hagan caught their breath. Kachelle's long red hair framed her beautiful face and tumbled carelessly around her shoulders complementing the colours in the tweed suit.

'I just have to have this,' she declared, though her mind shouted back at her, 'Where the hell could I wear it?'

'Mr McAlinden, the hat?' asked Miss Hagan, nervously.

'The hat, oh yes get the hat, please,' and Miss Hagan hurried off.

Within a few seconds she appeared with a trilby hat, exactly like a mans only daintier.

'I've never worn a hat. A head scarf is more usual for me,' Kachelle stated.

'Oh please try it on for me,' said Mr McAlinden.

Kachelle placed the hat on her head, but Mr McAlinden immediately removed it and replaced it at an angle and pulled it slightly down on the forehead.

'The image is complete. That's exactly the effect I have been looking for.'

'Surely you will not get many women in Ireland prepared to dress like this?' said Kachelle.

'Perhaps a few, my dear, but I'm interested in the American market and you could help me sell it to them. But we'll talk about that over dinner tonight!

'Oh I thought you meant over lunch now, I've a bus to catch!"

'Do you have to hurry home? Please stay, I need to talk to you, I'll cover your hotel expenses,' he added.

Kachelle looked into the small cubicle. She caught her reflection in the mirror. She had to admit she did look good, 'I hardly recognise myself,' she said to her reflection. While changing, she thought, 'I could stay here tonight. After all I do want to talk to him about the women knitting the Aran sweaters.' Fully dressed, she approached the counter with all the garments in her hands.

'OK, Mr McAlinden, I'll stay over. My own room in a hotel right here in Donegal town?'

'Yes yes of course,' he assured her. 'But please, will you do me one more favour? I'll get the trousers altered and will you please wear the complete outfit to dinner this evening?'

'If you like,' replied Kachelle, After all, I only have what I'm wearing now, as I was to return to Dungloe on the four o'clock bus.'

'Please, now go to the Donegal Arms Hotel, just across the street and book into one of their finest rooms and I'll contact you by telephone for dinner. All of these garments will be delivered to the hotel and your room by five thirty.' He caught Kachelle's hand and gently patted it.

Kachelle walked from the shop in a daze. She couldn't quite believe what was happening. Life sure was strange and wonderful! Before booking into the hotel, Kachelle bought a small flannel and a bar of scented soap, new stockings and a white crisp blouse with long sleeves and large cuffs with small pearl buttons.

The hotel took her breath away. Expensively decorated, warm and inviting and she had her own small bathroom. Kachelle quickly ran a hot bath, and soaked herself with her new flannel and soap. A small bottle of shampoo with the hotel's name on it was displayed at the edge of the bath. Kachelle's hair was normally washed with ordinary household soap so she indulged herself with the fancy shampoo. Relaxing, she lay still in the bath. 'This is what we need at home,' she thought 'instead of a tin bath in the front of the fire. Comfort, privacy- but a bathroom would simply look out of place in our house.' A sudden thought hit her. Instead of building a chalet bungalow to house the students why not build a modern house for herself, with a bathroom and modern kitchen, proper bedrooms for D.D, herself and the girls and Padraic Charlie and the baby, then the students could sleep in the old dwelling.

'That's it,' thought Kachelle, 'that's what I will do. Oh I can't wait to see the bank manager on Friday.'

Kachelle dried her hair in the thick luxurious towels, wrapped one around her and lay down on the bed. Soon she was fast asleep. A knock at the door awakened her. Pulling her coat on over the towel she opened the door slightly.

'Parcel for madam,' said a small boy dressed in a dark navy and gold uniform.

'Thanks, son,' and Kachelle quickly accepted the parcel. A small envelope was attached. 'Meet you in the lounge at 7.30. Tom McAlinden.'

By 7.15pm Kachelle was completely dressed. Her hair, shining with lights of copper and red, curled playfully about her face and shoulders. She felt fresh after her bath and sleep. The trousers now fitted perfectly, highlighting her small hips and neatly rounded bottom. Kachelle had left off the nylon stockings as her suspender buttons had shown through material. If anything, the trousers were even more comfortable without nylons. The new white blouse highlighted the tweed material and the boots and hat completed the picture. The tweed skirt lay unnoticed in the parcel.

'Who are you?' Kachelle asked herself in the mirror. 'Is that beautiful woman really me?'

She toyed with the hat in her hand. It seemed daft wearing a hat indoors but then it seemed daft her here at all.

'What the hell,' laughed Kachelle, 'you only live once,' and she tilted the hat sideways and down just as Mr McAlinden had done.

Kachelle knew she had turned heads as she walked across the wide hallway to the lounge, and she enjoyed the feeling. Mr McAlinden rose to greet her, appreciation shining from his eyes.

'A drink before dinner?' he suggested.

'A brandy and ginger please,' answered Kachelle confidently.

'A woman after my own heart,' he laughed and clicked his fingers for the waiter. Kachelle crossed her long legs, relaxed back to enjoy her drink, and to listen to Mr McAlinden.

'Oh please, call me Tom,' he said, 'and may I call you Kachelle? It is such a beautiful name'

They agreed on first names and Tom quickly set about relating his life story. An only son, he was determined to carry on the family business and modernise the complete stock. What he needed was a model to help sell his new stock and in his mind Kachelle was just that woman.

Kachelle choked on her drink.

'Me a model? You have to be joking!'

'No I'm not. Look at you. You're perfect. You have everything. You would model here for me in Ireland but your image will go mostly to America, on patterns etc. If you want to go to America I can arrange that also. I have many contacts there,' he explained. 'Look, let's dine and we will talk later,' and he gently offered his hand to lead her into dinner.

People in the dining room gasped in amazement as Kachelle entered the room. Tom missed nothing. A few elderly staunch looking Catholic women tutted in disapproval, but even they could not take their eyes off her.

'See, they can't even concentrate on their meal because you are so beautiful, so different,' he explained. 'Now tell me about yourself.'

Over the meal Kachelle talked about her life on the island, her children and her plans for the future. Tom had not failed to notice her rough hands and chipped nails.

'A diamond in the rough,' he thought to himself.

'Have you never thought of leaving the island?' he asked

'Never! It's my home. I was born there, as were all my children.'

Tom quickly noticed that Kachelle never mentioned her husband. Something was not right. If he had a woman like Kachelle he would not let her out of his sight.

'Enough about me. Now who knits your Aran sweaters? How much do you pay? Do you supply the wool?'

'Whoa, whoa,' he laughed, holding his two hands up in front of him. 'One question at a time. Why do you want to know?'

Kachelle explained the hard life experienced by the island women. They were all excellent knitters with patterns passed down through the generations. If he supplied the wool and paid a decent wage she would encourage them to knit the finest sweaters he would ever see.

'Just imagine,' she whispered leaning closer, 'American buyers knowing that women of Arranmore island sat by turf fires in winter knitting sweaters, or perched on the rocks bleached white by the hot sun as they twirled their toes in the golden sands in summer with the dark blue ocean splashing gently about their feet.'

'My, but you certainly have a way with words.'

She could see that he was caught. The image she had described would certainly help sell his Aran sweaters in America.

'Done!' and he reached forward and shook her hand. 'I'll supply all the wool you need and I'll pay a fair price, a decent price per sweater knitted.'

'And for those who are unable to knit due to old age, but have a skill of dying the wool various colours of the Donegal tweed, what will you pay?' she declared.

'Same as those who do the knitting, Kachelle. With you in charge, our business can't fail! Now let's toast the Arranmore Aran knitters. By God I'm glad I met you today.'

Tom went on to explain that he had recently taken on a new partner in America to help market patterns for women using Donegal tweed.

'Please, Kachelle, model for me. You are just what we need. Why, you could more than hold your own with any of them film stars. Maureen O'Hara couldn't hold a candle to you!'

'Nonsense, Tom,' answered Kachelle, 'I'm a housewife and mother. I have a family!'

Again Tom noticed no mention of her husband.

'You are a born business woman, Kachelle. Look at the way we have just agreed to the Aran knitting. You have a clear, quick thinking mind. The Americans might never wear the bloody sweaters - just to own one, knowing it was knitted by the island women is enough. You're a genius! Look, all you would have to do is wear the suits and hats just like you're doing now. I'll arrange a photographer and you will travel to different locations for outdoor and indoor photographs. I'll pay you 100 punts per modelling session!'

Kachelle gasped. 100 punts for just having her photograph taken! This was hard to take in.

'Listen. Enough for tonight. Sleep on it and let me know. The others are going back into the lounge. Let's join them and enjoy ourselves. Enough business for now.'

Kachelle agreed. Settling herself comfortably in the lounge she removed the hat and jacket, opened the waistcoat and sat back, enjoying her brandy.

'You're the finest looking woman in the room Kachelle, God gave you more than looks. He gave you brains - use them,' and Tom patted her knee. He was about to continue speaking when someone at the end of the room began playing gently the piano and some one else began to sing.

After several more brandies, Kachelle couldn't believe how much she was enjoying herself. Any other evening she would be tucked up in bed, tired after a hard day's work. Here, people were only starting to come out and enjoy themselves. This is how the other half lives and yes, she admitted to herself she wanted more evenings like this. She was awakened from her day dream by Tom calling someone to sing, 'I'll Take You Home Again, Kathleen,' his mothers favourite song.

'Look no further, Tom,' she offered. 'I'll sing it to you, in appreciation of a beautiful day.'

Rising unsteadily to her feet, Kachelle brought a hush to the room with her rendition of the song. When she had finished, Tom with tears rolling down his face, kissed her cheeks, which were soft and smelt sweet, and thanked her profusely. The crowd begged for more and Kachelle obliged with The Three Leafed Shamrock of Ireland and The Rose of Tralee. She caught the look of admiration and appreciation in Tom's eyes. He looked so proud of her. In an instant, the memory of singing in London and Padraic Charlie's dark embarrassed look came to mind. Here was a man, one she had only just met, but one who looked up to her, was proud to show her off and compliment her.

CHAPTER 17

Next morning Kachelle awoke to breakfast and fresh flowers being delivered to her room.

The note with the flowers read:

'My star will not travel to Dungloe by bus. My car is at your service. Thank you for last night. Meet me in the lounge at noon. Regards Tom.

'How sweet,' thought Kachelle as she tucked into a large Irish breakfast of bacon, egg, sausage and black pudding with thick buttered wheaten bread and a large pot of tea. 'This is the grand life!' she said to herself as she carefully wrapped the tweed suit and hat for collection.

'Kachelle!' called Tom as he came forward and clasped her hand. 'Did you sleep well?'

'Out like a light,' laughed Kachelle, 'but I think the brandies helped!' Tom was amazed. Even with a late night Kachelle was as fresh as ever.

'Now please sit and listen to me, dear,' said Tom. 'Have you thought about modelling for me? I'll pay 100 punts per session. You drive, so I'll arrange a car for you. It can at stay at Burtonport and you will not be bothered with old buses. It will not take up all your time. I'd love to see you every day but I understand you have family commitments so even twice a month to model the garments. Oh please say yes,' he begged.

Kachelle's mind was in turmoil. What should she do? She hesitated slightly before answering.

'Tom, you're a dear. I feel you and I could be close friends. Can you leave it with me just a little longer? If you give me your telephone number I promise to let you know by this time next week.'

'I won't do a bit of good until I hear from you,' he fussed. 'Now please allow me to drive you back to Dungloe.'

'Yes, I would like that. I'll just go up and get you the suit I want to buy.'

'It is already purchased.'

'No!' exclaimed Kachelle in dismay. 'I really wanted it even though I am not even sure when I should wear it.'

'I got it, my dear, for you. It was made with someone like you in mind. It is already in the back of my car for you.'

Kachelle's mouth opened, but Tom placed his two fingers gently on her lips and ordered her to say nothing.

Kachelle climbed into the front of the luxurious, black shiny car. The smell of the tan leather upholstery engulfed her and she eased herself comfortably beside Tom, now conscious that her shoes and coat looked very shabby indeed.

Tom chatted merrily while he drove, pointing out many places of interest. The rain blew over the mountain tops, flattening flowers and scattering sheep. The sea in the distance stood up in defiance of the dark clouds and everywhere was soaking wet. Decaying cottages huddled at the bottom of the mountains. The harsh cold winds worried their roofs and ripped away thatch and tin. The cows were too fearful to bellow and moan. The road to Letterkenny was wild and lonely but Kachelle felt safe with Tom.

Tom deposited Kachelle in Dungloe and stayed long enough to enjoy a pot of tea with her. He kissed her cheeks again and bade her farewell, making her promise to telephone him within the week.

After he had left, Kachelle felt depressed. The room, though warm and comfortable, was lonely. She didn't bother with dinner that evening, retiring early. Memories of the night before crowded her mind and she felt herself resentful at having to return to the island.

Next morning Kachelle dressed herself in the tweed jacket and skirt, leaving to one side the trousers, waistcoat and hat. She did not want to overdo it and cause a stir in the small town of Dungloe. Her appointment with the bank manager was for 10.30am. At 10.20am Kachelle entered the bank neatly, expensively dressed and feeling a little nervous though she was not about to let the bank manager know this.

The bank manager invited her to sit down and listened carefully to Kachelle's plans. He listened and played with his pencil.

'Kachelle, I know the payments on the boat are being paid and the shop is holding its own and you still have a few pounds coming from America but even though you own the land, do you realise that to build a house of four bedrooms and a bathroom on the island could cost you in the region of £10,000? Materials have to be bought on the mainland and shipped across. Builders, plasterers, carpenters etc would have to live on the island or have a boat available to take them back to the mainland every day, that costs money. Have you anyone who would back you in the loan?, guarantee that if the payments failed, and I'm not saying that they will- your idea for the old house to be used by students is great I can see that working for you, but you just need that little extra. Would you consider perhaps selling some of the land?'

'No, no never,' cried Kachelle, 'that's for my children. I could never sell our land.'

'Well, think about it, perhaps a smaller house or getting a guarantor. What about your brother in law in America. Would he help?'

'I wouldn't ask him. Leave it with me. I'll think about it and get back to you.'

'Here, take my phone number, and if you can arrange anything just phone me and we'll discuss it again.'

Kachelle left the bank dismayed. She returned to her hotel. All her great hopes and plans were dashed. Perhaps she was aiming too high but the image of a modern home for her and the children pulled at her mind. If only someone could guarantee the money ....who? There was no one on the island who could help. She could never sell the land.

Then an idea hit her. Tom McAlinden, the biggest business man in Donegal! Sure 10.000 would mean nothing to him. But she had only met him; it didn't seem right to ask him. On the other hand, he needed her, as a model. What had he said- 100 punts per session? Two sessions a month was 200 punts, a session a week was 400 punts a month! God now she was getting carried away. Kachelle's mind was racing. What was she to do?

Kachelle ordered a brandy and ginger ale to be brought to her room and lit a much needed cigarette. By the time she had finished her drink, her mind was made up.

A girl has got to do what a girl has got to do! She lifted the telephone and dialled Tom's number.

'Tom, I'll pose for two sessions a month, more if you need me, but I need you to phone the bank manager in Dungloe and act as guarantor for me for 10.000 punts!'

There! She had said it.

'What on earth are you going to do with 10.000 punts?' enquired Tom.

'I'm going to build a new house for my family and have the Irish students live in my old home. Will you help me Tom?'

She waited with anxious breath.

'What about your husband, will he mind?' enquired Tom.

'Ah, he'll not even know. He's not interested in what I do. He has his son, and that's all he wants.'

Tom clenched his fists. He knew he was right. Things were not good between them. But Kachelle had mentioned sons. He must have misunderstood her.

'Tom, are you still there?'

'Yes, I'm here Kachelle, I'll always be here. Don't worry, I'll phone the bank manager. You build your fine house and I'll contact you later about the modelling. Take great care. I worry about you crossing the sea tomorrow.'

'Oh thank you, Tom. I really appreciate this. I'll not let you down. Good bye.' and Kachelle replaced the phone.

It was as easy as that. A simple phone call. Tom was such a dear. She would work hard for him and make her children proud of the finest and best house on the Island.

Half an hour later the bank manager rang and asked her to call in immediately to sign papers.

Kachelle stepped into the boat to make the return journey home. A gale scalped the waves, spraying foam. The wind rested for a while as if taking a deep breath, the dark black sea rolled in heavy, lazy, huge waves against the pier sending its iodine salted spray into the air over Kachelle's face.

The journey home would be rough. Kachelle held tightly on to her parcels and rolled with the boat. The rhythmic clanking of the old engine accompanied the whistling wind, drowned out all sounds of human voices. A curtain of hail swept across giving rise to red angry eyes, full of salt and sea spray. The little boat ducked and dived the incoming waves playing havoc with the travellers' possessions and stomachs. The island came into view. Kachelle stared backwards. The mainland was surrounded by a wall of dark black cloud, as if it had never existed.

Tom McAlinden stared out of his shop's window. His thoughts were of Kachelle. God grant her a safe journey. He hadn't prayed in years and now he was praying hard for a woman's safety, someone he had only met, yet he felt he had known her all his life.

There was no one waiting to meet Kachelle. She stepped off the boat and with head bowed she struggled against the wind and commenced her homeward journey. When she entered the cottage, the girls rushed to greet her. They had set the table and a large fire roared up the chimney. Padraic Charlie was in his usual chair with baby on his knee.

Only D.D was missing. Kachelle changed out of her clothes and distributed the presents. It was like a Christmas morning. The girls were delighted with the dresses and sweets. Philomena eagerly grabbed the magazines and Padraic Charlie settled the baby in his bed and lifted the out-of-date newspaper. D.D's fishing rod lay abandoned on the kitchen table.

When the children were settled for the night, Kachelle threw a sod of turf on the fire and spoke to Padraic Charlie of her plans. She did not mention Tom McAlinden and the modelling, concentrating instead on the women and the knitting and building the fine house.

'I don't know about the house. What we have is okay.'

'Times are moving on,' she reflected. 'This was alright for your Ma and Da. You want baby to go to college where he'll be mixing with a completely different class of people. What if he wants to bring friends home? You don't want them laughing at him calling him the poor island boy, now do you?'

'No, I want the best for him.'

'Well then, let's start by giving him a new home with a bathroom and electricity and telephone. Sure we'll have the whole island talking about our fine house, what do you say?'

'You're the one with the head for business. You see to it all. I'll run the shop like you said and you can see to everything else.'

'Fine,' answered Kachelle, patting her knee. 'We'll start tomorrow on your driving lesson. A new start for the children. I'll say good night.'

Kachelle was so excited about her new plans that she forgot to say goodnight to D.D. Little did she know that he had not even come home, choosing instead to stay with John Paddy as he visited the pubs, and later to help him stagger home.

'Ah, sure you're a grand wee fellow altogether D.D, always ready to help aul John Paddy. You stick with me and I'll make a man of you. You'll be a grand fisherman one day,' stuttered the old man as D.D helped him to bed.

Late nights were affecting D.D's school work but Kachelle was too busy to notice. When the school master sent for her, Kachelle would charm him with her smile, place several bank notes on his desk for school funds and ask him to be just a little more patient with her son. After a stage he just gave up. He recognised that D.D had a quick mind, was excellent at Irish History, the subject he most enjoyed, but all other subjects failed him. He could speak the Irish language, not write it.

'You'll get by on your wits,' he would say to D.D 'You're one of those who will always fall on his feet.'

When D.D asked what he meant by this he would shake his tired head and quietly said, 'If you fell into shit son, you would come up smelling of roses!'

D.D would just shrug his shoulders and smile innocently.

Kachelle quickly set about teaching Padraic Charlie to drive and within a few days he started out on his first shop delivery. The eldest girls helped keep house, mind the baby, collect turf for the fire, milk the cows and help Biddy Joe. D.D spent his time preparing for the fishing with John Paddy. He would put in an appearance in the evening, claiming he had already eaten, then slip away to his room. Within the hour he was off again to John Paddy.

Kachelle never checked on her son. Her time was taken up with planning permission for the house, contacting builders and the Gaeltacht authorities. She had already met with several of the island women who had placed Kachelle on a pedestal, she was their heroine. They were actually going to be paid for knitting. Something they had been doing all their lives! Kachelle was to travel to the mainland to collect the wool.

That summer Kachelle travelled to the mainland many times to make arrangements for all her plans. Tom McAlinden had kept his word and a dark green Morris Minor car awaited her at Burtonport. Kachelle was thrilled. When Padraic Charlie heard about it she simply stated that it made her independent for travelling to Dungloe and Donegal town for various meetings with builders etc......

'I got it quite cheap, and you know me, I never pass up a bargain,' and she smiled at him as the lie ran smoothly off her tongue.

Tom McAlinden met with Kachelle a month later. Over brandies and gin she thanked him sincerely for guaranteeing her loan with the bank. He assured her it was no problem. He was only too delighted to help and he was looking forward to the modelling session next day.

Kachelle posed in a dark red and blue pleated skirt and a snow white Aran sweater with a little red and blue check scarf at her neck. The back drop was Mount Errigal. The photographer assured Tom the photo shoot was perfect.

'There you are my dear, 100 punts deposited into your bank account,' smiled Tom. 'How soon can you model for me again?'

'Tomorrow if you like,' laughed Kachelle. 'Why, I have never received so much money for doing so little in all my life!'

'Told you you would enjoy this modelling,' joked Tom 'But seriously, can you stay on the mainland for another day?'

'I don't see why not. Everything is under control at home. You will be paying another 100 punts won't you?' she teased.

Tom longed to take her in his arms and tell her he would give her the world if she would let him but he sensed the time was not right. One day he would and he hoped and prayed that Kachelle would respond to him.

The following day Kachelle posed wearing an Aran sweater, a mass of twists, turns and bobbles with a dark green skirt. An Aran cap on her bright red curls complemented the outfit. This time the dark blue sea surrounded her as she casually lay against a large rock examining a piece of sea weed.

Tom knew before the photographer spoke that this picture would be perfect also. They travelled back to the hotel in Tom's car, talking and joking confidently with each other about the modelling session.

'You'll have to get the telephone installed, Kachelle. It's horrible not being able to contact you and talk to you,' stated Tom.

'It will come,' assured Kachelle 'but you will have to be careful of what you say. The postmistress is an interfering old busybody and I don't want my business told all over the island. You may write to me and let me know the date for the next modelling session.'

'Bring your new suit next time, Kachelle ,and we'll photograph that as well,' he advised.

Tom walked Kachelle to her car, kissed her gently on her cheek, and bade her farewell and safe journey home. Kachelle's car was packed high with long shanks of oily Aran wool for the island women.

The boat journey was uneventful, and this time Kachelle was met by a dozen excited women. Kachelle shared out the wool evenly and said she would call with them within a month. Various sizes were distributed and those who got a child's size were to knit two sweaters for the price of one adult one. No one complained. The women were only to glad to be able to earn some extra cash for their families.

Kachelle's housing plans were on target. Tom had helped speed up housing plans from Donegal Council, they had provided the architect and recommended a builder. The whole island was amazed at the thought of a new house being built. It was many a year since a new dwelling had been erected.

D.D would sit quietly at night in the corner of the pub drinking in every word of the old timers. It was here he got to learn their version of Irish history. He would listen to their double meaning jokes and laugh at auld John Paddy saying, 'A woman is like a garden, she needs a good digging now and again to keep her in place, but one should always use the head and save the feet for dancing!'

'Aye a woman's place is in the home, looking after her husband and children not running, all over the country doing what a man should do,' agreed all of the other men.

'Some women are too big for their boots,' offered another.

'Yeah, but she is a fine looking woman, I wouldn't mind - Ah!' exclaimed Micky John as he rubbed his left ankle.

'Leave it out!' stated John Paddy as he indicated D.D with a nod of his head.

D.D sensed that they were talking about his mother but said nothing. He was angry with her. Why couldn't she be like all the other mothers? He thought how much he longed for Padraic Charlie to put his foot down and control her so he was the boss. John Paddy had said that was the way it should be and yet when he caught some of the men stating that his mother was finest looking woman to ever walk the island his heart swelled with pride.

Within two years, Kachelle had her fine house built on the brow of the hill, overlooking the Atlantic Ocean and golden beach. The cemetery lay to the left and a fine view of the chapel and other dwellings lay to the right.

The older islanders were heard to say, 'It will never last. The first bad weather it will be blown down. It would have been better if she had built in the shelter of the hill, protected from wind and rain.'

Kachelle would smile at their statement. She had ensured a good strong foundation and had used only the best materials. Her home would stand for generations to come. Her house was for D.D.

Kachelle's family was growing up rapidly. Philomena was now almost sixteen, a pretty girl who had finished school and was content to help her mother with chores and the Irish students, Sheila was following in her footsteps but had surprised her mother by stating that her Aunt Mary Charlie in Glasgow had offered her a job learning to be a priest's housekeeper. Mary Charlie had secured this post after leaving the island. She had never married and had always kept in touch with Padraic Charlie. Padraic Charlie didn't seem to mind Sheila talking about leaving the island.

'You can rest assured she will be in good hands with our Mary Charlie' he had stated, yet advised Sheila to leave it for a year, promising to write to his sister about his decision.

The two younger children gave no trouble. Baby followed Padraic Charlie everywhere and D.D kept out of his road.

D.D was quite tall for his age with a head of unruly red curls, pale complexion and deep blue eyes. He didn't mix with young boys who attended the Irish college but loved to show off, repairing the boat to go fishing, pretending he knew it all and was much more aware of life than them. He would light his cigarette and blow circles in the air while they stood back in amazement. He was quick to sense who he could bully and who he could not. This ensured he always had money for sweets and cigarettes. Not that he needed it. John Paddy had treated him like a man, a working man. When the fish was sold at Burtonport John Paddy had given him a good wage with advice;

'Tell no one, son. That's yours. Never let anyone know what money you have. Always pretend you haven't any and believe me you'll get by. Never let your right hand know what your left hand is doing!'

So young D.D hid his money in the barn and was quite pleased with his growing stock. He was always glad when the students left. Winter was his favourite time, no students, no tourists. The island became his again, and now he could share a pint of stout with the aul ones. After all he was ready for leaving school.

When the other boys boasted about joining their fishing boat on leaving school he boasted about being a skipper of his own boat. After all, John Paddy worked for his family. Soon he would work for him. He would be Captain.

Kachelle failed to notice the nasty side of her son's personality. Kept busy with the students in the summer and with her modelling she had almost abandoned her family. The girls kept house and saw to all the chores and now enjoyed knitting the Aran sweaters and earning some money. The women of the island responsible for the knitting would gather in each other's houses and sit in a circle chatting and knitting away. The two younger children played together contentedly and D.D was rarely seen.

The fine house was now well finished and the telephone had been installed. Tom would now phone to inform her when there was wool ready for collection . This was code to Kachelle that a modelling session was planned.

It was a hot summers day in July 1958 when Kachelle casually opened a letter from America. Padraic Charlie was off on his rounds, the girls were playing with the baby down on the beach and D.D was somewhere.
'Dear Kachelle,
It is with great difficultly that I write to you. Kachelle, I need to see you, please. Oh my darling life is so unfair. If only we could get a second chance, turn back the hands of time, I would do everything so different. I would never have left your side. The joy we would have had rearing our son D.D and Philomena.

Kachelle I have been having a lot of trouble lately with my wound from the war. The bullet moved and has been causing me great pain. The doctors now say that there is a serious infection. I am being treated with drugs but there is great fear that if it moves again it will kill me. Oh God, Kachelle, please pray for me. Can you come and see me? I miss home so much. Me who couldn't wait to leave Arranmore and now I am breaking my heart to see my island and you once more.

'I'll pay for your fare. Please come. I need you. I love you Kachelle with all my heart and soul. Hug D.D and Philomena for me.

We are soul mates for ever.

Diarmuid Charlie.

Kachelle sank into the chair. Her beloved Diarmuid Charlie was dying! Oh God no! She cried, holding her head in her hands. A noise at the door made her look up.

'What's wrong?' demanded D.D.

'Nothing, nothing,' she answered, pushing the letter into her apron pocket. 'Nothing at all, just a little turn. Your mother isn't getting any younger you know,' and she gave him a weak smile. 'And to what do we owe the pleasure of your company?' She half-heartedy joked

'Nothing,' he said shrugging his shoulders. 'I do live here you know,' and he smirked cheekily at her.

'Come and talk to me,' she said, pulling out a chair.

'I'll take a mug of tea if you're offering,' he stated.

Kachelle smiled.

'Why he even talks like the aul ones,' she thought to herself.   Catching a side view glimpse of him while making tea, she suddenly realised just how much he was growing up.

You're not at all like your father, she thought. 'You're more like myself and you are going to be so tall.'

D.D accepted the mug of tea. His mother fidgeted in the kitchen drawers for a packet of cigarettes.

'Here, have one of mine,' he offered, challenging her to confront him about smoking. The cigarette was accepted and together in silence they smoked and enjoyed the tea. Kachelle's mind was in turmoil. What was she to do? How could she go to America? Life had settled down. For her to go to America could start Padraic Charlie off again. But her beloved Diarmuid Charlie was dying! D.D caught glimpses of his mother studying. Something was wrong. He would have to find out what.

'How's school,' she asked absentmindedly.

'I leave at the end of the month,' and he pulled a face.

'Leave?' she gasped.

'Well I am fourteen. Everyone else is leaving. You leave school at fourteen you know,' he fired back.

Kachelle stared at her son. Where had the time gone? Fourteen!

'I'm going to work full time on the boat with John Paddy,' he continued boldly.

'Sure you practically live with him,' she retorted.

'Well I sure as hell wasn't wanted here!'

'Don't you dare talk to your mother like that,' she shouted back.

'Truth will hurt,' he quickly said as he placed his cup in the kitchen sink. How he wanted to run to her, hug her tightly and tell her he loved her but John Paddy had said to admit you love someone was a sign of weakness and they could use it against you.

'I'll be needing long trousers now. Perhaps next time you're on one of your trips to the mainland you will buy me some. As soon as possible,' and he quietly walked out the door.

Kachelle lit another cigarette. The house was silent except for the tick of the large clock. Diarmuid Charlie was dying and her beloved son was so changed she didn't know him. Kachelle lifted the heavy handle of the large black telephone and pushed the handle on the side several times.

'Annie, will you put me through to Donegal Town 102?'

'How are you keeping, Kachelle?' the old postmistress enquired.

'Fine, Annie. I just need to order more wool. I'm in a hurry. Can you put me through please?'

Kachelle knew she would be offended by her answer but she was in no mood to talk

'Hello, Mr McAlinden. Kachelle McGinley here. I need more wool. I'll be on the mainland tomorrow can I call and collect it?'

Tom paused for a second. Kachelle had never phoned him before. She didn't need any more wool. Something must be wrong. Remembering what he had been told about the post mistress listening in, he replied.

'Fine, no problem. I'll have everything ready for you. See you tomorrow,' and he rang off.

Kachelle set about keeping busy. She didn't want to think about anything. When the girls returned all their chores were completed and a fine array of home baked cakes and pastries was proudly displayed on the kitchen table. The aroma of Irish stew filled their nostrils.

'Have we forgotten someone's birthday?' laughed Philomena as they all tucked in. Later as the girls sat around the radio listening to the old Irish songs Kachelle took stock of her family. They were growing up so fast. Philomena was the image of her father. Why hadn't she noticed before? Sheila talked constantly about Glasgow and working with Mary Charlie.

'Where's D.D?' Kachelle enquired.

'Possibly out with his girlfriend,' laughed Philomena and the others fell about laughing.

'Girlfriend? Don't make me laugh,' sneered Kachelle. 'He's only a child,'

'Pretty big child, Ma,' retorted Philomena, 'Sure he's leaving school soon.'

'D.D has a girlfriend!' chanted Kachelle's third daughter. 'D.D loves John Joe Mary.'

'Who did you say?' demanded Kachelle.

'John Joe Mary, Ma,' offered Philomena. 'Her granda haunts the lower beach. He was found drowned you know,' Philomena did not get to finish. Her mother had gone quite pale.

'Ma, are you alright,' asked a concerned Philomena.

'I'm fine, I'm fine. See to the young ones for me, that's a good girl,' and Kachelle stumbled to the front door for air.

'Sweet Jesus no, not this on top of Diarmuid Charlie's letter. Not D.D and John Joe's daughter, not his granddaughter. An image of a pretty dark haired 'child of the fairies' with a swollen belly and Mary Anne stating the child was John Joe's flashed by her.

'D.D!' she called. 'D.D!', this time louder and more urgently.

'He's not here, Ma. Possibly at John Paddy's,' shouted back Sheila.

Kachelle strode out defiantly across the fields to John Paddys. On arrival, she got a glimpse of her son mending nets. He was wearing an old pair of long trousers. His sleeves were rolled up. He seemed taller and although scrawny, the frame work was there. He'd be a fine man.

'D.D, I need to talk to you,' she said flatly. D.D continued with his work.

'What about?' he asked quietly.

'John Paddy, can I have a few moments with my son, please?' she enquired.

'No problem ma'am,' and John Paddy touched his forelock.

'What's this about you having a girlfriend?' she demanded.

'D.D was quick to realise that she was concerned and took his time answering.

'What if I have? I am grown up, you know, or haven't you noticed?' he sneered.

'You'll stop this nonsense at once and come home now,' and she reached forward to take the nets from him.

'I am home, Ma. Where you live is not my home, never has been never will be!'

'Of course it's your home. I built it for you. Everything I've done, I've done for you,' she explained.

'And you want me to live in it someday and rear my family there?' he asked.

'Yes, yes of course, D.D, more than anything in the world.'

'Well, it will probably be an island girl I will marry then. Perhaps even John Joe Mary,' and he smiled sweetly at her.

'No, no never,' she shouted. 'Anyone but her. Now, you'll stop seeing her at once!'

D.D's heart jumped with delight. She feared him seeing John Joe Mary. He couldn't care less whether he saw her or not but if it worried his mother he would see her all the more. 'Don't get mad get even' he thought and couldn't prevent a little smile at the corner of his mouth.

'D.D do you hear me? D.D, you won't see her any more, and we'll talk again,' she offered.

D.D. shrugged his shoulders, said nothing and continued mending the nets.

CHAPTER 18

Kachelle tossed and turned all night. John Joe came back to haunt her memories again and again.

'Please God no!' she begged. 'Please don't let John Joe's family have anything to do with mine.'

Next day Kachelle sat beside Tom, a brandy in one hand and a cigarette in another. She confessed all to Tom, confessed her love for Diarmuid Charlie and his request to see her.

'Look, read it for yourself,' and Kachelle sorted through her bag for the letter.

'Where did I put it?' she cried.

'Calm yourself ,my dear,' offered Tom. 'I did think something was wrong. You never spoke about your husband so I know you never loved him.'

Tom again wanted to take her in his arms and assure her of how much he loved her, but now was not the time.

'Do you want to go to America to see him? he asked quietly.

'I don't know. What will I tell Padraic Charlie?' she asked wearily.

'Kachelle it's your life. Live it for yourself. To hell with Padraic Charlie! If you want to be with Diarmuid Charlie I'll make the arrangements. Perhaps you'll allow me to accompany you?' he asked timidly.

'Oh Tom, that would be wonderful. Yes, yes of course I must go, we'll go. Please see to everything.'

Tom wrote Diarmuid Charlies name, address and the hospital title in his notebook. He advised Kachelle to lie down and rest and he would begin to make plans.

Unaccustomed to lying down in the afternoon, Kachelle tossed and turned, her mind in complete confusion. Tom had said it would take a while to arrange everything. Fear and the excitement of meeting Diarmuid Charlie again filled her thoughts but eventually she fell asleep.

When Kachelle awoke the room was dark and humid. She had just finished washing her face when a knock came to the door. Tom was standing there, agitated and pale.

'What is it Tom?' she almost whispered.

He entered the room and clasped her hands to his breast.

'My poor dear,' he repeated again and again. 'Please sit down,' and he led her to the end of the bed.

'Kachelle, your letter was posted over a month ago.' He hesitated; she nodded for him to go on.

'Diarmuid Charlie died two days ago!........'

'What?' pleaded Kachelle. 'No, no, I'm going to America to see him. We are, Tom, aren't we? He's not dead, please, please tell me no!'

Tom gathered her in his arms and stroked her hair. Kachelle sobbed her heart out. It was too late; he was gone. She would never see him again. For the best part of the night Tom held Kachelle while she sobbed on his shoulder.

The following day Tom, purchased a change of clothes for her and encouraged her to eat a little.

'You should phone home,' he advised.

'Why?'

'They will probably phone Padraic Charlie to tell him about his brother,' he said.

'Diarmuid Charlie never knew I had the phone installed. I was afraid to take a chance of telling him in case he would let something slip and the postmistress hear it! We'll probably receive a letter telling us. I'd best go home in case it arrives soon.'

Tom was about to say how long it took the last letter to arrive but decided not to.

Kachelle returned home the same day. Padraic Charlie was off on his rounds, the girls were down at the beach and D.D was nowhere to be seen. She had just finished her third cup of tea and sixth cigarette when D.D entered the kitchen.

'Did you get my long trousers?' he asked quietly.

'Oh sorry, love, I forgot.'

'Doesn't matter. I bought myself a pair in Dungloe.'

'You were in Dungloe?' she asked amazed.

'I am capable of taking the boat to the mainland, you know. You couldn't care less if I never got long trousers,' he pouted.

'It's not tha,t love.   I have been very busy.   I have a lot on my mind.   I'm sorry.   Look, we'll go shopping soon and I'll get you a new suit, shirts and ties.   None of the other boys will have a suit.   How's that?   We'll go soon.'

'Na, give me the money and I'll buy my own.   You owe me £2.10.0 for the ones I did buy!   John Paddy lent me the money,' and he stared at her shrewdly.

Kachelle opened her purse and placed three pounds on the table.

'There, take that, love, and I promise I'll get you a suit soon.'   Kachelle sank slowly into her chair and placed her head in her hands.   Her son stared at her, saying nothing.   Then lifting the money he quietly left the house.

The same evening Padraic Charlie returned early from his rounds and handed baby to Philomena, instructing her to bathe him and get him ready for bed.

Kachelle looked up in surprise at his entrance.

'He's dead,' he stated.

'What?' asked Kachelle, confused at him knowing so soon.

'I was on the mainland today to collect the goods and the Gardai approached me and said that a message had come from their head office in Letterkenny stating that Diarmuid Charlie died a few days ago.'

Silence descended.

'His wife had arranged for us to be told,' he continued.   'He's buried an all.   She'll probably write to us.'

'What do we do now?' murmured Kachelle.

'Nothing we can do.   He's dead and that is that!'

'For God's sake, he was your brother!' shouted Kachelle, 'We can at least have a Mass said for the happy repose of his soul!'

'I hope he's rotting in hell,' he hissed back at her.   'As long as the land is signed over to me I couldn't care less.

'You and the land. That's all you care about....'

Kachelle did not get finishing.

'What I care about is my son and my girls.   By the way, I believe his bastard is ready for leaving school.   Get him off to England soon.   There's nothing here for him.' and he turned his back and walked out the door.   Kachelle opened the lower cupboard door and poured herself a large brandy.

The following day, neighbours called at the house. Word had spread and Mass cards were starting to arrive. On the Friday a neighbour called to show Padraic Charlie and Kachelle the Donegal Democrat.

On the front page was a large photograph of Diarmuid Charlie in his soldier's uniform smiling broadly.

'Island War Hero Dies' read the caption. The story was of an island man who had made good in America and was followed by a photograph of his wife and family.

Later that evening when everyone was in bed, Kachelle sipped her brandy and stared at the photograph. About 12.30am D.D quietly entered the kitchen and sat beside her. He patiently waited for her to speak.

'Ah, he was a grand man,' she said. For over an hour she talked about nothing only her childhood days with Diarmuid Charlie and Padraic Charlie. For the first time in D.D's life he felt close to his mother. He took responsibility for lighting the cigarettes and between them they quickly smoked a pack of twenty. Kachelle was glad of his company. He made several cups of tea and placed sods of turf on the fire to keep them warm. For once, he was all hers. She neither needed nor wanted anyone else.

'Run down to my drawer in the bedroom and get us another packet,' she requested. 'And I'll make us a bit of toast. I bet you're starving.'

Feeling all-important D.D entered his mother's bedroom. A chest of drawers with three deep drawers stood in the corner. Kachelle hadn't said what drawer so he opened the first one. Nylons, pants and other items of underwear were neatly folded. The second drawer was night dresses and blouses. The third drawer contained other items of clothing, her aprons and at least ten packets of cigarettes.

Taking a packet for his mother and one for himself, D.D was about to close the drawer when a piece of white paper caught his eye. He removed it from her apron pocket. There was an American address on it. Knowing he had no time to read it, he placed it in his pocket and returned to the kitchen.

The aroma of freshly made toast filled the air and he and his mother tucked in. The sun was rising when Kachelle, a little unsteady after the brandy, decided to go to bed. She pulled him to her, hugged him tight and rubbed the top of his head.

'You're a good boy Diarmuid Charlie McGinley and I love you with all my heart.' Kissing both his cheeks she advised him to get some sleep and left him alone.

D.D quickly set about tidying the kitchen. His heart filled with pride. He loved his beautiful mother and she loved him. He took the brandy glass to wash it, swirled the last of the brandy around and then gulped it back. On reaching his bed he lay fully clothed with a wonderful sense of warmth and fell fast asleep.

For the first time in his life D.D stretched and smiled to himself. It was still early. Jumping up, he quickly entered the kitchen and took down the key of the shop. In no time at all he had packed the van for the day's business. A chore he knew Da hated to do.

'He'll get a lovely surprise,' he thought to himself and then quickly filled the old van full of diesel. By the time Kachelle had risen the baskets were full of turf for the day's cooking and heating and all of her children were gathered around the table enjoying their meal. Padraic Charlie entered the kitchen and turned on the radio for the day's news.

'The van is packed, full of diesel and ready to go,' commented Philomena.

'Thanks love,' said a surprised Padraic Charlie.

'I didn't do it,' said Philomena. 'I have enough chores to do around here. D.D did it all for you.'

Padraic Charlie scowled.

'Thank you D.D,' said Kachelle immediately. 'That was very thoughtful of you.'

'Well he is fourteen soon,' sang all the girls and they fell about laughing. D.D blushed.

Sheila talked quickly about the boys and girls who were due to leave school. A ceile dance was always held on the last day and everyone looked forward to going to it. Sheila continued rhyming off where everyone was going to work. Most of the girls were going to work in hotels on the mainland, others were going to Scotland and England to family and friends.

'What are you going to do D.D?' asked Sheila innocently.

'I'll work full time on the boat with John Paddy. We have all ready to go to salmon fishing. I can't wait,' he replied.

'I'm selling the boat,' stated Padraic Charlie. Kachelle stared at him. A silence fell over the kitchen,

'I have someone from Killybegs interested. They will be coming next week to see it,' and he lifted his head and made for the door. Halting, he stared at the girls. 'No one is to touch the van again,' he ordered. 'I'll do my own packing!'

You bastard! You bastard! Kachelle screamed silently to herself.

'Is that right Ma? Is the boat being sold?' asked D.D, and all eyes were on Kachelle.

'I don't know! Now out all of you and give my head peace.' Kachelle reached for the brandy bottle, D.D stood defiantly.

'Is my boat being sold Ma? I've told everyone I will be skipper of the boat. It can't be sold. John Paddy and I have everything ready to go salmon fishing,'

Kachelle studied for a moment. With Diarmuid Charlie gone, there would be no more money from America. Perhaps it would be best to get rid of the boat!

'If your father has decided to sell it, then he will sell it, son. Now go, go and do something and give me peace!'

D.D sought solitude. They couldn't do this to him. He would be the laughing stock of the island. He had boasted, felt good about fishing from his own boat. The other boys would laugh at him now. With no boat, there would be no fishing with John Paddy and there was no vacancy on any of the other boats with so many leaving school. He searched in his pocket for a cigarette. A full crumpled packet was produced and the letter from his mother's drawer.

D.D read with great interest Diarmuid Charlie's last letter.

'The joy we would have had rearing our son D.D and Philomena! 'Jesus Christ,' he exclaimed, 'Philomena and me are full brother and sister! Diarmuid Charlie is my Da! The bitch! No wonder Padraic Charlie couldn't stand him!'

Everything fell into place. Why he had to live with Biddy Joe and Granny McGinley. Why his 'DA' never bothered with him. Why he had shouted he had to leave the island at fourteen! 'That is why he is selling the boat,' he gasped. 'He doesn't want me around.'

Right now he hated 'DA' and most all her, the bitch who had caused this all.

John Paddy was right. All women were whores! In a mad rage he roared to himself.

'It's my fucking boat. I should be fishing it. There is no bastard from Killybegs going to take it. If I can't have it no one will,' and he stormed towards the boat.

No one was on board.

'Don't get mad, get even with the bastards,' he kept repeating to himself as he lifted the can of diesel and began sprinkling it all over the inside of the boat. Then he quickly slipped the boat's ropes from the pier, lit a match, dropped it on to the floor and quickly jumped ashore and with all his might gave his beloved boat a shove out to sea.

The boat bobbed gently on the waves and very slowly and hesitantly moved out from the pier. Black smoke started to pour from the wheel house. A small explosion was heard and great angry red flames licked their way out the windows and across the deck.

D.D sprinted away as fast as he could and headed for John Paddys. He casually entered the house and set about making tea. John Paddy slept the sleep of a drunkard. After calming down, D.D finished his tea, washed his hands thoroughly and began mending the fishing nets in the midday sun.

John Paddy crawled from his bed.

'Is that tae I smell D.D?' he roared.

'Stay where you are and I'll get you a cup.'

'I suppose you have half a day's work done son. God, what it must be to be young and fit! This aul body of mine is done. I should have been up giving you a hand.'

'Well you know what they say, John Paddy,' offered D.D. 'Get the name of an early riser and you can lie all day.'

'The truth be spoke my boy. You never said a truer word. Now, reach us those aul cigarettes.'

The old man and the boy sat drinking tae and smoking, making great plans for salmon fishing.

Within the hour, several children came running across the fields shouting loudly.

'In the name of Jesus......' began John Paddy but he never got to finish.

'The boat is on fire! The boat is on fire!'

D.D dropped his cup and helped John Paddy to his feet.

'Run son, run and see if anything is wrong. Run quickly now, I'll catch you up!'

D.D and the children ran to the small pier. A crowd of islanders, including his mother and sisters, had already gathered. The boat was ablaze. Black billowing smoke filled the sky causing people to cough and choke.

'She's drifted out too far. It's too late to do anything,' commented the older men.

John Paddy finally made it up to the top of the hill. He fell to his knees on seeing the sight.

'Holy Mother of God protect us,' he prayed.

Then a silence fell as everyone stood quietly watching the scene. After an hour some of the islanders started to drift home. D.D sat with John Paddy saying not a word. Young and old men started to shake their heads in sympathy.

'Terrible, John Paddy, and you ready for the salmon.'

'I've had my day of fishing. It's young D.D who is losing out. He is a hell of a good fisherman, I've taught him all I know, but there will be no fishing for him this year!'

The younger boys, who were leaving school with D.D offered their sympathy also. D.D played the martyr role to the hilt. Deep down he felt quite pleased with himself.

'Are we fully insured?' Padraic Charlie asked Kachelle over the tea table.

'Of course,' she stated and added, 'Some are saying John Paddy was careless with the gas stove. He is getting on, you know. Thank God it didn't happen when anyone was on board.'

'Just get the insurance sorted out. It was being sold anyway,' and Padraic Charlie lifted the baby up in his arms and took him outside for a walk.

Kachelle reached for the brandy bottle. D.D entered the kitchen through the back door and quietly lifted the Donegal Democrat with Diarmuid Charlie's smiling photo and returned to the barn where he studied his fathers face and read again and again about his life in America. Later, he tore out the sheet, folded it neatly and placed it with his hidden stack of money, and the letter from America.

The last few days at school were agonising for D.D. The other boys talked constantly of the salmon fishing and of girls. The 'end of school days' ceile dance was approaching. D.D had travelled to Dungloe and purchased a suit, shirt, tie and new shoes. For the first time he had his hair cut by a proper barber and he insisted on wearing it teddy boy style, like the Rock and Roll singers on the British record labels that Dan Tom's brother sent from England.

At night the young ones would gather in Dominic Paul's house and play records that Dominic Paul's brother sent from England. The fast moving rock and roll music would fill the air and set their feet tapping. Dominic Paul would talk of his brother learning to jive with a girl and the next time he would be home he would teach Dominic Paul and his friends to jive.

'Can you get us any beers before the dance?' asked one of the boys to D.D.

'No problem, I can get us all the beer we want and more,' answered D.D confidently.

'Can you get us a girl?' joked another.

'Sure you wouldn't know what to do with a girl,' sneered D.D and the group fell about laughing.

'I wouldn't mind finding out!' shouted another and soon they were roaring and singing a double meaning song about a girl who helped her boy find out what to do.

'Are you buying another boat?' D.D asked Kachelle as she walked to the pier to travel to Dungloe.

'No, I have no plans to,' she answered.

'I might as well go to America then,' he replied.

'Will you stop this nonsense about America? Look what America got Diarmuid Charlie.'

'Aye, if he had stayed here, things would have been very different, wouldn't they Ma?' he asked her, staring her full in the face. Then he calmly turned left at the cross roads and left her to continue alone.

He knows, thought Kachelle, but was puzzled as to how he had found out. Losing Diarmuid Charlie's last letter bothered her. She tried hard to remember what was in the letter, but the shock of reading he was dying seemed to have blocked the rest of the letter out.

Maybe I will buy another boat when the insurance comes through but then D.D is very young to take full control of the fishing and John Paddy's fishing days are over.

Kachelle's thoughts were in complete and utter turmoil. Something was going to have to be arranged. She needed desperately to keep D.D at home. He was stubborn enough to leave and go to America and she couldn't bear that.

'You're not really with us today, darling,' offered Tom.

'I'm sorry. I have so much on my mind; I'm finding it hard to concentrate.'

'O.K. We'll call it finished for today,' and Tom nodded to the photographer to stop shooting.

'Come on, Kachelle, we'll go somewhere comfortable and over a few brandies you can tell me all about it!'

Kachelle accepted Tom's offer by simply linking his arm.

'So you see,' she finished later, 'I don't know, Tom, whether to buy another boat or not.'

'Would D.D consider going to college to further his education for another three to four years?' he enquired.

'Definitely not! He has always hated school. He would certainly laugh at the idea. Besides he would not have the qualifications to get into college.'

'Don't need qualifications. Money talks at the end of the day, Kachelle. I know the Christian Brothers who run the college in Bundoran, I could get him in there.'

'Thank you, Tom, I am very grateful but alas, D.D would never go!'

For the next few minutes they sat together in silence.

'I have a very good friend who skippers a large fishing vessel in Killybegs. He would have crew for this year but I could certainly get D.D signed on for next year, that is if nothing else turns up on the island,' suggested Tom.

'The island boats are family boats. It is rare for a place to be offered out. If I could just stall D.D from leaving until next year I'm sure he would join the crew at Killybegs. Thank you, Tom, you're a wonderful man,' and she reached forward to kiss him on the cheek.

Without thinking Tom sought her mouth and kissed her long and hard.

'I'm sorry, my dear, I should not have done that. But I have wanted to for so long. I love you, Kachelle, loved you from the first day we met. I have prayed hard that you will love me too!'

'I do love you, Tom. No, please, hear me out. I love you. I am not in love with you. There is a big difference. I'll be honest with you, I don't think I will ever be in love with you. Oh I do hope this doesn't spoil our friendship. Right now I really need you!'

Tom patted her head.

'Thank you for being honest. At least you love me. I will always be there for you, Kachelle. Who knows, perhaps some day when you are thinking a little clearer you will find yourself in love with me. I'm a patient man. I can wait.'

They wrapped their arms around each other and embraced gently.

CHAPTER 19

D.D was ready for the end of term dance.

'Oh my God, you look a right sight,' joked John Paddy. 'A new suit, must have cost a fortune. I never had a new suit, you know. I got my Da's after he died. Sure you only wear a suit to get married and after that only to funerals. Sure you look grand, son. You would think you stepped of the American boat. You'll have every girl in the island after you. They'll be thinking you're loaded with money dressed like that. Go on now. Pay no heed to an old man like me. Off you go and enjoy yourself.'

D.D took the small narrow roads, with the grass growing down the middle, to the school house. No crossing fields today in case he would ruin his suit. He adjusted his collar and straightened his shoulders. He felt uncomfortable and dressed up.

The boys will get a shock when they see all the beer I have stacked away for today, he thought to himself, and a smile of cockiness arose on his face.

On arrival at the school house, all the others turned to stare at him. They had never seen D.D in long trousers before. The dark green suit with the purple shirt and the tie left them speechless at first, until someone commented on his hair. Within a few seconds they were all falling about laughing. D.D's outfit made him stick out like a sore thumb. The rest of the boys wore new coarse hard wearing long trousers with thick black belts and open neck white shirts.

'You bastards, you'll get none of my beer,' he snarled and within seconds a fight had broken out. D.D fought with anger like a terrier dog. He lost control completely, taking on at least four other boys.

The school master arrived and on seeing the sight cancelled the dance. Now twenty pairs of angry eyes were on D.D.

'It's all your fault, McGinley. We're sick of you, you spoil everything, go and get lost, you bastard,' were some of the comments to be heard.

On hearing the word 'bastard' D.D. let fly again, pinning an older boy down while he hit him repeatedly with his fist about the face and head.

'Be off with you,' roared Father Connolly who had just appeared on the scene. He lifted D.D up by the scruff of the neck and shook him.

'McGinley! I might have known. Get yourself away from here and I'll have a word with your mother and father.'

'Fuck you,' roared D.D to the priest. A hushed silence fell over the school yard, McGinley had used bad language to the priest! Such a thing had never been heard of before.

'I'm not afraid of you,' yelled D.D and he swung his right arm at the priest. The priest blocked his swing.

'Attack a man of the cloth, would you? I could bring the curse of God on you, young man, but for the sake of your father I won't. Now I warn you again be gone!'

D.D stared him defiantly in the face, breathing heavily. For a moment the priest felt a panic rise within him. This young man was not going to back down. Something was going to have to be done or he would lose credibility among the young ones watching.

'Come on, school master, no need to cancel the dance. In, in everyone, and enjoy yourselves.'

The delighted crowd forgot about D.D and cheered, quickly making their way into the school house.

Father Connolly joined them, leaving D.D to stand alone. A soft rain had started to fall and D.D fought hard to hold back tears. Turning quickly he raced across the fields, until he reached the spot where he had hidden the beer. He drank hard and fast. Still in a fit of temper he tore off his coat and flung it down on the muddy ground, jumping up and down on it and cursing everyone. The shirt on his back was ripped in several places. The new shoes he fired across the field. Feeling sorry for himself he settled down in the rain to continue drinking.

John Joe Mary made her way to the where D.D had hidden the beer. She knew he would be there. Looking up at her through drunken eyes he demanded what she wanted.

'I love you D.D,' and she sat beside him and cuddled him. He offered her a beer.

'No I shouldn't, Mammy will be angry,' she protested.

'Fuck them all! If you're not going to drink with me, fuck off,' he shouted.

John Joe Mary reached for the bottle and settled down beside him. He snuggled close for warmth and laid his head on her ample bosom. It had been a long time since anyone had held him close. He moved closer. Placing his hand on her knee he started to explore under her skirt.

'No D.D, Mammy will be angry,' she cried.

'Are you my girl or not? If not, get to fuck home and don't talk to me again!'

After a lot more beers, followed by fumbling and loosening of clothes D.D threw his leg over John Joe Mary and pinned her arms high above her head.

'Tell me you love me,' he demanded.

'I love you, D.D, I do,' John Joe Mary repeated again and again.

'You are all a pack of whores, pack of fucking whores. She's a whore. My Da is not my Da! Fuck you,' and his thrusting and swearing continued until he finally collapsed on top of her. For a while they lay silent.

'We can get married now,' said John Joe Mary quietly and innocently. D.D looked at her in disgust and fear. Her clothes were wet and muddy. Her heavy black knickers were caught around her right ankle.

'Fuck you, I'm not marrying anyone. If you tell anyone what we did I'll kill you. Do you hear me? he roared shaking her shoulders violently.

'OK! OK!' she wept. 'But I love you D.D,'

'I don't care. Now fuck off home and don't ever talk to me again.'

D.D kicked at the second crate of beer bottles.

'Fuck the lot of yous,' he roared as he fired the last of the full bottles at the nearest rock, then stumbled across the field to John Paddy's.

'In the name of God,' exclaimed John Paddy on catching sight of him. Moving quickly for his age, he caught D.D just as he was about to fall and half carried him into the house.

'My Da is not my Da,' he kept saying over and over again. 'Do you hear me John Paddy?' he laughed, 'My Da is not my Da, my uncle is my Da!!' And he started a laugh which turned quickly into tears.

John Paddy worked quickly to settle him down. With a rough towel he dried his head and shoulders, and got him into bed.

'I'm a man now John Paddy aren't I? I've left school, going to go salmon fishing only I burnt the fucking boat,' and again he convulsed with a mixture of laughter and tears.

'You're drunk young man. You don't know what you're saying. I'll have a good talk to you in the morning.'

'I'm a man now, I had her I did, John Paddy. Fucking bitch says we'll get married I.......'

But before he could finish John Paddy slapped him hard and ordered him to sleep. Never having been chastised before D.D was about to answer but thought twice and fell back on the pillow whispering,

'I love you John Paddy. You have been like a Da to me.' And he passed out.

'Poor kid,' whispered John Paddy as he rubbed the damp red curls. 'We'll have a good talk in the morning!'

Next morning D.D awoke with a splitting headache but pretended to John Paddy that he was fine.

'What happened, son?' asked the old man.

Perhaps it was hearing the word son that encouraged D.D to open up and he poured his heart out to John Paddy.

'Well now,' said John Paddy as he placed four heaped teaspoons of sugar into a large mug of tea and handed it to D.D. 'You listen to me, son. Listen hard, because if you don't there will be a lot of things you will regret.

'First the boat - fuck that, it is gone. The insurance will cover that, sure they all think I was at fault. I don't give a damn for one on this island and you can be the same. Never, and I repeat never, admit you set the boat on fire, now are you listening?' D.D nodded. 'Never tell anyone. Not even the priest in confession. Regarding your first experience of a woman. It had to happen some time. You deny that, or you'll find yourself shacked up for life taking orders from a woman. Oh, I'm telling you, women are so clever son. Just waiting to snare you. Every one of them is a conniving whore. Sure if you eat a plate of beans how do you know which one will make you fart? If she appears with a story about having a wee one just you say what I've said. Wasn't it Eve who tempted poor Adam? Sure all women are Eves. Never trust any woman.

'Now number three, your Da. Don't be angry with Padraic Charlie. If he's not your Da, so what? It's hard for a man to accept another man's child. I imagine even worse if it is his brothers! He always loved your Ma but he was always in Diarmuid Charlie's shadow. Oh Diarmuid Charlie was a charmer, and you take note son, you catch more flies with honey than you do with vinegar. Don't be angry with Padraic Charlie. Give him some respect.

'Well your Ma is your Ma, no matter what. You have wanted for nothing and sure she worships the ground you walk on. You have to accept the ways things are. As you have said, you're a man now, so just put everything behind you and get on with your life. As for Father Connolly, many's a time I felt like giving him a dig in the mouth myself.'

'Aye, I guess your right,' answered a deflated D.D and pulled hard on the cigarette.

In no time at all the whole island knew about D.D going to hit Father Connolly. The old folk blessed themselves on hearing it and said that no good would come of it. Parents warned their children to stay away from him as he was no good. Others simply commented 'Blood will out. Sure he isn't a real islander. His Grandma was a tramp from the mainland , a blow in.'

Kachelle waited until she could get D.D alone to talk to him so it was several days after the incident before she could relay her plans about fishing in Killybegs.

'Why do I have to go away to fish, Ma?' he asked, while studying her face the whole time. 'Sure the insurance money will replace the boat.'

'I will get you your own boat some day, son, but it will have to be when you are older. I want you to help me prepare this winter for the students next year. The old house needs to be thoroughly cleaned and decorated. You could help deliver the wool to the knitters and there are a thousand and one jobs to do around here. Next season you can sign up with the best skipper in Killybegs and after a few years we'll talk about a boat of your own.'

D.D stared at her long and hard. 'Thanks for nothing,' and he tossed his lighted butt of a cigarette towards her and left the room.

'Oh God,' she prayed silently. 'Guide me to do what is right for him. I only want to keep him with me as long as possible.'

Unknown to Kachelle the decision of what to do with him was taken out of her hands.

D.D seemed to have settled down. He no longer went to Mass. He continued to spend his nights in the pub with John Paddy and filled in a part of his days by working on the old house. Kachelle completed a few more modelling sessions and was planning her last one before the winter really settled in when Tom announced that his partner in America was planning to visit and wanted to meet her.

CHAPTER 20

At the end of November 1958, Kachelle was relaxing with Tom in his home when a visitor arrived at the door. Voices were heard and the maid escorted a gentleman into the living room.

Kachelle's heart pounded in her chest. She couldn't understand why, but he was the most handsome man she had ever seen. Tall, with broad shoulders, he had salt and pepper hair and beard and piercing, large brown eyes. He rushed forward, and taking Kachelle's right hand brought it immediately to his lips and kissed it. Kachelle found herself blushing and dry mouthed.

'You are more beautiful than your photographs,' he said in a rich, deep American drawl. Tom instantly recognised there was a spark between these two.

'She likes what she sees. I'm going to lose her,' he thought.

Kachelle found her voice.

'Really, Tom, aren't you going to introduce us?'

'Yes, yes of course. Kachelle, may I present Francis Flattery, my partner in America, better known as big Frank.'

Kachelle felt slightly weak and sat down. 'Two F's in his name' is what Biddy Joe had said in her long ago reading of the tea leaves. She studied the figure before her.

'I would like to get to know you better,' she thought to herself and tried to peel her eyes away from him.

Just as Biddy Joe had said, so it happened. Frank and Kachelle became friends immediately and by Christmas they were having a full blown affair. Kachelle had travelled to the mainland before Christmas and when a gale force storm blew up on Christmas Eve morning, she was forced to stay on the mainland for four days. She wasn't unduly worried. Philomena knew where the presents were. All groceries had been left in, they could cope without her. Kachelle spent every second with Frank, not noticing that Tom had disappeared off the scene.

'This is real love,' she would whisper to Frank. 'I'm not walking, I'm floating and I don't ever want to come down. I feel for the first time in my life I am in love. I thought I loved Diarmuid Charlie, and I did but it didn't feel like this. I would follow you to the end of the earth, my darling.'

'I feel the same about you. I adore you. You are my queen. I loved you from the first time I looked at your photograph. Please, Kachelle, let us not let anything stand in our way. Your family are grown. Your youngest has his father. Mine are all grown also. Let's claim what is left of our lives for ourselves. Will you think it over?'

Kachelle didn't need time to think long or hard. She had missed one opportunity, she would not miss another. Padraic Charlie had Baby, Sheila would soon be off to Glasgow. D.D was going to Killybegs and she was sure Philomena would look after her fairy child, and keep house.

'I don't need to think it over. I would follow you to the ends of the earth, my darling.' and she snuggled closer to him.

Kachelle returned home on 29th December. Philomena and Sheila talked incessantly about the storm at Christmas.

'It's no good, Ma,' said Philomena suddenly. 'I'm sick of this way of life. The storm meant there was no electricity, no telephone, no boats able to go out. I'm leaving!'

Kachelle stared at her in disbelief. 'What?' was all she could say.

'I'm young, Ma. I want to see new faces, do new things. I've accepted a job as a junior maid in the Bundoran Arms Hotel. I start on the 7th of January.'

'I'm going to Glasgow to Mary Charlie,' chipped in Sheila. Dad says it is okay. So I'll be away also, but I'll come home at holidays.'

Kachelle was about to answer by saying she couldn't care less if she came home or not but bit her tongue. With Philomena gone who would help look after baby and their fairy child. Oh why couldn't she call the child by her proper name, Elizabeth, and Baby was now far to old to be called baby any more!

'Dad has agreed that we can both go,' Philomena stated firmly. Kachelle stared at her two daughters. They were very young and pretty. They had a right to live their own lives, but what about her and Frank?

'Oh and by the way, Ma, John Joe Mary's Granny wants to see you urgently,' said Philomena.

Kachelle put her coat on and left the house quietly. A bitter December wind tore at her. With her head bowed she strode boldly to the other side of the island, her thoughts only of herself and Frank. On arrival at John Joe's house, Kachelle suddenly thought as to why Mary Anne would want to see her. Kachelle was shocked at her old friends appearance. Biddy Joe looked younger than her.

'Mary Anne, it is good to see you. It has been too long. It's hard to imagine we live on this small island and I haven't seen you in years.'

'Don't fret,' said Mary Anne comfortingly. 'You have been a busy woman. Look at the fine business and family you have built up. I'm sorry for having to send for you. Especially in this cold weather. Kachelle, you have been a good friend to me. I might not have said anything, but I know there have been times you have not charged me for the goods, and even left a few pounds as if it was my change.. I'm sorry to bring bad news to your door.'

'Bad news? What bad news?' enquired Kachelle.

'Do you remember when John Joe died, you saw my dark haired girl, my little girl of the fairies I called her, so you remember I told you she was expecting John Joe's child?'

'Yes I remember meeting her,' answered Kachelle slowly.

'Well,' went on the old woman, 'She had a little girl and we called her John Joe Mary!'

Kachelle's heart beat faster and her head ached.

'She was friendly with your lad D.D, called him her boyfriend.'

'I never heard him mention her,' lied Kachelle.

Mary Anne lifted Kachelle's hand in hers.

'Kachelle, she is pregnant and tells me it is D.D's.'

'No, no that can't be true! He's too young to be her.....'

'Calm yourself love, I'm not out to make trouble. She tells me it was the end of term ceili dance. They were both drinking beer. She claims she loves him and is going to marry him.'

'That is impossible......' began Kachelle.

'To be honest, she is a bit of a wild thing. I need your help, Kachelle. As you know John Joe Mary is just not right. I don't want men using her. There's a convent in Dublin where young girls stay to have their baby and they live there afterwards with the nuns. Can you help me get her into this convent? Then I know she will be safe.'

'Yes, yes of course,' said a grateful Kachelle. She never once questioned if the child might not be D.D's. Kachelle was just so glad a fuss would not be made. 'Leave it with me,' she offered.

'As soon as possible, please, and I don't want Father Connolly or the whole island knowing.' pleaded Mary Anne. 'I'll say she has gone to live with my sister in Cork.'

Kachelle assured her that she would arrange everything and prepared for the journey home. Her mind was numb. With the girls talking about leaving and now this, everything was moving too fast for her.

Before returning home she stopped off at John Paddy's. D.D was sitting at the side of the fire, a bottle of stout in his hand. John Paddy lay sleeping on the settee.

'D.D what have you done? Do you realise that John Joe Mary is saying you are the father of her child? Are you planning to ruin your life completely?' The questions came thick and fast.

'Sure if you ate a whole plate of beans, how do you know which one makes you fart?' he retorted, 'John Joe Mary has had plenty of fellows.'

'You bastard,' she shouted, striking him across the face.

'Aye that's right ma, I'm only a bastard, that's one thing you can be sure of!'

'I'm sorry! I'm sorry! I didn't mean to hit you. I'll make it up to you. Look we'll get you a boat. You'll have it by spring. John Joe Mary is going away for good. Her Granny has asked me to arrange everything......No one will know. You have worked hard on the old house. We'll go together and choose a boat soon, is that okay with you?'

'Aye, that will do fine, and it will be my boat not his,' and he indicated his head towards the door. Kachelle knew he meant Padraic Charlie.

'Only yours, I promise,' and she quietly left John Paddy's.

On returning home, she found that the young ones and the girls were in bed. She poured herself a stiff brandy and settled down to wait for Padraic Charlie to return home from his rounds. She did not have long to wait. Quietly she busied herself making him a sweet mug of tea.

'So you're home then,' he stated as he entered the kitchen.

'Yes I couldn't get in because of the storm I..'

But she did not get to finish her sentence.

'No doubt your fancy man, Tom McAlinden, gave you a marvellous Christmas, you whore!'

'How dare you! I'll......'

'You'll do nothing. I know about your bastard and John Joe Mary. It is bad enough he goes to hit the priest but he gets a fairy child in the family way. How would you like it if happened to Elizabeth? A letter arrived from America today. We would have had it before Christmas only for the storm. Diarmuid Charlie has left me all the land.'

'No, never,' she shouted at him. 'He would never do that!'

'Well he has. Read it for yourself. After all we were brothers, and blood is thicker that water. You're only a blow in! I want your bastard of this island right away. I'm beginning to doubt if he even is Diarmuid Charlie's.'

'How dare you!' and Kachelle fired the sweet cup of tea at him.

'The girls are leaving. I gave them permission. Your bastard is leaving also. It is your place to take care of Elizabeth and Baby now. No more running to the mainland. If you don't agree I'll tell the whole island about you and your fancy man and about John Joe Mary's condition. Even you wouldn't want to ruin your children's reputation. He can't live here now. The other Islanders will shun him. The worst thing a man can do is to get his way with a fairy child, even you know that.'

Padraic Charlie left the kitchen and Kachelle alone. She stared about her fine modern kitchen. Her fine house didn't seem to matter now. Her children were leaving and there would be no future for her and Frank.

'Why me, Jesus?' she asked the Sacred Heart picture as she sat alone.

By the end of January, Philomena and Sheila had left. John Joe Mary had moved to a Magdalene convent in Dublin and Kachelle had cried on Frank's shoulder after telling him she could not go with him. Frank was returning to America in February and Tom was devastated because Kachelle was cancelling all modeling contracts.

'As sure as God, you never know what is going to happen from one day to the next,' she told herself. Her hardest task of all was talking to D.D.

Kachelle sat in the kitchen while Elizabeth and Baby played on the rug. D.D had just entered, excited at the prospect of the two of them making plans to buy a boat.

'D.D' she began, ' you're all grown now and I have something to tell you. As you know Diarmuid Charlie died and before he did he made a will. The old house and land belongs to Padraic Charlie. The land this house is built on belongs to Padraic Charlie. But this fine house is mine. It will one day be yours. I intend to buy lots of land here and leave it to you. Land is important son. You might not understand now but you will some day.' I will be contesting Diarmuid Charlies' will, but before she could answer Padraic Charlie entered the kitchen.

'I see he's still here,' he said to Kachelle, ignoring D.D completely.

'I have a name you know. I'm Diarmuid Charlie McGinley,' shouted D.D.

Padraic Charlie faced him and for the first time took a long hard look. He was his brother's son all right. Not so much in looks, but the in the way he held himself, always ready for a fight.

'The girls are all making their way in the world. Are you man enough now to do the same? It is time you moved on, off this island!'

Kachelle rose quickly from her chair to go to his side and speak. D.D put his hand up in front of her. 'He doesn't know about Philomena, poor bastard,' he thought.

'Is that what you want?' he quietly asked the man he had believed for years to be his father.

Padraic Charlie simply answered, 'Yes.'

D.D stuck out his hand and offered it to Padraic Charlie. Taken aback Padraic Charlie hesitated at first, then took the young man's hand. It was the first time the two of them had ever touched. Padraic Charlie instantly recognised the rough hands of a fisherman.

'I will respect your wishes. Thank you for rearing me. I will never bother you again. Good bye, Ma,' and he turned to leave the room with his mother crying after him

'No, D.D, please come back!'

Kachelle raced after him, all the time calling him to come back. D.D strode on, ignoring her pleas. Soon he was lost in the vast darkness. Kachelle sank to her knees and cried the tears of a mother, demented.

D.D packed his belongings in an old rucksack. He entered the tiny shop at the pier to buy cigarettes. The other boys of his age hung about the shop talking about the fishing season to come. How D.D envied them. Acting the hard man he played a great part, pretending to be excited about going to England!

'Great money to be made at the tunneling work,' he informed them. 'At least £500 a week.' D.D related stories he had heard from the aul ones in the pub.

Shouting his good byes, he pushed the rucksack on his back and headed for the pier as if he hadn't a care in the world. Biddy Joe! He suddenly felt he had to say goodbye to Biddy Joe.

When he entered the kitchen she was quick to take in the rucksack. 'The time has come,' she thought to herself.

'I'm leaving,' he said, a slight tremor in his voice which he hastily excused. 'God but it's cold out.'

'At least have a cup of tae with me, son, before you go,' she offered.

D.D gratefully accepted the chair by the fire and was silent as Biddy Joe made the tea.

'Have you any idea where your're going?' she enquired

'Aye, to London. There's great tunneling work there. A couple of the aul ones gave me names and addresses to contact. £500 a week can be earned. It's tough work, but sure I'm tough,' he said as he shrugged his shoulders.

Tough? Biddy Joe thought to herself. You're as soft as butter, but you have to pretend to be tough.

Biddy Joe kept her thoughts to herself. They drank their tae in silence.

'You've read everybody else's, Biddy Joe, now read mine,' and he pushed his empty cup before her. Biddy Joe was about to comment by saying 'You're only a child,' but knew this statement would not be appropriate.

She turned the cup upside down on the plate and turned it three times. She prayed, 'Father, Son and Holy Ghost.' Then she settled back.

'I can see a journey.' D.D sneered. 'A long journey. I see work for you. You'll work hard, earn lots of money but you'll also play hard. Money will run through your fingers like water. You're going to have to watch your drinking, son. It could well get a grip on you. Ruin your life. If you keep a steady head, I see a wonderful girl for you. She will be Irish but she will have a different culture from you. She will love you with all her heart and soul. I see a beautiful home and a family, alas, not on this island. Try, son, to put your past behind you. If you don't, you'll end up very bitter and very lonely. I say again, I do not see any family for you for many years to come.'

D.D recognised that she was trying to tell him that John Joe Mary's child was not his.

'I've something for you, now that your all grown up,' said Biddy Joe. She rose and went to a small cupboard and lifted out a package roughly wrapped.

'Your Granny asked me to give it to you when you were all grown,' and she handed him the parcel. D.D tore it open. Large white notes of paper scattered about his knees.

'What is this?' he asked.

'Granny McGinley loved you. That was her life savings. Unfortunately it is all out of date. I don't know if the bank can do anything about it.'

'Just my luck again, Biddy Joe. Granny McGinley should have sent them to him in America. He was her favourite son. 'maybe'....he said slowly as he wiped his mouth with the back of his left hand while staring at the money. Biddy Joe interrupted his thoughts.

'You take care, son,' and she placed a small prayer and medal into his hand. Always keep these about you,' she advised.

'I'll pray for you everyday',

'Aye, Aye I will,' he answered meekly.

'Here take this also,' and she gave him a small sealed plastic see-through bag with some dark brown earth inside.

'What is this?'

'It's a little piece of home. So you'll always have your beloved island with you.'

D.D threw his arms around her, kissed her on both cheeks and whispered, 'I'm not away yet', and he gave her a cheeky wink. Taking several large notes he folded them in half and placed them in his inside pocket with the bag of earth, prayer and medal. Then turning he hurried out the door with the money in the wrapping paper, leaving his rucksack lying on the floor. Biddy Joe knew instantly what he was going to do and with tears streaming down her face she shouted after him,

'Don't do it son, you'll only get hurt more', but the fast blowing eastern wind carried her words in a different direction. Taking some holy water she splashed some after him and prayed to God to keep him safe.

DD ran as fast as he could back towards home, careful to take a different route so that he would not meet his mother. Bursting in through the back door, he startled Charlie and 'baby'. Thrusting forward Granny McGinley's package he said pleadingly,

'There, there it's for you. Granny McGinley left it all to me but I want you to have it. Biddy Joe didn't know what was inside. There must be thousands', and he wiped his nose on the sleeve of his jacket. Padraig Charlie sat in disbelief. The money, his money was lying in his lap. DD's steel blue eyes held Padraig Charlies silently pleading for him to ask him to stay at home.

'We could buy a boat. Fish it together', he offered and rubbing the top of four year old 'baby's' head he suggested, 'Wouldn't that be fun, us all fishing?'

After an uneasy silence Padraig Charlie lifted 'baby' up in his arms with the package held firmly in his right hand and flatly stated, 'This will buy him the best education so that he can skipper his own boat. You better hurry, time and tide wait for no-one'.

DD squared his shoulders, ready for a fight.

Fuck you, you bastard! his mind squealed as he bit down hard on his lower lip, drawing blood so that the words could not escape. Nodding his head in agreement and inhaling noisily through his nostrils with temper he walked slowly out the back door with 'baby' crying in his ears.

'I want DD; we go fishing. I want DD'.

Taking to his heels he strode purposely at first, only to find 'baby' chasing after him, crying on the wind to wait for him.

'Go home, go back', he roared while lifting a small pebble and firing it wide. The youngster kept running towards him crying out his name. DD stopped. He hadn't time for a scene. He needed to get away before anyone witnessed him crying.

'You and me go fishing DD please', begged 'baby' sobbing. He threw his chubby arms around DD's legs. DD rubbed the black curls on the child's head and after a few seconds he bent down and hugged him.

Padraig Charlie stood quietly in the distance watching the scene.

'You be a good boy and I promise you, cross my heart and hope to die', and he made the sign of the cross on his lips and heart.

'You and me will have the finest boat on Arranmore some day and we will be the best fishermen'.

'Promise?', begged 'baby'.

'Yes I promise, now please go home, Da is waiting for you', and he indicated with his head towards Padraig Charlie. DD rose to his feet and raced towards the pier with the youngster's cries ringing in his ears as he feebly attempted to follow him.

The small boat had cast off and was edging away from the pier, leaving a gap of almost three feet. Islanders stood on the small slippery pier crying and shouting prayers and advice to the young travellers, many of whom would never return home. DD sprinted forward and with a daring leap, jumped onto the small boat, rocking it violently. The girls squealed while the young men roared loudly congratulating him. Angry islanders shook their heads in disgust and could be heard saying, 'Mad as a bloody March hare; cheeky devil; might have got himself drown; never quit until he kills somebody'.

'Hi, McGinley, your travelling light', joked a boy of DD's age, drawing attention to the absence of a rucksack. DD ignored him. Standing defiantly at the bow of the boat he viewed his home. The island was growing smaller and was beginning to slip from view. Tears stung the back of his eyes, his throat sore from swallowing them, his heart beating loud with panic. He was leaving home. He was frightened.

'Oh God,' he thought to himself. I don't want to go. I want to stay and be a fisherman.

John Paddy's words rang out in his head,

'You can take the boy out of the island, but never the island out of the boy.'

He fingered Biddy Joe's small bag of earth and remembered he had some of granny's money.

'Fuck you all,' he called back to the island and then turning he joined the other travellers. Laughing and rubbing his hands together he sang,

'London, here I come.

'Right back where I started from.'

Sixteen year old Christine Paul pulled a small gold case from her handbag and began powdering her nose.

'Here, let me get ready for London too,' teased D.D.   He grabbed the small compact and pretended to be applying make-up to his face.   The young travellers fell about laughing.

D.D positioned the small mirror to the side of his face. He caught the last image of his mother on the islands highest point, beckoning him back.   But it would be many a year before he would return.

END